BLOOD AND ROSES

Tainted Hearts Series

#3.5

By Lylah James

BLOOD AND ROSES

Copyright © 2018 by Lylah James.
All rights reserved.
First Print Edition: February 2018

LIMITLESS PUBLISHING

Limitless Publishing, LLC
Kailua, HI 96734
www.limitlesspublishing.com

Formatting: Limitless Publishing

ISBN-13: 978-1-64034-311-5
ISBN-10: 1-64034-311-3

No part of this book may be reproduced, scanned, or distributed in any printed or electronic form without permission. Please do not participate in or encourage piracy of copyrighted materials in violation of the author's rights. Thank you for respecting the hard work of this author.

This is a work of fiction. Names, characters, places, and incidents either are the product of the author's imagination or are used fictitiously, and any resemblance to locales, events, business establishments, or actual persons—living or dead—is entirely coincidental.

Dedication

To Lyov, because once an Ivanshov man speaks, there is no stopping him. He wanted his story to be told. And then Maria started to whisper too.

I am powerless when it comes to them.

CONTENT WARNING

Not intended for readers younger than 18.

This book contains dark—and sometimes violent—depictions of the world of organized crime and sexual assault. Certain events might be triggers for some readers.

Author's Note:

Lyov's and Maria's love story was only meant to be a short story, but once they started to speak to me, I couldn't stop them. Their story turned out much longer than expected, and here we are. *Blood and Roses* should be read after *The Mafia and His Angel*. This is the fourth book in the Tainted Hearts Series

Blood and Roses is a tragic love story. If you have read *The Mafia and His Angel,* then we all know how this story ends. Maria's and Lyov's love isn't sugar-coated, and their ending is written exactly how it is meant to be.

Tainted Heart Series Reading Order:

The Mafia and His Angel: Part 1 (Now Available)
The Mafia and His Angel: Part 2 (Now Available)
The Mafia and His Angel: Part 3 (Now Available)
Blood and Roses
The Mafia and His Obsession: Part 1 (Coming Soon)
The Mafia and His Obsession: Part 2 (Coming Soon)

Chapter 1

Lyov

The gun went off, loud in the silent night. His screams were heard as another gunshot sounded. Blood seeped on the cold, hard ground as he writhed in pain.

"You are really stupid if you thought you would make it out alive," Isaak growled behind me. I chuckled, because my bleeding captive was *really* stupid.

"Please…" he begged.

I *tsked* at the coward…and thief. Stealing more than tens of thousands of dollars from me would only lead to one end.

And his end would ultimately be death.

I squatted down beside him, tapping his head with the back of my gun. He stared at me with wide, frightened eyes. Poor thing. I wondered if my cold heart felt bad for this bastard's ugly demise.

I cocked my head to the side, thoughtful. *Do I feel bad?*

Ha. Fuck no.

I enjoyed his fucking pain. Best thing that could happen after a shitty day. Maybe I could sleep better tonight.

"I don't know if you're lucky or unlucky that I caught you in Russia. Did you think Solonik would help you escape?" I asked, pressing the barrel harder into his temple.

He winced and shook his head. Well, tried to shake his head. I had him pinned against the hard ground. He couldn't move even if he tried.

"I'll go for unlucky then. Because I can kill you, have your blood splattered all over the ground and wall, and nobody would care. Nobody would bat an eye," I hissed in his ear.

I huffed at the thought. *What a stupid little thief.*

My eyes followed his twitching legs, where the two bullets had pierced the skin. I was tempted to torture him some more. Unfortunately, I had a meeting to go to. Something more important at the moment.

"I'll let you go this time," I said with a shrug. Standing up, I nodded at the end of the alley. "Go on, now. Run before I change my mind."

As expected…he did.

He limped toward the end of the dark alley, his legs mostly useless. I could almost smell his fear from where I was standing.

So pathetic.

I glanced at Isaak, who was leaning against the wall, a cigarette between his lips. He smirked and shook his head. I smiled too because the best part was finally here.

Raising my gun, I pointed at the back of the boy's head, my sight secured on the spot. He didn't notice the gun. He didn't see his death coming.

Only because he was desperate to live—to escape.

Too bad for him.

My finger latched against the trigger, and I pulled it without a second thought. He dropped to the floor soundlessly, his body unmoving.

I walked over to where his dead body lay and kicked his feet. Nothing. His face was turned toward me, his eyes still open, looking at me lifelessly.

The fear in them was still there. I could also see the shock, the way his pupils were wider than before.

His mouth was opened, and trickle of blood dripped past his lips. Shaking my head, I turned away from the man. Isaak pushed away from the wall, coming toward me.

"I'm surprised they always fall for that line," he said mockingly, staring at the unmoving body. "Can't decide if they are either cowards or just plain stupid."

"I would go with stupid." I stuck my gun back inside my waistband and pulled my suit jacket over it.

Isaak scoffed before calling for clean-up. He rattled the address quickly before cutting the call off. "They'll be here in five."

We walked back to the black bulletproof Mercedes-Benz, its windows tinted for privacy. Absolutely nothing could be seen from the outside.

Pretty useful when you had enemies on your case every day.

"To the Royalist," I snapped as I got into the car. With Isaak in the front, the driver drove away without a single word. The drive wasn't long, the club just a few blocks away.

When the car stopped and my door was opened, I stepped out into the fresh air. The dark, cold night masked our faces as we entered through the big doors of The Royalist.

At the entrance, the guard nodded his head and slightly bowed in respect. It was something given to me freely, without even asking.

They knew exactly how to greet a Boss. As he straightened, his eyes glanced around us, making sure we weren't followed.

I walked inside with Isaak following closely behind. Several guards were stationed in the entrance hall. All of them nodded in my direction as I walked by.

The hall was lit by several really fucking expensive crystal chandeliers. We finally stopped in front of another door.

I raised an eyebrow at the guard, waiting for him to let us in. He swallowed nervously, rubbing the back of his neck.

He was obviously new.

"Is it only you?" he said in Russian, nodding behind me at Isaak. "And him?"

I glared and then snapped, "Yes. Do I need fucking permission before entering my own club?"

His eyes widened, his feet taking him a step back. "M-Mr. Ivanshov?" he stuttered.

"The one and only," I growled, taking a menacing step forward.

He shook his head fervently. "I'm sorry, Boss. I…"

With a flick of my wrist, I shut him up. His mouth closed quickly, his jaw almost snapping. His body trembled slightly as he opened the door. I could see trepidation on his forehead when he realized who he was actually talking to.

Did Solonik really hire this boy? What a joke.

As soon as I walked through the door, warmth filled my body. The room wasn't chilling like the halls. No, it was warmed by the fireplace and a heater.

The large banquet hall was designed for royalty. Couches, chairs, and tables were around the room. The middle was empty, a huge gap. The biggest chandelier hung in the middle of the ceiling, making the entire room glow.

The men talked and laughed amongst themselves, glass of wine in their hands, expensive suits adorning their bodies.

Without a second glance, someone could tell that these men were the wealthiest ones, made from filthy money. And I was amongst them.

Not just part of them…I was the Boss. The King.

Everyone's attention was drawn to me as I walked further into the room. Valentin Solonik came forward with a huge smirk.

"Lyov, finally!" he said loudly, clasping me on the back as if we were old friends.

Instead of speaking his mother tongue, he spoke English, so everyone in the room could understand.

We were a mix of Mexican, Russian, Japanese, and American. I could also spot a few Middle Eastern men.

"I almost thought you weren't coming," he continued in the same thick English accent. He tried hard, but his Russian accent was still present.

"And miss the event of the year? I don't think so," I replied drily. Unlike Valentin, my English accent was perfect. While Solonik took care of the business in Russia, my base was in the States. I sat on my throne in New York, where I had ruled for years.

Valentin nodded, handing me a glass of wine. "Enjoy the evening then," he said with a wink before sauntering back to the guests he was attending.

I took my seat on one of the couches, facing the middle of the room. Isaak sat down beside me, finishing his glass in two large gulps. "I'm going to need more than one glass if we have to get through the night," he muttered.

I huffed, taking a sip of the expensive wine. I would have chosen vodka or whiskey, but these were the nights we turned classy. Or we tried to.

It was all about appearance. At the end of the night, most of us would walk away with a couple of million in our pockets, while others with the *goods* in their arms.

My eyes flitted over to the door across from me. It was closed...for now. Glancing at the clock, I saw that it was close to midnight.

A few more minutes and those doors would open. That was when the fun began.

Chapter 2

Lyov

"Gentlemen, welcome. The evening is about to start. I am honored to have all of you here. Tonight, surprisingly, is hosted by me," Solonik said with a small laugh.

Each year this event is hosted by a different group. This year it was Solonik's turn. I had never hosted it before. And never fucking would.

I was snapped back into the present when the door opened. There was utter silence for a moment, and then the murmurs started.

Men laughed, some snickered, others smirked at the sight in front of them.

The Royalist wasn't just any type of club. Not just anyone could get in.

Actually, it wasn't even a club.

More like a ring. The most well-known and successful sex and slave cartel ever established. One that nobody could bring down even if they tried.

Many did, but only their dead bodies made it

back home.

Removing my eyes from the men around the room, I glanced at the door. My gaze found the women piling in.

I counted in my head. Twenty-five in total. The girls were between sixteen and twenty years of age.

All of them were naked, their bodies on full display, stripped bare of their dignity. They had nothing left.

Only a black lace mask adorned their faces. They wore their hair down, falling behind their back as they entered the room.

All twenty-five of them stood in the middle of the room, their backs straightened rigidly.

Solonik clapped his hands, and they fell to their knees almost instantly, mere puppets to this game.

They knelt on the floor, their arms stretching out in front of them with their palms on the cold, hard ground. They arched their backs as they pushed their asses up in the air in total surrender.

"The slaves have joined us, so our evening can begin. We have a wide collection—different colors and sizes," Solonik introduced.

He walked to the first girl, his shoe touching her bare ass with the softest touch. She didn't dare move or even flinch. She stayed completely immobile, like a frozen statue. "The finest ass and pussy you will ever find. All of them well-trained. You can sample some of them before the bidding starts."

This was where our money came from. Our largest revenue. We could make up to more than ten million dollars in one night. The exchange went so fast—in the blink of an eye.

Buy and sell. Use and then discard.

That was what happened during these trafficking nights.

The slaves would do anything at our bidding. We were the Masters. They were the pets. Plain and simple.

"Enjoy the night," Solonik finished with a slight bow to his guests. Turning his head toward me, he nodded and walked back to his chair.

That was when I noticed the single girl, kneeling at his chair in the same position as the others. The only difference was that she wasn't with the rest of the slaves. She was with *him.*

"Are you bidding tonight?" Gavrikov asked, coming to stand beside me. He was another boss, part of Bratva. Someone else I trusted with my life.

"You know damn well I don't. I'm here to watch and make sure everything stays under control," I hissed.

"Just asking, man. You attend these events every year, yet you leave without a single bid. Nobody questions you because you're *The Boss*. But be careful. You don't know when the snake will strike," he replied back, tipping his glass against mine before leaving.

My gaze moved back to the girl beside Solonik. I couldn't see her face. Her cheek was pressed against the marble floor, her dark hair cascading around her shoulders and face.

For a brief moment, I wondered what she looked like. All the other slaves had stood up and were parading around for the salivating men.

But she…she stayed kneeling and hidden, an exquisite statue. It tempted me to get a closer look.

Finishing my wine, I placed the glass on the table before standing up. A woman came in front of me, her head bowed down. She started to kneel at my feet, but I quickly stepped away, pushing her toward Isaak.

He grunted in annoyance but caught the girl nonetheless, almost gently wrapping his arms around her. Women were his weakness.

I walked over to Solonik, whose eyes were trained on me. His fingers wrapped around the girl's neck in a possessive hold. I huffed, fighting the urge to roll my eyes at his weak show of possession.

You could possess someone without even touching them…they could be yours with a single gaze. You did not have to have a hold on to them to show ownership.

As I got closer, he cocked his head to the side in question. I nodded toward the kneeling slave. "She is not up for bidding?" I asked, raising an eyebrow.

Solonik chuckled. "Not now. She will be last. But not for sale. She is only available for the night, under some strict rules."

"She is yours?"

"For now. Until I can get the highest buyer. For now, I'll just enjoy her until I decide otherwise," he muttered drily, his fingers trailing down her spine.

She stayed unmoving, which only made me step closer. I wanted to see a reaction from her. Anything…just a small glimpse. Not a frozen sculpture.

"Are you bidding tonight?" Solonik asked,

crossing his ankles. He lounged back against the couch, tugging at his tie.

"No," I snapped back.

Yes.

Fuck! Frustrated at the sudden thought, I raked my fingers through my hair. I tried to suppress the growl that threatened to escape.

My gaze slithered back to the girl. Solonik noticed, and he smirked.

"You are boring, Lyov. Enjoy the night for once. There are plenty of samples for you to choose from," he said, waving his hand around the room.

I followed his movement, my eyes finding all twenty-five girls, but none of them had my attention.

Not like the tempting vixen kneeling beside my feet.

When I didn't answer, Solonik sighed, looking like he was deep in thought.

"I will let you borrow my slave. One blowjob. She gives the best ones," he finally stated, nodding toward the girl.

My eyes widened, and I raised a questioning eyebrow. He shrugged, lacing his fingers behind his neck. "Sharing is caring, Lyov."

My gaze burned into her skin as I contemplated Solonik's proposal. My length hardened at the thought of her taking it deep down her throat, sucking me dry.

With her ass in the air, I thought of fucking her in this position. Perfect posture to take me deep inside her cunt, I adjusted my cock in my pants and licked my lips.

"Is there a deal?" Solonik asked, snapping me out of my sweet, filthy thoughts.

It would be so easy to say *yes*. Just take her, use her…my body welcomed the thought, but my stupid brain fought against it.

I did not touch the slaves. That was my number one rule.

I did not fuck them. Number two rule.

Do not touch the slaves. Third rule.

Do not fucking touch the slaves. Fourth rule.

These types of events, no matter how tempting they could be, made my stomach churn. It was dirty, depraved, and utterly disgusting.

I might have been a part of the human trafficking ring. I might have been the watcher…to make sure everything went smoothly. But I had never participated before.

I had never taken a woman against her will.

Did that make me a better person? Fuck no. Just because I didn't touch them, it did not make me better. I was far from better.

I was their fucking worst nightmare. The Devil in disguise.

I just had my rules to keep myself in line.

"No. There is no deal," I said stiffly. Removing my eyes from the naked girl, I walked away.

It was hard when all I wanted to do was throw her body on the ground and take her right there, let everyone watch her scream in ecstasy with my cum dripping from her wet pussy.

There was just something about her. The way her face was hidden, almost like she was forbidden for me. And she was. That girl belonged to someone

BLOOD AND ROSES

else.

It only made me want her more. She became more tempting in my eyes than those other slaves who could easily become mine.

I made my way back to the couch to see Isaak missing, only to find him a few feet away speaking quietly with Gavrikov. There was a slave kneeling at his feet, his hand softly caressing her hair.

He always had a soft spot for the slaves. Isaak hated these events, even more than I did. But he had no choice but to play along, another Master in the game. And he played it well.

I sat back on the couch, my legs stretching out in front of me. My head hung back as I stared at the ceiling, waiting for this long night to be over.

My eyes closed, blocking away the screams of the slaves as they were whipped and fucked raw. The shouts of pleasure as the men came. The slapping of skins against each other as they fucked the girls into submission.

This was going to be a looong night. Just what I needed.

Where was my bed? And a bottle of vodka?

Yeah…back in my hotel.

I rubbed my forehead tiredly, tugging at my tie in frustration. Another scream sounded against the walls, this one filled with so much pain.

It was always pain.

No pleasure for the slaves. Very few had the chance of experiencing an orgasm. Only if the Masters were generous and liked the pussy or ass.

My eyes were still closed when I felt a hand on my thigh. I jumped, my heart thumping faster for a second. My fingers gripped the frail wrists, holding them still against my thighs.

I kept my eyes closed for a second, breathing through my nose. I was already hard and throbbing, desperate for release. It would be fucking impossible to push whoever this was away.

Swallowing hard, I opened my eyes...only to have my breath stolen from me.

Bluish-steel colored eyes.

The most beautiful blue eyes I had ever seen stared up at me.

She wore a black lace mask, very similar to the others, except hers had black beads hanging around the front.

She was kneeling down at my feet. Her posture submissive. Her naked body full on display, only the black mask covering half her face.

She stared up at me with those striking doe eyes. Her black hair, so long, so smooth, fell down behind her back in beautiful waves. Her perfect pouty lips painted a deep red.

The mask only made her look...more exotic...more tempting.

My legs opened wider against my will, and she shifted closer, her body resting against my inner thighs.

This close, I saw that her eyes were rimmed with black eyeliner and smoky eyeshadow, which only made her blue eyes pop out more. They were the only thing I could stare at, completely lost in them.

My hand tightened around her wrists, my fingers biting into her soft skin. She didn't flinch in pain like I expected her to. Instead, her eyes stayed glued

BLOOD AND ROSES

to mine.

She licked her lips, slowly and so fucking sensually that my cock jumped at the sight. I hissed out a harsh breath, my mind going wild at the possibilities laid out in front of me.

She was a tease. The look of an Angel but the temptation of a minx. So tempting that even the Devil would fall for it...in her trap.

I leaned my head down, my nose touching her jaw as I breathed in her smell. *Roses.* She smelt of fresh roses, like she had just bathed in them.

Her head tilted back in surrender as I dragged my nose down her neck, filling my lungs with her smell, driving myself wild with her.

My senses were lost as I pulled her even closer to my body, between my parted legs. When my gaze found hers, she stared at me with such innocence, I was rendered speechless.

Even though her voice was not used, those eyes spoke everything. They held pain and innocence...something they were all robbed of.

This slave, she was the true definition of beauty. So enticing that it was impossible to deny.

My lips dragged against her neck, following a path to her ear. I nipped at her earlobe, teasing her slightly. A touch barely there. "You look like an Angel...so fucking exotic," I whispered roughly in her ears.

She shivered, a slight tremble in her posture, and I smirked.

So fucking perfect. Absolutely perfect.

I released her wrists and pulled away, watching her closely. My eyes avoided Solonik and everyone else.

I didn't know why this slave was kneeling at my feet when I had refused Solonik's proposal, but right now, at this moment, I wasn't going to complain.

As soon as I released her, her fingers moved upward toward my zipper. She purposely avoided my gaze as she pushed the zipper down.

"What are you doing?" I asked, clearly knowing her intention. She wasn't allowed to speak unless spoken to.

"Let me serve you, Master," she whispered softly. Her voice almost drowned in the screams around the room, but I still heard it.

The voice of an Angel.

Nobody could speak so softly. Nobody could make those words sound so damn sweet as they did coming from her lips.

Without thinking, I unbuckled my belt. She licked her lips, her hands slightly trembling on my thighs.

When I pushed my slacks and my boxers down a little, her eyes jumped to mine.

The corner of my lips turned up a little as she swallowed hard. I raised an eyebrow, waiting for her to move.

And she did not disappoint.

Taking my hard, pulsing length in her hand, she wrapped her fingers around me, pumping it up and down.

I hissed, my hips slightly bucking upward when she tightened her hold. With confidence like no others, her eyes still on mine, she bent her head down.

Her tongue came out and licked the head, tonguing the drop of cum there. "Ah fuck!"

She stared at me, watching my reaction as her lips parted and took my cock inside her wet, warm mouth. She sucked me deep, her tongue tracing the veins pulsing around my dick. Her head bobbed up and down, taking me deeper each time as I hit the back of her throat.

She didn't fight against the invasion. No, she welcomed it, taking as much of me as she could.

No longer able to fight with myself, I let instinct take over. My fingers wrapped around her hair, gripping it tight. My knuckles dug almost painfully into the back of her head as I dragged her forward, taking control.

She relaxed in my hold, surrendering completely as I fucked her mouth exactly like I wanted. Deep, fast, and rough. Without any control because I was a beast unleashed.

Her teeth slightly grazed the underside of my hard length and I hissed, my hips bucking upward violently. I tugged at her hair harder, thrusting in and out of her mouth as if I were fucking her pussy.

Her mouth opened wide for me as I dragged her mouth over my cock. Thrusting inside one last time, I held her head firmly as her mouth wrapped around me.

Holding her still, I forced myself down her throat. "Swallow it all," I ordered, my voice husky with my own desire.

And she did, her throat worked up as she tried to swallow every last bit of me. Some dripped down her chin, following a path down her bare tits. My eyes openly gazed upon her stunning features.

She licked me clean, and I slipped out of her mouth with a small pop. Her tongue pressed out, between her parted lips, catching any remains. With hooded eyes, I dragged a finger over my cum that covered her chest.

Pushing the wet finger past her lips, I watched her lick it clean. Her eyes fluttered closed, and she whispered, "Thank you, Master. I am honored to have served you."

For a small moment, my heart stuttered.

I didn't want her to call me *Master*. Only because it did things to me…it made me think of very depraved things I wanted to do to her. Surprisingly, I wanted my name from her lips.

With that angelic voice, I wanted her to say my name.

I had already broken one rule tonight.

Do not touch the slaves.

Too late for that.

But I was about to break another rule.

Do not buy the slaves.

By the end of the night, this little slave was going to be mine. Only mine.

Chapter 3

Maria

I stayed silent. My body locked tight, refusing to move any muscle. A frozen picture in time.

I dared not to move my eyes up. I dared not look up at this strange man with a strange voice.

The way he spoke was with authority, his voice deep and rough as it caressed my body.

I stayed kneeling down beside my Master as this new master spoke. They were talking about me, I knew that. I could feel their eyes on me.

My skin crawled with disgust. I hated it when they gazed upon my naked body, stripped bare of everything. Even my dignity. My pride.

I had nothing left.

Nothing belonged to me anymore.

I was wholly his. Every part of me belonged to him—my *Master*.

And I hated every single day of it.

I wished, prayed, and hoped for my Prince Charming to come. Maybe he would come on a beautiful white horse. He would look at me with love and sweep me away. He was going to save me from the bad men. We would ride off in the sunset, toward his castle.

And there, he would love me with his whole heart.

We would live happily ever after.

But it was only a dream. A fantasy I built up in my head so I could stay alive.

When my Master touched me, I closed my eyes and pretended he was my Prince Charming.

I kept pretending. Every single minute of my life, I pretended this was not my reality.

But sometimes it was hard. When the pain got too much, when the screams would not stop, I could not hide anymore.

When it felt like my insides were being ripped open, I could not hide. I had to face my reality.

And it was yet another day. I was naked again. Most of the time, we were kept naked.

They said it was for easier access. For them to do whatever they wanted with our bodies.

We were told to bear our marks—their marks—with pride. When our bodies were blue and green, we bore them with pride. We paraded around, showing how good our Masters were to us.

The process repeated. Day after day. Night after night.

Some of the women have been here since they were children. Others when they were only teenagers. But no one was older than twenty.

I was taken eight months ago.

Eight months ago, I was eighteen years old.

BLOOD AND ROSES

Two months ago, I turned nineteen.

Every month, Master reminded me of the date I was taken. It was our anniversary.

I kept counting the months in my head, trying not to lose that small glimpse of the outside world. Desperately trying to keep hold of the string of what was left of me.

Unlike what Master thought, I had not lost my sanity yet.

I was still very much alive.

He thought I was dead.

He thought I was the perfect slave.

He thought I was just another pet. Another doll to play with. Another puppet with whom to do whatever he wanted.

But I had not lost my hope yet.

He thought he owned me.

But he was wrong. So, so wrong.

He might own my body.

But my soul…my thoughts…they were mine.

He could not take that away from me. My soul did not belong to him. My thoughts did not belong to him.

And my heart…it would never be his.

"She is yours?"

His voice snapped me back to the present. Not my Master.

But *him*.

For an unknown reason, I almost forgot all my training and wanted to lift my head up.

I wanted to see him. To see the man whose voice had caused things to happen in my body.

After so long, I felt something. A strange shiver

down my spine.

After being numb for so long, he made me feel something.

What it was, I didn't understand.

"For now. Until I can get the highest buyer. For now, I'll just enjoy her until I decide otherwise," Master muttered drily, his fingers trailing down my spine.

I fought the urge to retch. Every time he touched me, I had to fight against myself. I had to remind myself that I was the perfect pet.

I had to accept this touch. No matter how much I hated it.

The man was silent for what felt like a very long time.

And I felt suddenly desperate for him to speak again. For him to gift me the power of his voice to silent my demons.

"Are you bidding tonight?" Master asked.

"No," the man snapped.

From my position, with me still kneeling and my forehead pressed against the hard floor, my eyes widened.

Nobody would see this small action. It was my secret.

My breath stuck in my throat. Was he not part of this cartel? Did he not buy slaves?

I listened to them talk. Master suggested the man have a night with me.

My body tightened, waiting for his response.

When he refused, I let out a small breath. So small that nobody would notice.

Was it disappointment? Or relief?

BLOOD AND ROSES

I did not how to feel. Even though I have not laid eyes on this man yet, he was making me feel out of control.

Did he not want me?

Master's friends always wanted a night with me when they visited. They would say I was their favorite. That I was beautiful.

Did that man not find me beautiful?

I felt ashamed when I realized I cared. His thoughts suddenly mattered to me.

Swallowing past the lump in my throat, I closed my eyes. I inhaled and exhaled. My muscles stayed locked as he started to walk away.

His warmth faded, leaving me numb and cold again.

Master touched my neck, caressing my back. The soft touch did not last long before his nails dug into my hips, leaving his mark. I always bore his mark.

Even my weak body felt used to it now. His beatings. The endless hours of torture.

It was painful. It hurt more than I could describe, but all I had to do was shut my mind and float away to a magical land with my Prince Charming.

His hands moved upward to my neck, and he gripped it hard. Master pulled me to my knees, but I kept my head bowed down, my eyes on the floor.

I wouldn't dare to look up. It was a mistake I had done many times. But just like a lesson was learned for every mistake, I learned my lesson too.

In a much harder way.

Master always found ways to hurt me. New creative ways, he liked to call it

His breath was close to my ear. I didn't flinch

when he licked down my neck, leaving a wet trail.

Disgust rolled off me in angry waves, yet I could do nothing.

"I want you to go there and suck his dick in that pretty mouth of yours. Make him feel good. And then I want you to come back with your mouth full of his cum."

His words were crude and angry. Dangerous and commanding.

So I did as I was commanded. For he was the Master and I was the pretty doll at his service.

There was no changing that. No matter how much my mind fought it.

No matter how much I hated it.

Getting on my hands and knees again, I kept my head bowed. He slapped my butt, and with his silent permission, I crawled toward the man.

I was halfway across the room when I realized I didn't know *who* the man was. I didn't know who I was crawling to, who I was supposed to pleasure.

It was forbidden to look into the eyes of a Master…not until we were commanded to. In that small moment, I broke the first rule.

My head tilted slightly upward, my gaze quickly scanning the room. My heart drummed wildly against my ribcage, scared that I would get caught and be punished.

All that fear and panic disappeared the second I laid eyes on the man in front of me.

He sat on the couch, only a few feet away from me. His legs were stretched open as he settled against the seat, his head tilted toward the ceiling. I could tell his eyes were closed.

BLOOD AND ROSES

My eyes tracked his movement when he tugged at his tie, almost frustrated. My breath caught in my throat and my heart accelerated again.

I did not realize I was crawling again. This time with my destination in mind.

My eyes were glued to this man. I wasn't even sure if *he* was the one. My body and mind were disconnected. It felt like an invisible pull, making me reach for him.

As I grew closer, my breathing became harder.

I felt...nervous.

My crawling halted when I was only two feet away from him. So very close. One more step and I could touch him.

But I couldn't move.

This man...he was big. I could see his muscle definition through his clothes. With his long legs, I guessed he was over six feet tall. The couch he sat on looked dainty and small compared to him.

His suit stretched over his wide chest and I gulped. My eyes went to his fists that rested on his thighs. He clenched and then unclenched his fingers.

I looked up at his face again, his eyes still closed. A few strands of his dark hair fell on his forehead, like it was stubborn and didn't want to stay in place. It looked like he hadn't shaved in a few days. The dark stubble gave him the perfect rough look.

He looked far from a gentleman.

The air around him felt colder and more intense. Even with his eyes closed, his body laid back, he spoke dominance.

His authority was loud and clear.

My Master—Valentin—was nothing compared to this man.

My Master would force his dominance on me.

But this man...without a single word, he let the world know he was the King. The master. The judge, jury, and executioner. He held all the power, and everyone else danced to his tunes.

This man...was dangerous.

He was no Prince Charming.

He was the devil in disguise.

And I had already fallen in his trap.

Swallowing my fear, my panic, and disgust, I continued to crawl forward. The seconds ticked by as I reached his legs.

My body settled between his thighs, moving effortlessly and as elegantly as I was taught. My breathing was silent, my movement slow and featherlight.

I touched his thigh.

His hand snapped forward, his fingers wrapping around my smaller wrist. My breath stuttered to a stop. My heart hammered with no control. The first touch pushed me over the edge, and I was falling...falling in the deep, dark abyss.

His hold tightened, and I knew that with a single touch, he could easily break my wrist. But he didn't.

I felt his eyes on me. My skin burned from his intense gaze, and I was so very tempted to look up...to stare into his eyes.

His thumb pressed against the inside of my wrist, and without realizing it, my head moved upward.

Our eyes met.

And the world stilled.

BLOOD AND ROSES

I was robbed of my words. I was robbed of my thoughts.

Everything and everyone froze…nothing mattered.

Only our eyes, gazing into each other. I could see my reflection in his pale grey eyes.

My naked body was visible through his eyes, and everything ended.

I saw my shame, his eyes a mirror to my soul.

I could see me…a dirty slave. Owned by another man.

With one look, just like seconds ago, everything froze…my world shifted and tilted. Reversing and finding its place again.

For a brief moment, I had forgotten who I was. But I saw myself through his eyes, and it was enough reminder.

This man wasn't my Prince Charming.

And I wasn't his sweet love.

He was a Master.

I was a slave.

And I had a job to do. A command to follow. A man to please.

Then I would return back to my place, next to my Master's feet with my mouth full of this man's cum.

I licked my lips. His eyes followed my movement, and I knew I had his full attention.

With ease and after countless times of doing this, I blinked up at him. My stomach rolled, yet I kept my focus on the task.

But being the Devil, he played with my mind again. He pulled me into his trap again.

Instead of just pushing my face against his crotch and forcing me to take his manhood like all the others, he leaned down.

His head was next to mine, his nose slightly touching my jaw. The softest touch, so sensual…so beautiful…so right.

His nose trailed down a small path, touching my jawline and my neck. I felt his breath against my skin, causing a slight shiver.

When he breathed me in, my eyes fluttered closed.

Why did I not feel repulsed by his touch? This man was affecting me…changing everything I had ever known.

My world and his were crashing together, the lines aligning and fitting together without our permission.

He dragged me closer. His thighs spread wider to accommodate me. My body pressed against his, and I melted in his embrace.

In this moment, nothing else mattered. Not the depravity of this action, nor the disgust I felt just seconds ago.

He shifted slightly, and our eyes met again. We stared silently at each other. His gaze held nothing…it was empty. A black void. Mine spoke everything loudly.

Could he see my truth? My reality?

Did he care?

Our gaze broke apart when he leaned down again. His lips touched my skin, placing kisses along the path of my neck to my ear. My body felt warm and flushed, a strange feeling building up in

BLOOD AND ROSES

the pit of my stomach.

When was the last time someone touched me so gently? When was the last time a man kissed me so softly?

He nipped gently at my earlobe, and I almost gasped. His touch was so featherlight, making me want more.

He teased me, and I craved more.

"You look like an Angel…so fucking exotic," he whispered roughly in my ear.

I shivered, a slight tremble that I knew he would notice immediately.

But there was no stopping it. His words changed everything. The same deep, rough voice as before. This man who was holding me…was the same who refused me.

You look like an Angel…so fucking exotic.

An Angel?

He thought of me as an Angel?

My cheeks heated, and my body tingled.

Nobody had ever called me an *Angel* before.

I was slave to everyone else.

But this stranger…this Devil called me Angel.

Instead of ripping my soul apart, he was giving me pieces of myself.

So I would return him the favour in the only way I knew how.

As soon as his fingers released me, I moved to his zipper. My eyes avoided his, not wanting to see my lost dignity in his.

"What are you doing?" he asked.

He knew the answer, yet he wanted me to speak. Something I was forbidden to do. I only replied to

Master, and until he gave me permission to speak, I was not allowed to utter a single word.

My Master was strict with his own rules. Fear slithered down my spine, but yet again, I pushed it away.

I broke a second rule.

"Let me serve you, Master," I whispered so softly, for his ears only.

The moment the words were out of my mouth, he started to unbuckle his belt. Instinctively, I licked my lips again.

My hands trembled on his thighs, feeling strangely nervous. He pushed his slacks down until his hard length was visible.

Oh. He was long, thick, and *hard*. The crown of his shaft was almost an angry purple, telling me he was ready for my mouth.

My eyes snapped to his. The corner of his lips turned upward in a small, knowing smirk. He waited.

He didn't push. He didn't demand.

Finally, my gaze moved down to his jutting manhood again. A very impressive size and length. There were already white droplets on the head.

I gulped and looked up at him. It seemed I couldn't keep my eyes off him. The pull he had on me was different, a little unsettling. But through the nervousness, I *liked* it. With our gaze on each other, I bent down and licked the length.

He hissed and swore loud. I watched his reaction, mesmerized by the sight of unadulterated lust on his beautiful face as I took him in my mouth.

My lips wrapped around his length, sucking him

deep. My tongue traced his pulsing veins, and his hips bucked upward, pushing himself deeper in my throat.

I didn't fight against the invasion. For the first time, I welcomed it. I took him in my mouth to give him the pleasure I wanted.

His fingers wrapped tightly around my hair, his knuckles digging painfully in my scalp as he pushed me harder and deeper down his cock. He gripped my hair tight, taking absolute control.

I relaxed against his hold, surrendering to him. He fucked my mouth, taking what he wanted.

He growled low in his chest, and my nails dug into his thighs.

It was dirty. Deep. Rough. Fast.

But he made something that I hated with a passion so sensual. I pulsed between my legs and pressed my thighs together.

Something was happening to me. He thrust in and out of my mouth, forcing me to take all of him. One last thrust, he held my head down on his cock.

I had no warning as he filled my mouth.

"Swallow it all," he ordered, his voice husky with his desire.

Without a second thought, I did. Without thinking of the consequences, I swallowed every single drop, pleasing him with every lick and swallow.

My throat worked against the effort, some cum dripping down my chin. His eyes traveled down my breasts, following the wet trail his fluid was leaving.

After giving him one last lick, he released my head and pulled away. I licked my lips, making sure

I had gotten everything.

For some strange reason, I wanted to please this man.

His eyes were hooded with need as he dragged a finger up my breast and pushed his cum back into my mouth. My lips wrapped around his finger, sucking it clean.

Was he happy? I wondered if I pleased him.

My eyes fluttered closed when he dragged his wet fingers against my lips.

"Thank you, Master. I am honored to have served you."

A soft whisper. Months and months of practice had drilled this in my head.

Always thank the Master for honoring us with their cum.

I hated him. I hated thanking them for making us dirty and ugly.

I was so lost in the moment...in *him*...that I forgot who and where I was.

A slave. I was a slave.

Don't forget it. Never forget it. Don't lose yourself.

I had to remind myself again. Over and over.

No matter how beautifully dark this man was, he was the Devil. No better than any other man in this room.

No better than Valentin Solonik.

I felt him touch my chin, tilting my head up. My eyes stayed closed, refusing to give him the small glimpse into my soul.

"Look at me."

My eyes snapped open at his order.

I am a slave. He is a Master.

Don't forget it. Never forget it. Don't lose yourself.

If I did as I was told, my punishments would be less. If I pleased them, I would have a good night of sleep.

If they liked me, I would get to eat some bread and cheese.

If my screams of pain were their new favorite music, I would get water.

I am a slave. He is a Master.

He was not my Prince Charming.

Don't forget it. Never forget it. Don't lose yourself.

His grey eyes stared down at me, his head cocked to the side. His curiosity burned my skin.

His warmth was hurting me. I no longer wanted it.

"Why did your eyes suddenly turn empty, pretty Angel?"

His words caressed me…and then cut through my skin, forcing their way into my heart.

I was falling into his dark trap again.

My lips pressed together, refusing to answer. He raised an eyebrow, the tip of his finger gently tapping my chin.

"Are you refusing to answer me?"

I swallowed and wanted to close my eyes. But his intense gaze wouldn't let me.

Shaking my head, I kept silent.

"Then answer me," he demanded quietly.

Our faces were mere inches apart. He leaned forward, our breaths mixing together, our lips almost touching.

"Speak," he said again.

I didn't. What could I say?

Small moments of stubbornness, just like this one, have always gotten me into terrible punishments.

But they were all worth it.

I showed them, silently, that they would never control me fully. My mind was still mine. My heart and soul still belonged to me.

"I want to hear that beautiful voice again."

My heart cracked. The play of his words was music to my ears.

Beautiful voice.

He thought I had a beautiful voice?

Did I have a beautiful voice?

My lips parted against my will. I wanted to hear my voice. I wanted to hear the beauty he was speaking of.

Master taught me that I was ugly. Everything about me was dirty.

But the Devil...was saying something different. So very different.

Confusion clouded my mind as I breathed, ready to speak. For him. Only for him.

But my words never made it past my lips.

"I see my slave has served you well."

I closed my eyes at the sound of Master's voice. He was back. And he just shattered the small world the devil and I had built together.

The man released his hold on my chin, and I immediately felt his loss. Inside my head, I curled into myself harder, hiding away.

BLOOD AND ROSES

My eyes snapped open when he touched me again. His gaze was still on mine as he caressed the top of my head. He combed his fingers through the length of my black hair.

My heart stuttered at the sweet touch. Too sweet for the devil.

His palm cradled the back of my head, and he pressed me down until my cheek was lying on top of his thigh.

My body was still between his legs, still cradled in the safety of his embrace. He stroked my cheek now, and my body relaxed. My eyes closed as I melted into his warmth.

I never wanted him to stop touching me.

The world…every single ugliness in it vanished into thin air.

I floated far, far away…in a magical land.

Where the devil was my Prince Charming.

Where we lived happily ever after.

But all of that came to screeching halt. Too quickly I was snatched away from my happily ever after and dragged back into the dark abyss.

A bottomless pit that I kept falling into…with no one cushioning my fall.

My ears registered his voice, his words…his demands.

"Go the bedroom. I want you on the bed, waiting for me."

Chapter 4

Lyov

I hated the way she cast her eyes away. I hated how she suddenly closed off, as if finally realizing what happened between us.

I didn't want her ashamed. That was the last thing I wanted, and being the fucker I was, that was the only thing I accomplished.

What did I expect? Fuck her pretty fuckable mouth like a starved beast and expect her to fall right into my lap?

And in a place like this? Where other women's and men's screams could be heard?

The look in her eyes glassed over, and I just knew she wasn't with me anymore.

The moment between us was broken.

She looked down, focusing on something besides my face. I quickly fastened my pants again before touching her chin in an attempt to bring her pretty blue eyes on me again.

"Look at me," I ordered, my voice still a little

BLOOD AND ROSES

gruff from my recent orgasm.

Her eyes snapped up, and I almost smiled. The effect I had on her was undeniable.

I had her in the palms of my hands, no matter how much she fought it.

"Why did your eyes suddenly turn empty, pretty Angel?" My question was a whisper, only for her ears.

A small widening of her eyes told me that my words hit her right where I'd aimed. Her tattered heart.

But her lips refused to move, refused to answer me. She refused to give me her angelic voice, and it just made me want it more.

I wanted this forbidden moment.

"Are you refusing to answer me?" I questioned slowly, using my Master's voice.

She was, in fact, forbidden to speak to me unless Valentin gave her permission. But then again, I was also a Master. The owner of this fucked-up cartel. It didn't matter what Valentin's rules were.

My power was greater than his.

And I would use it, however I wanted, to have this Angel.

Even if it was fucked up...even if I were pushing for something so wrong, it felt *right*.

By the end of the night, I would own her. Mind, body, and soul.

No one else would say otherwise. Not even her. It wasn't her choice. Not anymore.

"Then answer me," I demanded again.

When she only stared at me, blinking slowly, her face a little flushed, I asked again.

No answer.

I wondered if she was scared. Of me?

My heart tightened a little bit at the thought. Unlike the others, I didn't want her fear. I didn't want her tears or screams of pain.

I wanted her moans of pleasure as I fucked her with my tongue. My fingers. And maybe if she was a good girl, I'd give her my cock.

I wanted her voice...her lips turned up in a smile. How would her laugh sound?

Were my words making any difference, or was she too far gone? She didn't look like the other women here. The way she'd looked at me, I saw that her resolves were not fully broken yet.

Valentin Solonik hadn't clipped her wings yet. No matter what he believed, if she had the freedom, she would fly. She would soar higher into the sky if only she could.

They taught her that she was nothing. But I wanted to prove her wrong. I wanted to show her the beauty of intimacy. The pleasure of a man and woman mating.

I wanted to give her warmth.

I wanted to make her feel.

Her thoughts only of me. Her lips wording my name. Her heart beating with the need to please me. And in return, I would give her whatever she wanted.

Give and take. A balance of power.

It was a quick thought, a brisk yearning, my cold heart opening just a little to make place for hers.

She had me captured, my attention all on her. The Angel holding the Devil in chains.

She was the captor. I was the captive.

She was the Master. And I was slave to her warm blue eyes that held so much pain.

I saw her lips moving, but no words could be heard. My lips turned up in a small smirk, knowing I had finally broken through the barrier.

She wanted to speak. For me.

I waited as she tried again, but it was too late.

Our moment was broken by a third voice. One that I wanted to forever cut off. If I ripped his tongue out, then he wouldn't make any sound.

"I see my slave has served you well."

Only sad part was that I couldn't do it. Not yet, anyway.

He was too big of an asset to my business to kill him off.

After all, everything was business. Everything was a game to play.

And I needed to play this game carefully so that the final move was mine.

I looked down at *my* slave to see her eyes closed, a look of regret washing across her face. I knew if her eyes were open, I would see the pain there.

She was just as heartbroken that our moment had vanished.

I mentally huffed. *Not so fast, little Angel.* Our moment would never be broken, not until I decided so.

Releasing her chin, I saw her shoulders slump down. Ah, I got a demanding slave on my hands. It appeared she didn't like when I wasn't touching her. *Don't worry, Angel, I don't like it when I'm not touching you, either.*

My palm cradled the back of her head, and I pressed down until her cheek was lying on my thigh. She let out the tiniest sigh that anyone else would have missed. But I didn't.

I felt everything from her. The slight shiver. The small sigh. And I didn't miss the small tilt of her lips.

Her body was cradled between my legs as I stroked her neck and then her cheek. She sighed again, and I felt her body going limp, relaxing against my touch.

She gave me the one thing everyone else wanted but couldn't have.

Her submission.

And it was now more potent than ever. It had been fought for, and I won. Fair and square.

"You sent her to me?" I asked quietly, so as not to disturb her.

My eyes made contact with Solonik's, waiting for his answer. He nodded with a dirty smirk, like he'd won something.

He moved forward, coming closer to *my* Angel. His foot lifted up as if to touch her, but I swiftly moved, so her body was safely hidden in my embrace.

The tip of his shoe made contact with my leg instead, and I watched his eyes widen in surprise.

He stepped back, an eyebrow raised in question. "Yeah, I sent her to you. I thought maybe you need some relaxation. But unfortunately for *my* slave here, she broke my rule."

He *tsked* in fake disappointment, but I could tell that her breaking the rules made him excited. What

BLOOD AND ROSES

a sick fucker.

"What rule?" I demanded, getting angrier with each passing second.

He wasn't laying a hand on her. If he as much as dared to do so, he would have no fucking hands by the end of the night.

Unfortunately for him, I always kept my promises.

"She was ordered to come to me with her mouth full of your cum. I see that's not the case anymore," he drawled lazily.

My throat worked up as I tried to stay seated. Fury built inside of me, as well as disgust, as I fought against the urge to puke all over his expensive shoes and suit.

"You know what happens when a slave disobeys. She will need to be punished. And what a great night to punish her. We have everyone present. May this be a lesson learned for all the other slaves," he continued slowly, watching for my reaction.

And I gave him one.

"No," I said firmly, stopping his tirade of useless words.

He sputtered, his eyes moving back and forth between her and me. "What do you mean?" Solonik hissed, his face turning a deep shade of red. "She is mine! I can do whatever I want with her."

"No, she isn't," I replied calmly while he completely lost it.

His lips curled in distaste. "Are you fucking serious right now? Lyov, she sucked your dick. That's all. Don't act like she's carrying your fucking child."

41

"She is not yours. Not anymore," I continued over him.

She was never yours to begin with.

"Like hell! I own her," he bellowed.

My eyes moved back to my Angel, only to see that her eyes were closed, like she had fallen asleep. *Good.* I didn't want her to witness this.

I stared up again, and everyone's attention was now on us. Well, it was about to get nasty for Solonik.

"I'm buying her."

My voice was loud and uttered clear for everyone to hear. There were gasps and mumbling around the crowd.

For years, this business had been operated, and I had never touched a slave, let alone buy one.

But there is always a first for everything.

All I knew was that I wasn't leaving The Royalist without my blue-eyed Angel.

"No. I'm not selling her," Solonik said, his fingers curling into fists.

My fingers continued to caress her hair as I regarded Solonik. He looked like a man possessed.

Too bad for him, I was a man's worst nightmare. If I wanted something, I'd take. And I wanted *her*.

"Too bad. I'm buying her. Let's do this the easy way. Either I walk out of here with her and you gain a couple of million, or we solve this the hard way. And trust me, Solonik, you don't want to choose the second choice." I spoke low but just loud enough for everyone to hear.

He had the ultimatum, and it was his choice. But whatever happened, I was walking away the winner.

BLOOD AND ROSES

"I'm walking out of here with her. Either you take the money, or you become a poor man overnight. Choose wisely. I am being *very* generous here."

"Solonik, you don't want to test Ivanshov," Gavrikov called out, laughing quietly. "Tonight is not the night. Give him the girl and let him make you a rich man. What more do you want?"

Behind Solonik's back, he nodded, letting me know I had his support.

"It's not an easy buy, Lyov. She is my most prized possession. You do realize what you are asking me to give up, right?" he hissed, looking down at my Angel.

I wanted to gouge his eyes out for even looking at her.

Not giving him an answer, I only leveled him with a glare. He released a long breath before tugging at his tie. "She costs a lot. You can't afford her. Not in one night."

Nice try, bastard.

I raised an eyebrow while chuckling quietly. "I'm sure I can afford whatever price. You seem to forget who owns this place, Solonik."

He stayed quiet, looking at me with hateful eyes. I stared back, with much more loathing in mine.

"How much? One million? One point five? That's more than anyone would give you," I bargained.

All I wanted was to get the fuck out of his place. Yet here I was, bargaining the price of my Angel.

But she was priceless.

Only I knew that. Everyone else thought she was

an object to be bought.

But I saw her with wings, flying…laughing.

Loving me.

My eyes widened at the thought, my breath stuck in my throat.

No. What the fuck, Lyov?

Keep her. Fuck her. Give her what she wants. But never love her.

I couldn't love or be loved.

A cough brought me back to the present. Solonik smirked and then laughed. "You got yourself a good one, Lyov."

My brows furrowed in confusion as I waited for him to elaborate.

"She is a virgin."

The world stilled. Everything halted to a slow pace and every noise faded away.

I could only hear the sound of my breathing and the roar of my blood rushing through my ears.

My eyes were drawn to her as she used me for comfort. My fingers were still stroking her cheeks, Solonik's voice still vibrating through my ears.

She is a virgin.

Impossible! How could she be a virgin? In a place like this?

The first thing she would have lost when she came to a place like this would be her virginity. Then her dignity. And lastly her mind.

I looked back at Solonik, and I just knew…he wasn't lying. He wouldn't lie about this.

Remembering the shy look, the innocence in her gaze, I realized that my little Angel was untouched in places that only I would touch now.

BLOOD AND ROSES

Mine.

My heart was surprisingly at a steady pace, but every instinct in me was roaring for her.

Territorial.

Possessive.

All fucking mine.

The need to claim her hit me harder than before. The beast within me yowled with possessiveness.

The realization had lust, intensity, and every other fucked-up emotion coming to the surface.

I welcomed them, embraced them.

Just like I was going to embrace *her*.

I swallowed past the lump in my throat, finally finding my voice again.

"How much?" I asked simply, desperate to get this over with.

"Two million," he said loudly.

Everyone went silent at the price. Not even a virgin cost that much. Solonik was pushing it, hoping I would say *no*.

The maximum price for a virgin was one point five. And not a lot even went for that price.

Two million...it was out of the question.

Solonik knew that. He smirked triumphantly, crossing his arms.

What he didn't realize was that whatever price he would have laid on the table, I would say yes.

She was *mine*.

And God forbid anyone refused me...they wouldn't like the consequences.

"Fine," I said.

He lost his smile, his arms falling to his side. "What?" he sputtered.

45

Isaak hid a laugh behind his fist while Agron and Gavrikov snickered.

"Nice one, Lyov!" Agron called out, winking.

"But I want to check for myself." Turning toward the blue-eyed Angel, I gripped the back of her neck.

A possessive hold to show her exactly who was in control. Not her. Not any of those disgusting bastards staring at her naked body like it was theirs to look at. And sure as hell not Solonik.

"Go the bedroom. I want you on the bed, waiting for me."

Chapter 5

Lyov

I watched her slowly coming back, her eyes fluttering open. She lost her smile as she gazed up at me with soulless eyes.

I had to bite back a curse, knowing that in some ways I had hurt her already fragile heart. She thought I was no different than those bastards lusting after her body.

The problem? I actually wasn't better.

Only because I didn't only want her body. I wanted her everything. Until she had nothing left to give.

I was selfish that way.

Did it matter? No. I wanted her…so I would take her.

This Angel quickly became an obsession that was going to break me in the end. She was both light and darkness.

Me? I was only darkness. Our two worlds were about to clash together in the only way it could, and there was no going back.

The moment I had laid eyes on her, she belonged to me.

She slowly moved from between my legs, her gaze still on mine, silently begging. My finger trailed down her cheek, softly caressing her skin. Her face moved with my hand, like a kitten seeking warmth.

My thumb brushed over her lush lips, and she blinked up at me, the moment broken yet again. Her eyes went to Solonik, and she swallowed in fear.

I tapped her chin, wanting her attention back on me. I was her only concern now. No one else mattered.

I was her everything. Her whole fucking world.

"Go," I said simply.

Her training finally kicked in at the authority in my voice. Her head bowed down, giving respect like she would give any Master.

I didn't need her bowing down to me. We would talk about that later.

Right now, I just wanted to get her out of everyone's sight. Giving her the smallest respect and dignity back. It wasn't much, but it was the only thing I could give. For now.

The moment she stepped out of this place, her whole fucking world would change. The lines breaking, reversing, and then aligning again. New rules to play by.

She was about to learn what it meant to be *mine*.

Her hands went to the floor, her ass in the air as she prepared to crawl to one of the bedrooms. My voice stopped her movement.

BLOOD AND ROSES

Actually, it stopped every fucking movement around the room. Dead silence. Nobody moved. No sound. I was pretty sure they stopped fucking breathing too.

"Walk," I demanded, my voice coming out harsher than I intended.

The red blinding fury was building up every passing second. Seeing her crawling on her knees just made me want to shoot someone and cause a blood bath.

Her legs were slightly shaking as she stood up, her eyes purposely avoiding Solonik. The slow walk to the bedroom was excruciatingly painful. It was too late when I realized that making her walk was the worst decision.

Her bare body was full on display, her blinding beauty for everyone to see.

When the door closed, I released a long, shuddering breath that I hadn't realize I was holding.

Solonik turned to me, his lips curled in anger. "You're going to regret this," he hissed.

"No, I won't. And you won't, either. You will be a richer man by the end of the night. It's time to party, Valentin," I said, getting off the couch.

After fixing my suit, I winked at him. "Enjoy the rest of your night."

I know I will.

Keeping those words to myself, I marched toward the room where my Angel had just disappeared.

No seconds were wasted as I opened the door and walked inside, making sure to lock it behind me. Nobody was disturbing us tonight.

This moment…it will only be ours. Away from all the depravity of the world. Away from all the harshness…our reality.

Just us.

My eyes met darkness, and I blinked in confusion. My hand moved blindly across the wall, trying to find the light.

When I finally did, the room was instantly illuminated, and my eyes fell upon the beauty waiting for me in bed.

Our connection was fast. Breathtaking almost. One that left me confused and reeling.

My mind was playing games with my heart.

I had a choice. Fall into her trap or play the game like a master in disguise.

My gaze moved up her body, taking in everything laid out for me. She was on her back, her legs pressed together, with her arms on either side of her.

She was stiff, looking so small and scared. Like an Angel laid out for a sacrifice.

In her mind, this was a sacrifice. I was just the Devil. The one who was going to rob her innocence.

Little did she know.

I took a step forward, finally making my choice. Smiling at myself, I took another step.

With each step, my heart beat just a little faster…harder. With each step, I fought against the urge to claim her.

I watched her chest rise and fall with each breath. Her fingers curled into fists at her sides as I approached. Her eyes stayed on the ceiling,

BLOOD AND ROSES

purposely avoiding me.

She was scared.

I wondered if I could get her excited by the end of the night.

My lips tilted up. That wouldn't be hard to accomplish.

Stopping beside the bed, I only gazed into her face. She swallowed nervously, still not meeting my eyes.

The black mask was covering her real beauty, and I wanted it gone. I felt her suck in a deep breath when I bent forward, my fingers latching around the corner of the mask and slowly removing it.

Slowing uncovering her for my eyes.

The mask fell on the bed beside her hips as her eyes fluttered close. Her long lashes cast shadows on her cheeks.

She was...beautiful.

Breathtaking.

Sensational.

Exquisite.

Angelic.

I was at a loss for words as my eyes caressed her face. Everything was fair in war...and this game was won by me.

Poor Solonik. If only he had realized what he just lost...and what I just gained.

Slowly, not to startle her, I sat on the bed. She stiffened, her eyes pinching closed. Leaning closer, I reached forward, my fingers hovering over her cheeks.

Not touching, not moving...yet it still felt like I was caressing her.

Her warmth called to me as I finally and slowly caressed down her cheek. Unexpectedly, her eyes flew open, and she blinked up at me in surprise.

"Hi," I whispered, sounding so fucking stupid.

She only stared at me, looking confused. "You are so beautiful; do you know that?" I said softly, still touching her face.

Slowly, her head shook *no*.

"Well, you are. It pisses me off that nobody ever said that to you, but you are so fucking beautiful," I continued, still staring into those blue eyes.

While she remained silent, they spoke volumes. They told me everything I needed to know.

It was so hard ignoring the ache that was currently resting between my legs, when all I wanted to do was take what was *mine*, but tonight was going to be different.

"I'm not going to hurt you," I whispered, leaning just a little closer. "That's not why we're in here."

She cocked her head to the side, waiting. "I want you to speak…say something. I want to hear your voice again," I finished.

This time it was me waiting…for her.

She opened her mouth and then snapped it shut, her eyes flying to the door in panic. My body moved quickly so that I was between her and the door, so that I was the only thing she was seeing.

"Solonik's command doesn't matter anymore. You don't have to worry about him. Ever," I growled, the anger fueling again.

A ghost of a smile lit her lips before it was quickly gone and she was staring at me in suspicion.

Great…just great. She didn't believe me. Of

course, she didn't believe me. I just bought her. Well, not yet...but still.

My hand moved up, moving a few stray strands of hair away from her face. "You have nothing to be scared of."

It was the truth, and now I just needed her to believe me.

I moved forward so I was lying down beside her. With an arm around her waist, I turned her toward me so we were both lying side by side, facing each other.

Her naked body pressed against my fully clothed one, and I fought back a groan as my dick jumped forward in excitement.

Settle down, junior. Now is not the fucking time!

Her breathing came out harder, her palms now resting against my chest. She stayed frozen, stiff as a board, as I struggled with my own self-control.

Leaning closer, our foreheads now touched—a soft touch that had her eyes widening. I wondered, when was the last time she experienced a gentle touch?

"Will you speak? For me?" I asked, entwining our fingers together, our hands now against my chest.

What was it about her that piqued my interest so much, I didn't know. She was intriguing, and I wanted to uncover every single layer of her.

An unpredictable connection that was shifting the lines of my world.

It had nothing to do with her beauty, or what was between her legs, and was being offered to me on a silver platter.

It had everything to do with her mind.

Because I knew…she was very much alive. She just needed a little nudge and her wings would open wide, ready to fly.

"What do you want me to say, Master?"

My eyes widened before I quickly got myself under control. "You spoke."

Confused eyes met mine. "You commanded me to," she whispered, fear creeping its way into her eyes. "I am sorry, Master. I shouldn't have spoken. It is my fault."

"No!" I snapped.

Her body flinched, and I mentally chastised myself. "No," I continued more softly. "I want you to speak. But only if you want to. It has to be your choice."

"I am for your pleasure. What you want me to say, I will say."

Her turbulent eyes told me that was the last thing she wanted…*to only be for my pleasure.*

"Tonight is different, little Angel," I started, letting her go. She laid on her back again, and I propped myself on my elbows, still staying close so our warmth was mixed together.

"How so, Master?" she asked quietly, almost shyly.

"First, don't call me Master," I ordered, leveling her with a look that held no discussion.

She nodded speechlessly, looking quickly to please me.

"Good girl," I returned, running a fingertip down her naked side.

Her breathing accelerated again, and my eyes

were drawn to her chest. Her nipples were erected with cold air, but now her skin was taking on a rosy color, her whole body blushing in the most beautiful way.

Fuck! My cock throbbed painfully. I could take her right there, and she would let me.

I could fuck her virgin pussy, and she wouldn't utter a sound. She would be all mine...

So damn tempting. A perfect sight that almost made me come in my pants like a horny teenager.

But I still willed my cock down.

"What's your name?" I asked, moving my eyes to her face again.

She licked her lips, her gaze shifting away for a small moment. "Master named me Rose. Sometimes I am slave 367."

My heart stuttered as she spoke about herself for the first time. She didn't give me the answer I wanted...Instead, she gave me the answer every other fucker out there was given.

Master named me Rose. Sometimes I am slave 367.

How many times had she repeated those words?

"No," I breathed, leaning forward so she had no choice but to look into my eyes again. "Your real name. What's your real name?"

She swallowed, while the pain reflecting from those gorgeous blue eyes broke my heart. I was a bastard, a thief, a killer...yet one tiny woman I just met had the power to make me feel...to break me.

"It is forbidden," she whispered so softly that I almost missed it.

"Will you not grant me this wish?" I asked, my

finger trailing up her side again.

With my lips hovering above hers, I whispered, "*Please.*"

She stared at me silently, her luscious lips parting.

"*Maria.*"

A single word with a single breath…so softly spoken. A whisper that made it to my ears.

Maria.

Fuck, even her name was beautiful. How was that possible?

"Maria," I breathed, our lips inches apart, yet not touching. "You have a beautiful name. It suits you," I continued when she stayed strangely quiet.

She ducked her head down shyly but not before I saw her smile.

"From now on, you will only be addressed as Maria."

Her body stiffened. I could feel her pulling away from me, her mind shutting down quickly. The windows were closing, leaving me outside in the dark.

"It is not allowed. Master will never accept it."

Her broken whisper made me want to rage. For her sake, I took a deep breath, and I tried to speak as gently as I could.

"Solonik does not matter to you anymore. What he thinks is not your problem anymore. He no longer commands you," I said through gritted teeth.

Her head snapped up, almost hitting me in the process. With wide eyes, she stared at me in confusion.

My arm went around her waist, pulling her

BLOOD AND ROSES

closer, holding her captive. "You should only care what I think now. What I want. Everything else does not matter. From now on, my words will be the only thing that you listen to, not any other fucker out there."

Her eyebrows furrowed for a moment before her eyes lightened. "You are my…Master now?"

Ah, fuck this shit!

My jaw tightened as I gritted my teeth, but I gave her the answer she wanted. It was part truth anyway.

"Yes."

Her breath was stuck in her throat before she let it out in a loud whoosh.

"You are mine now, *Maria*."

I purposely used her name, watching her reaction. She surprised me when her lips tilted up in a small ghost smile.

"I like that," she breathed gently, our eyes clashing together.

It didn't matter which part she liked…whether it was her name or the fact that I proclaimed she was mine.

But in a matter of seconds, her quiet, sweet acceptance broke every fucking self-control I fought against. The urge to claim what was mine hit me harder than before.

My fingers dug into her hips, not so hard as to leave pain, but enough to let her know who was in control. Our lips were close, only inches apart.

I stayed above her, not moving. She breathed, watching me through half-lidded eyes. My other hand came up to her cheek, my thumb stroking the softness gently.

"I didn't plan for this. I didn't come into this room for this, but I can't seem to stop myself, little Angel," I said, my voice huskier than before. I should have been a better man and stopped this.

But every single sensibility was gone. There was no point controlling my body or the fiery lust coursing through my body for this woman.

So I turned off my mind and focused only on what was next to me.

I focused only on her.

No self-control. I let myself go as my lips made a slow descent toward hers.

She stopped breathing as our lips touched. Or was it me who stopped breathing?

It didn't matter though, because the second our lips touched, a jolt of electrifying desire shot through me.

The connection was fierce and electrifying. Scary yet it felt so…right.

My lips moved over her, tentatively at first, until I wanted more. I pressed harder just a little bit, and she gasped so softly, her lips parting.

It gave me the perfect move. My tongue slipped past her lips, tasting her. She was slow, her hands creeping up to my arms, holding onto me for dear life.

And I let her.

I let myself be her anchor while I drowned in her.

Every touch, every breath…every swirl of my tongue jolted my heart into beating faster. The lust became fiercer until all I felt was her.

When her lips moved against my own, the world slammed to a stop. And then it was spinning wildly, driving me crazy.

She was kissing me back, her lips tentative, slow, inexperienced, gentle but a kiss nonetheless.

I froze, letting her control the kiss. Her mouth feathered over mine. Even through the layer of clothing, I felt her nails biting into my arm.

This felt so much more.

Her touch moved upward slowly, tracing my arm up to my neck. Against my own will, I was moving with her.

My fingers trailed up her naked body as I started kissing her again. Her tongue met mine, dancing together, kissing, mating, loving.

Our bodies fell together, the pieces falling into place. It was strange…my mind refusing to accept it, but my heart welcomed it.

Stupidly, without thinking, I let my heart be in control this time.

My hand slipped behind her neck, pulling her upward, the kiss deeper and harder now.

She moaned.

A soft croaky moan coming from deep within her broke every single control. The beast was unleashed as I pushed her on her back, my body looming over hers.

A predator trapping his prey.

I didn't give her time to think before I claimed her lips again, wanting more of everything.

I wanted to draw her moans from her throat, wanting to hear her sound of pleasure. Pleasure that I was giving her.

Sucking on her lower lip, I pulled it between my teeth, biting softly. She moaned again, her body moving restlessly underneath mine.

My eyes opened to find hers closed, her head thrown back as she savored our kiss. Maybe her first kiss.

My lips left hers. "I didn't plan this, Maria. I wasn't going to touch you, but *fuck*, I can't stop myself. I want you so fucking much," I panted with each breath.

Her eyes snapped open, but I was kissing her again, drinking in her gasps and moans.

"Do you feel it? Do you feel me?" I growled, putting her body closer to mine.

My knees pushed her legs apart, my lower half settling between her parted thighs. I thrust my hardness between her legs, wanting her to feel *me*.

She pulled back, her body shaking, her red swollen lips parted, yet no sound was made.

Only my clothes separated us…my cock from her pussy. It would be so easy to take her, fuck her right there, have her virgin blood on the white sheet, showing everyone that she was mine.

But this wasn't about me.

How could it be about me when I had someone as divine and exquisite as Maria underneath my body, her mind and heart willing?

Her breathing came out in harsh pants as my hands moved over her body. My fingers trailed over her right breast, my thumb circling the erect nipple.

Her back bowed, her eyes widening in shock. "You feel it," I rasped.

With my eyes still on hers, I bent my head down

BLOOD AND ROSES

and took her nipple between my lips.

I tongued the tip and then sucked it, watching her every reaction. She didn't disappoint.

Her lips parted, eliciting another moan. I circled the tip with my tongue, my teeth lightly grazing it.

"Oh," she whispered, her hands going to my hair.

Her body moved with mine as she pushed her breast into my mouth, demanding more.

I chuckled against her skin, giving her whatever she wanted. My lips moved to the other breast, same attention given.

Cupping her other tit, I squeezed just a little before pinching her nipple, toying with the tip.

It drove her crazy, the mixture of my fingers and lips. Cold and warm. I gave her both.

"Do you like that, sweet Maria? Do you like having someone suck on your tits?" I said, our eyes meeting.

She stared at me with a hooded expression, her mind filled with desire. Her breathing turned into gasps as my fingers trailed down the swell of her breast, cupping it and then moving lower.

I trailed her ribs, my touch featherlight. My touch left her wanting more, and that was exactly what I wanted.

I wanted her to want me…to beg me.

I continued the pattern downward as my lips moved upward to her neck, sucking on the skin, torturing it with my kisses. Biting down on her soft skin, I left my mark.

She screamed…not in pain. Far from it.

"Have you ever had someone finger fuck you?" I

asked, my voice sounding harsher even to my own ears. "Have you ever had someone play with your clit, make you gush all over their fingers?"

She moaned in response, her head thrashing to the sides as my fingers moved lower. Down her hips, then her belly button, teasing her gently there.

And then down, right over her pussy. "What about a man's mouth? Have you ever had a man's tongue fucking your pussy? Deep and rough…making you come with just a flick of his tongue over your rosy clit?"

"Wh…what?" she gasped, her back leaving the bed again as I continued to torture her nipple.

I pulled away slightly, seeing that it was now a deep red color. Beautiful. Just fucking perfect.

"I'll take that as a no," I whispered huskily before meeting her eyes. "But then again, there is always time for *firsts*."

She could only stare at me, her chest moving up and down with each harsh breath. I smirked at her beautiful sensual expression, and my body moved lower.

Her fingers dug into my shoulders as my mouth hovered over her pussy. It glistened with wetness. I trailed my finger up her slit and then showed her my wet finger.

"Is this your first time too?"

She gasped, her mouth falling open. "Another first, Maria." Chuckling, I sucked the finger into my mouth, tasting her.

"Wet and sweet. But not wet enough," I said with a raised eyebrow. "We will have to rectify that."

With wide eyes, she watched me dip my finger to her core again. My thumb circled her tiny nub, and she let out a strangled cry, her head falling back against the pillow.

She squirmed under my touch, her hips moving of their own accord. Her body was begging me.

Her moans told me *yes*.

So I gave her what we both wanted.

She cried out when my mouth covered her core. Her hips bucked upward, her fingers tugging harder at my hair.

I placed a hand over her stomach, pressing down and stopping her movement. Holding her immobile for every torturous swirl of my tongue.

I licked her from top to bottom, tonguing her wetness like a starving man. The sweetest I ever had. I sucked her clit, my teeth slightly grazing.

Her legs opened wider for me, and I smirked against her quivering wetness. I dragged another moan from her, loving her breathless sounds

I traced different patterns, creating a road map with my tongue. She fucking loved it and begged for me.

"Please."

A soft whisper I almost missed.

Her body was tight as a bow-string, waiting for me to give her the release she desperately wanted.

My fingers spread her lips as my tongue coaxed her hard nub. It hardened under my ruthless attack. She creamed more, and I licked it up.

"Fuck, you taste so good, Angel. I could have you for breakfast, lunch, and dinner and I would be a happy man," I rasped against her inner thigh.

Her nails dug into my neck, and I returned my lips to where she wanted me.

I slipped a finger inside her, just the tip. My gaze moved upward as I gauged her reaction.

Her head was thrown back in desire, her eyes pinched closed. I pushed just a little deeper as her thighs trembled. She was tight as I slipped my finger out and pushed the tip in again.

She is a virgin.

Well, we were about to find out the truth, Solonik.

I continued to lick her as I pushed a finger in again.

Her thighs locked around my head, moan after moan spilling from her.

Just a little bit deeper…I watched her tight core suck my finger in. I could hear how wet she was, and her scent was fucking intoxicating.

My tongue latched around her clit, sucking hard just as my finger met with the resistance I was looking for.

Virgin.

Maria screamed, her orgasm hitting her by my voiceless command. She gushed into my mouth, and I licked up every last bit of cream she gifted me.

Removing my finger, I pushed my tongue in. Not far, but enough to draw another orgasm from her as I pressed my thumb over her clit.

Her whole body was shaking, and I heard quiet sniffles. My head snapped up, and I realized she was no longer holding onto me.

Her hands were pressed to her face as she

BLOOD AND ROSES

sobbed. Pulling away from her spread thighs, I wiped my chin with the back of my hand.

Her legs fell lifelessly on the bed, her body languid. But her crying pulled at my heart strings.

It fucking *hurt*.

Quickly moving so that I was lying on my back, I pulled her into my arms, her body a blanket over mine.

She curled into my embrace, hiding her face into my neck. Her tears were endless as I soothed her. Sweet words and gentle caresses.

"You were so good, Angel. So beautiful. So perfect. You amaze me," I whispered in her ear. "You are perfect."

Time passed, and I didn't know how long we stayed like that. I had gotten the answers I wanted, but my sweet Angel was left broken in my arms.

When her tears finally diminished, I nudged her chin up. Our eyes met. Her blue ones were filled with tears, looking so fucking beautiful. She took my breath away.

"Did I hurt you?" I asked softly, wiping away her tears. She pressed her cheek into my palm, and I smiled.

"No," she whispered back, her voice a little croaky.

"Then why are you crying?" I pushed just a little bit.

"Because I have…never felt this way," Maria answered slowly, gazing up at me with soft eyes.

"And how did you feel?"

She stared silently. I stared back, waiting.

Finally, her lips parted, and she spoke.

And yet again, she knew exactly how to spin my world around.

"Alive."

My throat closed up, but she continued.

"Beautiful. Treasured. Special."

She touched my cheek gently. "Many men have touched me, yet nobody has ever made me feel this way. They would only take…never give. But you? You gave me something instead of taking."

Our foreheads touched, our lips millimeters apart. "Thank you," she whispered.

She was thanking me…yet I was no better than them. What a cruel world this was. Sometimes the monsters are right there in front of our eyes and we don't see them.

And just like that, Maria was blinded.

I was betraying her. I was feeding her lies, yet I couldn't bring myself to stop.

I wanted that look in her eyes, the one telling me that I was everything. I wanted that look for however long I could have it.

And I was not ready to lose it yet.

So I let my Angel believe this lie. I let her believe that I was different.

Our lips touched in the softest kiss. It was one that was achingly slow. My hardened cock was still aching and begging for attention, but I refused to focus on it.

"The night is almost coming to an end," I said as we came apart for air. Her eyes glassed over with pain and sorrow before closing.

"Don't worry, little Angel. This is not the end. It's just the beginning. You're mine now. Tonight is

BLOOD AND ROSES

your last night here. I am taking you away."

My voice got her attention, her eyes opening again. Giving her a small smile, I placed a kiss on her forehead, letting my lips linger there for a moment longer.

"Let's get out of here," I muttered, helping her out of bed.

I kept a hold on her wrist. With her behind me, we walked out of the room. All eyes were on us, and Maria moved closer, hiding behind me, using me as her shield.

Solonik came forward, his mouth opening in protest. The anger in his eyes was undeniable.

Raising a hand, I stopped him before he even started. I didn't have time for his bullshit.

"Two point five. Take it or leave it. I don't care. But I am leaving here with her. This is your only option," I stated slowly with a raised eyebrow.

His mouth fell open at the price. "Two point five million?" he sputtered.

That was more than he demanded. But sometimes we had to play their own game to win.

I stayed silent, waiting. Although I was losing patience with each ticking second.

"Fine," he finally accepted.

Hallelujah, asshole. His acceptance meant nothing to me. I would still take Maria away, even if he hadn't agreed.

He turned to the audience, raising his wine glass. "My slave has been sold for two point five million dollars. As of now, she is in the keeping of Master Lyov Ivanshov."

He paused, looking at me from the corner of his

eyes. "Well, that is until he decides to sell her off after having his little fun. Who wouldn't want a virgin pussy?"

There was some laughter. Others snickered.

Isaak looked ready to commit murder. Agron and Gavrikov were just watching the scenes silently, taking everything in like they always did.

I didn't miss Maria's small gasp, the way her fingers tightened around my arm. I held her wrist tighter, putting the smallest pressure.

"I'm out. Enjoy the rest of your night, gentlemen," I announced loudly.

Turning to Solonik, I leveled him with a glare. "The money will be in your bank by sunrise."

Without waiting for his reply, I was already pushing Maria toward the door. But being the annoying bastard that he was, he stepped in front of me.

"Wait," he muttered with a small smirk.

He snapped his fingers, and I saw a woman coming forward...with a fucking leash.

"Rules are you can't leave the building without having the slaves on a leash. It's for protection, Lyov. I thought you would know better," he chastised with a small fake frown.

I looked at the leash, my disgust clear as day. There was no point hiding it.

"I don't need one," I said loudly, bringing everyone's attention to us.

"What do you mean? There are rules. The leash is to keep them under control," he hissed.

"I hate repeating myself, but I will, because you're probably fucking deaf. I said I don't need

BLOOD AND ROSES

one," I continued just as calmly.

I released Maria from my tight hold in proof. She stumbled back slightly in shock, and I took a step forward, away from her.

"I don't need a fucking leash to keep *my* slave under control," I said, taking another step away from Maria.

Another step toward the door. Another step away from her.

"My words are enough," I announced to everyone.

Watch and learn, fuckers.

"I don't need a leash for her to follow me. I don't need a leash to command her. Words are enough."

Without turning around and with my back still to Maria, I placed my hand out, palm up and waiting.

"Come here, Maria."

Silence. Everyone froze. And they watched.

They watched as I taught them the art of dominance.

Feet shuffled closer, and I felt her warmth coming closer. And finally, she placed her palm in mine.

My fingers intertwined with hers, and I pulled her closer into my embrace.

"And that, gentlemen, is how you command your slaves. If you need a fucking leash to be in control, then you are no fucking *Master*. To a slave, her Master's words are law. A *real* dominant's words will always be enough." I talked for the room while holding my Angel closer.

"You just need to know how to be one. Having a leash around their pretty necks doesn't make you a

Master. If *that* makes you in control, then it makes you a coward. It makes you weak."

"So, gentlemen, don't be cowards. Learn the true art of being in control. And that's the end of the lesson. Enjoy the rest of your night," I finished.

Without waiting for any reaction, I made my way out. With Maria's hands in mine, we walked out of the door together.

It closed with a loud bang, leaving us in the cold, dark hallway. Quickly, I removed my suit jacket and draped it over my Angel's body, hiding her the best I could.

I hated having her parade around naked, but it was the only way. If I had covered her before, it would have been suspicious.

Now, we were alone. Fina-fucking-lly.

"The car is waiting for us outside. It's going to be a little cold. I'm sorry, you'll have to bear with it for a few seconds," I muttered.

She didn't reply or make a single sound as I swept her up into my arms. Cradling her close, we walked out toward the waiting car.

I made quick work of getting inside and settling Maria on the seat. Taking my seat, facing her, I watched her reaction.

She looked outside the window, staying strangely quiet. Maria pulled the jacket closer to her body, holding it tight like she never wanted to let go.

And I didn't want her to let go.

"You're safe," I muttered in the silent car as it started moving.

She continued watching outside, her eyes

BLOOD AND ROSES

moving with each tree, light, and passing car. My little Angel looked entranced, her eyes twinkling in the dark as each light reflected into her blue orbs.

"You saved me," she said quietly, still not looking at me.

You saved me.

Oh Angel, if only you knew the truth.

I saved her for my own selfish reasons. Yet another monster in the dark, waiting to devour her.

Finally, she turned toward me. Her face soft…everything about her soft. Her shoulders drooped low, like thousands of pains had finally left her.

In her mind, she was free.

With our gazes on each other, her lips parted to speak. "Master…" she started, but I quickly moved forward.

She gasped, reeling back in surprise, but I had already gotten her into my trap. My fingers grasped her chin, a little more roughly than intended.

My touch kept her in place, her wide eyes on mine as I spoke.

"I have told you before, and I will tell you again, little Angel. Don't call me *Master*," I said roughly, my lips close to hers. "Lyov," I muttered.

She stared at me, confused, her body trembling slightly.

"You are *mine*. I think it's time I introduce myself."

Maria blinked, waiting.

"The name's Lyov. Lyov Ivanshov."

"Lyov," she whispered oh so softly.

Fucking beautiful.

71

Pretty Angel, I didn't save you. I just captured you.

Chapter 6

Maria

There were no words to describe what I was feeling. It was strange, the way my heart was beating faster. I could feel my pulse raging in my neck, right below my ears. It was harder to breathe, sitting in such close proximity with Master.

Lyov. Lyov Ivanshov. That was his name. He wanted me to call him by his name, yet it felt weird to call my Master by his name.

I felt like I wasn't submitting any longer.

The thought made me sick. If I weren't submitting, then what was I going to do?

What was *he* going to do with me?

Wasn't that why he bought me? To be his slave, serve him, worship him, like the whore everyone wanted—needed.

My eyes stayed on the window, watching the world swirl by as the car sped along the highway. I was finally seeing the outside world after eight long months.

Only eight months but it felt like an eternity.

Eight months since I was taken away from the sweetness of home.

Eight months since I was stripped of my dignity and innocence.

And eight months since I became a slave, no longer holding the value of a human being. I became a toy. One that could be played with and then discarded when I wasn't needed any longer.

My gaze shifted from the windows toward the man who saved me. His eyes were already on me, watching me so intensely that I shivered.

His grey eyes looked like a soulless pit of blackness in the dark. He looked dangerous. Vicious. Like an animal stalking its prey, holding it still with its gaze.

In this case, I was the prey and he was the predator.

My heart accelerated, and I felt tingles down my body. His heated eyes didn't waver from mine.

He held me in the palms of his hands, and I was a willing captive, falling deeper into his trap.

I had no chains around my neck, yet it felt like I was chained to him. His words. The way his gaze touched my body wordlessly, it had me captured. My mind, my heart, my body. And my soul.

He didn't have to touch me to assert his ownership.

I was *his*. With a single gaze, I became his.

The moment our eyes met in that room, with me kneeling between his legs, I became his.

I should have fought it, but I couldn't. The feeling brewing inside of me, the way my stomach twisted—*butterflies*—all those feeling became stronger with each passing second.

It felt like so much more.

When he touched me…there were no empty promises. When he spoke, he meant every word. Every word held a meaning. Whether it was good, bad, light, or dark. It meant something to my already fragile heart.

He touched me to give me something nobody had ever given me…without asking anything in return.

I gave, and he took.

He gave, and I took.

A balance of power.

A slave and a Master. I should have been doing the bowing, kneeling at his feet. Yet he bowed for me.

He didn't force his dominance. It was given to me, and I accepted it.

I willingly submitted to him because he earned my submission.

But now that I looked at him, his dangerous eyes tracking me, drinking me in, I wondered…was it all a game?

He was a Master. One of them. I was most likely not the first girl he bought.

Did he kill the others? When he got tired of them, did he discard them like a used toy—like they meant nothing?

Did he steal their innocence and then sell them? My previous Master did.

He wasn't any different, was he?

My brain was in a constant battle with my heart.

I wanted to believe he was good.

He saved me. He smiled at me with soft eyes. He held me gently. He kissed me sweetly.

This Master desired me, not as a slave, but as a woman.

You were so good, Angel. So beautiful. So perfect. You amaze me.

Such beautiful words for a slave who didn't deserve them.

I was dirty—filthy. A whore. A *slave*.

"What are you thinking so hard about?"

I flinched at the voice, so hard, so sudden in the silence of the darkened car.

When he placed his hand on my knee, I flinched again. A small tremor caused my body to feel cold and then hot. He dragged his hand up, caressing my leg until it rested on my thigh.

He touched burned my skin, and my gaze flew down, watching his rough hand on my naked thigh. It looked so big, manly, and so dangerous there.

The touch could have appeared innocent. But it wasn't. It spoke of so much more.

The hold he had on me…it said that he was claiming me.

His hand tightened just a little, a warning. My eyes went to his, and he raised an eyebrow, waiting for my answer.

While my previous Master didn't like it when I would speak, Lyov Ivanshov was trying to hear my voice every time.

Clearing my throat, I answered him. "Nothing, Master. I am just grateful that you have saved me."

"You think I saved you?" he questioned darkly.

BLOOD AND ROSES

His hands moved up, stopping when he reached the hem on his suit jacket. I internally smiled. He had given me his jacket. One of the sweetest things a Master could have done.

I nodded. "Yes, you have. My previous Master wasn't a good man. But you are."

He chuckled low in his chest, a tiny smirk on his face. It made him look dangerous but very handsome. I liked it.

"You think I'm a good man?"

I nodded again. He was. Better than the others. Maybe it was a childish thought, but he had proved himself to be better so far.

You are safe.

He had whispered those words to me, and my heart had skipped a beat. It was that moment when I decided that he was a good man. My mind was in denial, but my heart…it believed.

So I was going to trust my heart. I was going to believe my Master—Lyov.

And I was going to serve him with all of me—mind, heart, body, and soul. I was going to become his favorite so he wouldn't discard me.

Releasing my thigh, he sat back into his seat. I instantly missed his touch and felt cold again.

He gave me warmth…I loved it.

And now I craved it.

Master shook his head slightly, a smile on his face. Like he was having an inside joke with himself. I liked his smile.

It made him look young and happy.

I wanted him to smile more. I wanted to make him smile.

"I will be a good slave to you, Master," I whispered softly.

The air around us shifted and changed, almost instantly. It felt colder. Darker. Angrier.

Master lost his smile.

No. No. No.

I whimpered, hating it. Because I realized that I must have said something wrong. And he was going to punish me.

Wasn't that what they always wanted?

They didn't want good slaves. Good slaves didn't get punishment.

Masters loved to give punishments, so they wanted bad slaves.

He moved forward in a flash, grabbing my chin and holding me roughly. "You will never call yourself a slave again. I don't want to hear that word from you. Is that understood, little Angel?"

Master looked so angry. Furious. His beautiful eyes crackled with intensity, and I almost cowered back.

I nodded mutely, submitting, giving him what he wanted.

He closed his eyes, breathing in and out, like he was trying to calm himself. When he opened his eyes again, they looked softer. His touch turned gentle. He caressed my skin, his fingers moving sweetly over my cheek.

"You are an Angel, *Maria*. And you will address yourself as such," he continued quietly. The words were softly spoken, but I heard his command. "Is that understood, little Angel?"

I nodded, although it didn't make sense. "You

BLOOD AND ROSES

want me to call myself Angel?" I asked in return, confused.

He smiled then, another beautiful smile. "I want you to think of yourself as an Angel," he whispered, his lips so close to mine.

"Okay," I answered quickly, wanting to please him. I wanted to make him happy…please him in whatever way he wanted.

"Good girl," he praised with another caress, his fingertips featherlight on my neck.

My own lips lifted up, smiling. He made me smile.

"You have a beautiful smile, Maria. I want to see it on you every day."

My heart soared at his words, and when he smiled wider, I felt suddenly giddy. *He* was making me giddy…*happy*.

His words were my safe haven, and I drowned in them, wanted them desperately.

I will always smile for you, Master. Promise. Forever. Until my last breath.

When he pulled away this time, I didn't feel cold. I still felt warm. His words stayed with me through the whole drive.

My eyes started to get heavy, tiredness making its way into my body. But I didn't want to sleep.

I didn't want my eyes falling away from the man who made me happy.

I blinked, trying so hard. My body grew heavier, and when he noticed, he nodded his head. "Go to sleep, Maria. I will wake you up when we get there."

When I didn't move, he sighed and quickly

unbuckled his seatbelt. My eyes widened when he switched seats and came to sit beside me.

Drawing me closer into his body, he pushed me down until my head was lying on his lap. I breathed out, my body going limp.

It felt nice…perfect. It felt *right*.

His fingers were in my hair, playing with the strands. He caressed my cheek with his other hand. "Sleep."

This time it was a command.

Closing my eyes, I did as I was told.

Chapter 7

Maria

I was being shaken awake the next time I came around. My eyes opened tiredly before I jumped up in fright.

When I met grey eyes, I felt myself relaxing.

"We're here," he said.

Master opened the door before pulling me out. He didn't let my feet touch the ground before he was swinging me up in his arms.

He walked us into what appeared to be a hotel. Confused why we weren't in his home, I stayed quiet.

It was Master's decision.

When he reached the room, he let me down and steadied me when my legs wobbled a little.

"We're stopping here for today," he explained, staring into my confused eyes.

I nodded and smiled. "Okay."

Master walked further into the room and started to unbutton his shirt, pulling at his tie roughly. I waited at the door, watching and suddenly feeling very nervous.

He pulled his shirt from his pants and looked back at me.

"Come here, Maria."

My body glided toward him like it wasn't my own anymore. Standing in front of Master, I waited.

He brushed my hair out of my face and leaned forward. My lungs constricted as I struggled to breathe when he placed a kiss on my forehead.

His hands smoothed down my shoulders, and when cold air hit my flushed skin, I hissed.

The suit jacket fell on the floor, and I stood in front of my Master, naked. He could see everything. But his eyes stayed on mine, trapping me.

Finally, he pulled away, nodding behind me. I turned away and saw that the door was opened to a bathroom.

"Get in the shower," he ordered roughly, his voice sending shivers down my spine and the rest of my body.

"You want me to clean myself, Master?" I asked quietly.

"No. *I'm* going to bathe you."

Oh.

My heart fluttered, and the butterflies in my stomach increased.

"I'm going to clean you so that there is no trace of another man on your body," he continued in the same rough voice. "So get in the shower and wait for me."

I scurried into the bathroom, my heart wild, my mind crazy. He affected me in ways that nobody

BLOOD AND ROSES

ever had.

He was different. He made me *feel* different. And I liked it.

I liked feeling like this.

Following my training, I knelt down on the floor of the shower. The perfect position while waiting for my Master.

Maybe it was seconds, or even minutes, but it felt like so long. Finally, my eyes saw his feet as he joined me in.

His hands went under my arms, and he pulled me up. "Lesson one. The only time you will kneel is when you have your mouth full of my cock and you're gagging on it."

My eyes widened, and I sucked in a deep breath. "And right now, Angel, you don't have my cock in your mouth. So, no kneeling. You don't kneel, ever. Unless I tell you."

His lessons were different, but I liked them.

I nodded. He smiled.

Placing another kiss on my forehead, he whispered, "Good girl."

He reached behind me and turned on the water. It was cold at first when it cascaded around us, and I flinched.

Master chuckled quietly, bringing me closer into his body. I finally noticed that he was naked too.

He felt hard against my stomach, his body firm against mine. I should have been scared, but I felt strangely safe. When the water turned hot, I sighed in contentment. It felt so good.

I missed warm water and warm showers.

After wetting my hair, he shampooed it. Master

ran his fingers through my hair strands, massaging my scalp. So sweet. So gentle.

When he was finished with my hair, his hands moved to my body. I stood stiff for a second, feeling his hands moving across my flushed skin.

"Relax, Maria. I'm not going to hurt you," he said against my neck, placing a soft kiss there.

I nodded and forced myself to relax. But when he started to massage my body with the soap, I didn't have to force myself any longer.

It just happened. I released myself into his care.

He caressed my body, from my neck to my toes, washing me—cleaning me.

Giving me back the smallest dignity that I had lost.

When his hand reached between my legs, I closed my eyes. But he didn't hurt me.

Just as gently as before, he washed between my legs. It felt wrong. I didn't have a chance to think about it before he stood up and kissed my forehead again.

"You're a good girl, Angel. I'm proud of you."

My eyes snapped open to see him staring at me intensely. "You're clean now. Perfect. Your body is all flushed and so beautiful."

He bent his head, his lips teasing my ear. "And *mine*."

His.

I didn't notice when the water was off, but the next second, he was wrapping a towel around my body.

Helping me out of the shower, he dried me off. I watched him as he wrapped another towel around

BLOOD AND ROSES

his waist.

Master walked out of the bathroom, leaving me alone. When he walked back in, he was carrying something in his hands.

"Arms up," he ordered.

Instinctively, they went up. He pulled a simple black nightdress over my head.

I looked down my body, now fully covered.

He clothed me, shielding my shame from others.

"All done." He smiled. "Our food is waiting for us. After you eat, I need you to sleep. I will wake you up when we are departing again."

Grabbing my hand, he pulled me into the bedroom again. Master sat me down on the couch and handed me a plate filled with food.

I gasped, my eyes widening.

So much food. How?

Our eyes met, and he swiped away a single tear that trailed down my cheek. "You need to eat, Angel. Lesson two. From now on, you will have three meals a day. A plate full, not like you were being given before. You can have some snacks in between. Whatever you want. You will never go hungry again. Is that understood?"

I nodded speechlessly. Because what could I really say?

His lessons—his rules made no sense.

But they were his rules, so I would follow them. Not only because he was my Master, but because I wanted to.

We ate quietly. I kept my gaze on my lap, but a few times our eyes would meet. And every time I smiled. He would smile too and then nod toward my plate, silently telling me to continue eating.

Sometimes he would give me a piece from his plate, telling me to try it because it tasted good.

It was hard to eat so much. My stomach wasn't used to taking in so much food at once.

Master must have understood, because he took the plate from me. "Are you full?" he asked.

Nodding in relief, I sighed happily.

"Good. Go to sleep now," he said quietly.

I stood up, not needing him to tell me again. Kneeling on the floor, I went to lay down in the position I always slept in.

Suddenly, I was being lifted roughly from the floor. My head twirled in confusion as Master carried me to the bed and dumped me there.

I bounced on the soft mattress, a startled gasp escaping past my lips.

He was angry? I must have done something wrong again.

"You sleep on the fucking bed, damn it!" he snapped loudly.

His glare bored into my body. "I swear, if I find you sleeping on the floor again, I will take you over my fucking knees and spank your ass red until you can't sit down for days. Is that understood?"

Cowering back in fright, I quickly laid down on the bed. "Yes, Master. I'm sorry. Please forgive me."

"For fuck's sake," he hissed, closing his eyes. He pinched the bridge of his nose, and I heard him taking in deep breaths.

I peeked up at him through my lashes as he opened his eyes again. He looked back in control.

BLOOD AND ROSES

Placing a knee on the bed, he bent over my body so our faces were only inches apart.

His voice sounded calmer when he spoke, and my heart settled. "Lesson three. You sleep on the bed. Always."

I nodded. And he did it again, another kiss on my forehead. "Good girl."

Good girl.

I smiled. I was starting to like it when he said that. It made me feel better, like I had pleased him.

"Lesson four. Don't call me Master. I have said that before, and I will say it again. *Do not* call me Master. I am Lyov. You call me by my name from now on."

I nodded, and he smiled this time. "Say it. Say my name," he demanded.

"*Lyov*," I whispered shyly, my heart drumming loudly, my pulse erratic.

This time he kissed me softly—so soft and sweet—on my lips. "Good girl," he whispered back.

I liked it. I liked it so much.

He was pulling something deep from within me. He was tugging at my heart strings, making me feel.

I liked his name. I liked my Master. I liked my Lyov.

"Good girls get rewarded. Bad girls get punished. If you are a good girl and follow all the rules, you will get many rewards," he murmured.

"I will be good," I replied.

He smiled and kissed my forehead this time. "Go to sleep, Angel."

I closed my eyes, still smiling. He settled down beside me, pulling me into his arms, holding me to him.

My heart felt full.

Lyov saved me.

Just like I had dreamed of before. He came for me, swept me off in his arms, and carried me out of hell…toward our castle.

Maybe this was my happily ever after.

Because Lyov…he was my Prince Charming.

Just like I dreamed of. Just like I wanted.

I found my Prince Charming.

Chapter 8

Lyov

I watched her sleep, her breathing even in her deep slumber. Her chest rose with each intake of breath, and I was almost mesmerized by the sight.

My eyes were only on her—she was all I could see.

Instinctively, my arm tightened around her waist, pulling her closer. I needed her as close as she could be. In her sleep, she made a little soft sound in the back of the throat. Almost like she enjoyed being closer to me.

Wanting to feel her skin against mine, I slowly hitched her nightdress up. My hand found its way underneath the dress, and I pressed my palm against her bare stomach, holding her firmly to me.

Her skin felt warm and soft as I caressed her stomach, loving the feel of her under my hand. Maria turned around in her sleep, her body now facing me.

She looked so peaceful with her eyes closed and

her face soft with sleep. My heart felt a little lighter knowing that she was safe now, safe with me and away from those who had hurt her.

Whatever happened tonight—it fucked my head up.

Her actions, her words, everything was based on what they imprinted in her mind. They forced her to believe that she was less and only for our pleasure.

It was going to be fucking hard to change her. To make her human again. But I was going to make sure she had all the broken pieces again. I would glue her broken soul together so she was whole again.

Nobody was going to hurt her. Never again. No fucker was going to lay his dirty hands on her again.

I will be a good slave to you, Master.

I was almost so fucking tempted to march back into The Royalist and rip his head off. Solonik broke her before I could even have her. And now all I had left were the pieces. Some gone, some scattered, some broken.

I had focused on my instincts when I took her out of there. In the car, it took everything in me not to take her, claim her exactly like I wanted.

Fuck her deep, so she could feel me days after. So she knew that I was the only one she should ever concern herself about.

It is hard for a man not to take what is his, when it's only an arm away.

When Maria moved in my arms, getting restless in her sleep, she brought me back into the present.

My gaze whispered over her face. She looked like a porcelain doll, her black hair so shiny and

BLOOD AND ROSES

beautiful, her skin white, so soft that it almost felt like velvet. Her lips were pink and ripped, like she had bitten on them for too long.

I placed a kiss on her forehead when a whimper escaped past her lips. Her eyebrows furrowed like she was in pain, and I soothed it out with my lips.

She burrowed deeper into my embrace and let out a sleepy sigh. Her distress was gone, replaced with an almost content look. She was...safe. And she knew that.

In my arms, she would always be safe. Even in her sleep, I would keep the demons away.

Whatever I was feeling in my heart, none of it made sense. All I knew was that Maria was mine now. My little Angel.

And I needed her close to me. By my side.

I didn't care what it meant and what I had to fight with—she was *mine.* The minute I saw her, she lost her soul to the Devil.

Solonik might have let her go, but she had fallen into my trap. If she thought she was free—she wasn't.

I was going to steal her away from the rest of the world.

She escaped a monster only to end up in the hands of the Devil who controlled hell. The king of the underworld. And she was going to be my Queen, whether she liked it or not.

I was going to give Maria back her wings and then trap her again. Make her human so she could give me what I needed—what I craved. Her heart and her soul.

I began to lose track of time as I imagined what

it would be like to have her by my side. Having her in my arms, holding her close to my body, it only amplified my feelings—or whatever the fuck you call it—for her.

The darker part inside of me, the one that wanted to lose control so bad, seemed to be satiated with just watching her. For now. Until I would lose control and claim her.

When that happened, it was going to be a moment she would never forget. She was going to beg me for more, just like in that room at The Royalist. She was going to beg, and I was going to give it to her, gladly.

I wanted her passion and everything else that came with her. The fire and the burning.

I wanted her to look at me as if I were her world, the only one that mattered. My selfish needs were going to corrupt her, but I didn't mind at all. I had a feeling she wasn't going to mind either.

"Lyov."

My name snapped me out of my reverie, and I glanced down at Maria to see her staring at me. "What is it, Angel?" I tucked her hair behind her ear. This way her whole face was visible to me.

"Are you not sleepy?" she asked softly, her hand going to my chest. She didn't seem to mind that I was naked except for my boxers.

Instead, Maria chose to touch me, voluntarily. She glided her fingers up my chest until they rested against my neck.

A small smile appeared on her lips, like she enjoyed touching me. I knew I damn well loved it.

Her fingers moved over my cheek, palming my

BLOOD AND ROSES

face gently. "Are you okay, Mas—*Lyov?*"

Her sweet question was my undoing. Here she was, trapped by me, yet she was asking if *I* were *okay*.

"I am okay, Angel—just thinking. You should be sleeping," I whispered back. Our foreheads touched, and I kissed the tip of her nose.

She moved closer, her legs pressed against mine. Without thinking, I grabbed her thigh and hiked her leg over my hips, molding her body against mine. Maria let out a small gasp in surprise and licked her lips nervously.

Her eyes moved down, but our bodies were covered with the bedsheet. I knew she could feel my hard bulge between her legs, and I could feel how fucking warm she was.

My fingers bit into her hips, resisting the sudden urge to thrust against her heat. She swallowed nervously before burrowing her head into my chest...but not before I could see her cheeks reddening with a beautiful blush.

I smiled at her innocence, craving more of it. *Slow, Lyov. Take it slow. Woo the fuck out of her. Make love to her. And then you can fuck her.*

"Good night, Master."

"*Maria,*" I growled dangerously.

Her arm went around my waist, holding me tightly. I didn't know if it was in fright or if she was trying to hide into me, her way of escaping my wrath.

"I am sorry, Lyov," she whispered.

I took a deep breath, trying to control myself before I completely fucking lost it. "I will not repeat myself again, little Angel. This is your last warning. *Never* call me *Master* again. It's *Lyov* to you. Always."

What she didn't realize was that her soft whisper—when she called me *Master,* the beast inside of me loved it and wanted to claim her right there. I wanted to wrap my hand around her throat and fuck her tight pussy until she was screaming her orgasm.

My cock jerked at the thought, and I hissed. She froze in my arms, and I wanted to smack my head into a wall.

I had to rein myself in or I was going to lose her before I even had to chance to have her.

I took in a deep breath while my palm caressed her back in a soothing manner. After a few seconds, she finally relaxed, only to wiggle in my arms, trying to get herself comfortable.

My cock rubbed between her legs, and I internally swore.

"Stop moving," I snapped loudly.

She flinched, and I swore again.

Ah, for fuck's sake.

"Go to sleep, Maria. We have a long day tomorrow," I finally breathed out.

My little Angel nodded silently before closing her eyes. "Good night."

"Good night, Angel."

I stayed still, just breathing. I was scared to move, scared that I was going to come right there like a horny teenager losing his virginity.

Maria was long asleep by the time I finally relaxed and talked Junior Lyov down. It was the

BLOOD AND ROSES

hardest fucking thing I had ever done in my life.

When my eyes started drooping and sleep was beginning to claim me, I placed another kiss on Maria's forehead. There was this primal need inside of me, just to touch her and hold her. Just to feel the softness of her skin against mine.

My last thought before darkness took over was how badly I wanted to see *my* little Angel smile again. Not just a small smile on her lips. I wanted to see her smiling from her beautiful blue eyes.

I wanted to watch her soul smile.

Never had I thought about love or soulmates. A day ago, I didn't fucking care about it. I didn't even know what love meant, and I sure as hell didn't want it.

Love was a weakness.

But holding Maria in my arms, it didn't feel like a weakness anymore.

I felt powerful. In control. I felt alive.

It felt like I had found a new purpose in life.

My Angel.

***

"Did you miss me? Is that why you're calling?" the voice answered on the first ring.

"Good morning to you, too."

"It's actually still night here," she replied drily.

"Whatever, Lena."

"Well, what are you calling for? You do realize that you just disturbed my sleep?" she smarted off.

"You do realize that I am your boss, right?" I replied tiredly.

"Oops, sorry. I forgot. What can I do for you then, Mr. Ivanshov?" Lena continued. It was impossible to miss the sarcasm in her voice.

"I am bringing someone home."

I waited as my words were received with silence.

And then the screeching started. I took my phone away from my ear, only to hear Isaak chuckling from his seat across the room.

"Oh. My. God! Is it a puppy? Please tell me it's a puppy! You know I always wanted a puppy."

Hit her, Isaak mouthed while smiling.

My own smirk appeared. Lena was about to have a heart attack. But it was going to be worth it.

"No. It's a girl," I drawled.

Silence. Complete utter silence.

"So I need you to prepare one of the bedrooms. Preferably the one across from mine if you can. Order some clothes. She's going to need them. Small size. And other accessories, whatever the fuck females need," I continued.

Silence again.

"We will see you later. Have a good night, Lena. Enjoy your sleep."

I cut off the call before busting out laughing. Isaak joined me, and I wheezed, my stomach hurting.

"Did we actually get her speechless?" Isaak said through his laughter.

I nodded before taking a seat beside him. "I think so. She really needed to shut her fucking mouth. It looks like I finally found a way."

"Priceless!"

We were still chuckling when the bathroom door

BLOOD AND ROSES

opened. Maria walked out, now freshly showered. Her hair was in a bun, and she was wearing a dress that came down to her knees.

I had made Isaak order it the night before, knowing she was going to need some clothes to travel back home.

The dress was plain and simple, with only a small black belt around the waist. Tight around her chest but flowy from her waist. The color was a soft pink and perfect for Maria.

It really made her look breathtaking.

My beautiful little Angel.

"Are you ready, Maria?" I asked before standing up.

Without even asking her, she walked closer. My arms were still by my sides, fighting the urge to just pull her in my arms. But this was her choice. Her moment.

And she didn't disappoint me.

With a gentle smile, her cheeks blushing beautifully, she almost glided toward me. Maria stood in front of me, her head tilted back, her eyes boring into mine.

"I am ready," she said.

Her hand reached forward, and she grabbed mine. Instinctively, my fingers grasped hers.

"I am ready," she repeated again, more confident.

My lips stretched in a smile, finding it so hard to hide my happiness. *Good choice, Angel.*

I pulled her forward, and she fell into my arms, giggling. "Let's go home, then."

She nodded without saying a word, laying her

trust in the palms of my hands.

Our hands were clasped together as we walked out of the hotel, Isaak and my other men using their bodies as our shields.

The drive to the airport was silent. Maria's eyes were wide as she stared outside. I saw a hint of fear in the depth of her eyes, but every time I squeezed her hand in support, she would relax.

I loved her reaction to me. I knew she felt it, our connection. She felt it just as deeply as I did.

She spent her time looking at the clouds during the plane ride. We talked very little, only because we found the silence between us more comforting.

We reveled in it and fell deeper into each other during the silence.

When the plane touched down, I gently shook her awake. She smiled sleepily and held on to my arm as we walked out.

It didn't take us long to be back into the car, this time to my estate. Maria's new home. Now her sanctuary.

When the car came to its final destination, I helped her out of the car. She was mesmerized by the sight, like I knew she would be.

She stared for a long moment before I brought her out of her reverie.

"This is your new home," I said, bringing her attention back to me, where it should be.

"It's beautiful," she said, glancing back at the stone mansion.

"Do you like it?" I asked, my thumb rubbing over her cheek.

Maria nodded before smiling. "I like it very

much."

Her gaze found mine again, her blue eyes looking so bright in the morning sun. She pressed her cheek against my touch, like she wanted more.

"Before we step inside, do you remember the rules?" I asked, holding her gaze firmly.

She swallowed nervously before nodding.

"What are the rules, Angel?" I demanded.

"I will never address myself as a *slave*. I will never kneel, not unless you ask me to. I will always eat three meals a day, including snacks in between. I will always sleep on the bed. And never call you Master. I will always call you by your name, *Lyov*." She repeated the rules quickly, looking desperate to please me.

My heart felt light, and I couldn't help but smile.

"Good girl," I said, placing a kiss on her forehead. She melted in my embrace, and I held her to me. "Remember those rules, Maria. If you break any of them, I will be very displeased."

She shook her head. "I don't want to displease you."

My lips made contact with her right temple. "Good."

I held her, both of us completely lost in each other, before Isaak cleared his throat.

Slightly pulling away, I held her hand in mine. "Let's go inside, then."

We took a step forward, together. I saw my men; most of their eyes were on us. I saw the look they gave Maria.

The way I held her as she walked on my right, they just knew.

Their back straightened, their heads almost bowing in respect as we walked closer.

Behold your Queen.

Chapter 9

Maria

His arms were wrapped tightly around my waist, holding me firmly against his body. His embrace was strong and protective. I liked the way my body was cuddled into his warmth. Master—*Lyov*, he made me feel safe.

I couldn't remember the last time I felt safe, loved, or cherished. But in a matter of hours, he was able to make me feel all.

I liked the way his arm tightened around my hips as we walked toward the main door. My eyes took everything in. Lyov was a wealthy man, I knew that, but for the first time, I was truly seeing his wealth.

He was a powerful man.

Strong, dangerous, and deadly.

But compared to my last Master, it felt as if I would never feel his wrath.

It felt like I would forever be cocooned under the protection of his wings. Kept safe next to his heart, by his side. Never underneath his feet.

The front of the estate was gorgeous, and I found myself mesmerized. After being locked in cages and just a cold, lifeless room for so long, it felt nice to finally see something so majestic and beautiful in the sunlight.

A few men were lined up along the path to the door. They wore similar suits as Lyov, although Master's looked more expensive...and refined. It screamed he was the King and everyone else were just his puppets. His loyal subjects.

They were at his bidding. One word and everyone would run as they were commanded. Lyov had that type of power. I knew it the moment my eyes found him—sought him out between all those other rich men.

As if it were meant to happen. Meant to be.

He found me kneeling at Valentin's feet. His voice caressed over my skin, both burning and soothing me at the same time. And then I found him, my body calling out to his touch and wanting to feel the soft caress of his rough voice again.

Who would have known that a man like him could calm the screaming demons in my head?

Lyov could make my heart thump, like the wings of a bird flapping desperately to soar toward the sky. Only he could make my body flush red under his penetrating gaze instead of making my skin crawl.

As we walked toward the open doors, his men standing up straighter, their posture solid and unwavering—I felt safe.

We took a step inside, and the moment my feet

BLOOD AND ROSES

were past the doors and into the mansion, his lips grazed my skin lightly as he whispered in my ear.

"Welcome home, Angel."

Lyov had the power to make me breathless. And I starved for more of him. All of him. His words. His voice. His touch. His kisses. Everything that was him—I wanted it.

His lips moved down, and with so much gentleness, he kissed the side of my neck. A feathered touch. A kiss of devotion. A kiss with unsaid words. One kiss that could rival a thousand.

His lips lingered there longer than necessary, but I couldn't complain. My eyes fluttered closed, and I leaned more against his body, letting him feel me. I wanted the comfort he brought to my fragile soul.

I turned in his arms, and our eyes met. His grey ones heated me to the core as he gazed fiercely into my face, watching me as if I were the only thing he could see in this moment.

I had his sole attention, and he became the reason for each breath I took.

His full lips pulled up at the sides as he grinned down at me. The darkness that shadowed his face was swept off, and Lyov transformed from deadly to carefree. He was no longer Lyov, a King who owned those around him, to a simple man gazing tenderly down at me.

When I could no longer hold his eyes, mine dropped to his chest nervously. The way he stared at me, it did strange things to my stomach and heart. His hands gripped my hips, and he pulled me into his body, our fronts touching. He held me both firmly and preciously. It was a dangerous combination.

My hands instinctively went to his chest. His shirt was soft, and everything underneath it was hard. His strong muscles were firm under my touch, and I felt myself wanting more—to touch and see more of him.

His heartbeat was strong and sure, so much like *himself*—and so much unlike mine, which tripped with each breath I took.

I was nervous, he was calm.

I was unsure, he was confident.

I was shy, he was arrogant.

I was weak, he was strong.

We were opposites, yet when we touched, it felt like a jolt of lightning, a never-ending wave of pleasure passing through us. From the tips of his fingers to mine.

"Thank you," I whispered, still staring at the rise and fall of his chest.

With a finger under my chin, he tipped my head back. "For what, Maria?"

I took a deep breath and then let it out slowly. Nervousness clawed at my throat, and I suddenly found it hard to speak. Lyov stared at me expectantly, waiting patiently for me to continue.

With our eyes connected, I showed him my soul. I only prayed that he didn't steal it and drag it to the crimson fire of hell.

My lips parted, and I finally spoke again. "For bringing me here. You saved me. I don't feel…like I used to with my previous master. It's different. You are different. And you make me feel safe. I wish to be good for you, Lyov."

BLOOD AND ROSES

So that you never let me go.

Those words were left unsaid. A slave never made demands. We only listened and obeyed.

I was going to be everything he wanted and needed. Then he wouldn't think of leaving me. I would be his, just as much as he would be mine.

"It's cute that you keep saying I saved you, Angel. If only you knew the truth. I captured you. I am the devil in disguise, and the devil…well, he likes to play games."

His voice broke me out of my thoughts, and I stared up at him in surprise. He was no longer grinning, like a man with no worries in the world. Instead, he wore his signature smirk. The same one that made him look vicious. His grey eyes were laughing at me, but the darkness in there couldn't be mistaken.

His fingers lingered over my neck before drawing upward. His touch moved closer to my mouth. Lyov paused, and then his eyes went to where his finger laid, just inches away from its destination. He thumbed my lips roughly, and I trembled in his hold.

He brought his head down until our mouths were so close that I thought he would claim my lips. Instead, Lyov stayed there, letting anticipation lick its way into my body. His breath feathered over my skin when he spoke again.

"I am the devil in a pretty suit, sweet Angel. Remember that."

His voice was soft, caressing me—yet those words—they were anything but soft.

I should be scared. A small part of me was. After

months of being a slave and living in captivity, it taught me to doubt everything. It had instilled fear in me.

But with Lyov, the fear was mixed with something else. I couldn't figure it out. He made me feel. I didn't know what it was…but my heart skipped and my breath caught in my throat. My body moved on its own—moving toward him, even closer as I sought his warmth.

His smirk grew, and he chuckled low under his breath. His chest vibrated, and I liked the way it sounded. Rich and smooth. Dark and deadly.

Valentin was a handsome man. He truly was. His face was sculptured. He was tall, his build wide and strong, very much like Lyov.

But there was just something about my Lyov that held my attention and made me want more.

It confused me.

But I'd rather let Lyov do the thinking for me. I chose to place myself in his palms and let him take care of me. I gave him the power to become my everything, so I could be what he needed.

Because I trusted him. My reasoning might be naïve and weak, but I needed him. Our match wasn't ideal. It wasn't perfect. But I believed it was perfect for us.

For now. Until how long?

The thought broke through my delirious mind, reminding me of the future I couldn't see.

Even though Lyov told me not to call him Master, he was still one. Slaves are not kept forever. We are made to be bought and sold after being used.

BLOOD AND ROSES

I squeezed my eyes shut, refusing to think of this. No, Lyov called me Angel. I was his sweet Angel. My heart told me that we could never end. Me and him.

Yet...

A hand gripped my jaw, the hold gentle but commanding. A strength to my weakness. "Open your eyes, Maria."

My eyes snapped opened, and I stared up at Lyov. His eyes were narrowed dangerously, and his gaze swept over my face, intently watching my expression. My teeth nibbled at my bottom lips, nervous, scared, worried.

I didn't want to lose him.

Lyov seemed almost angry, but when he sweetly tucked my hair behind my ears, his eyes softened the slightest bit, but never losing that dangerous look on his face. His grip on my jaw didn't loosen, and he brought my face closer to his. I had to stand on my tip-toes until our faces were only half an inch apart. Our noses touched, and if I leaned a tiny bit, our lips would touch too.

"I can almost see the wheels turning in your head. The way you lost that happy look on your face, I don't like it. Whatever you're thinking, stop," he said. My heart fluttered and stomach clenched.

"If it makes you sad, then it does not concern you. Because, Angel, the only thing you should think about from now on is making me happy." Lyov growled the last part, as if the thought of me thinking of anything else other than him displeased him greatly.

"If I make you happy, then what happens?" I whispered as I fought the urge to cry. I felt unstable—drowning in an ocean of feelings I didn't comprehend.

"Then you will be happy too," he simply replied. Lyov cocked his head to the side with a thoughtful look. He released my face, and his hands went to my hips again. We fell into silence...and I liked it.

I could feel his men watching us. We weren't alone, but instead of pulling away, I melted into his embrace.

My voice was muffled in his chest when I spoke again, but I knew he heard it before his hand tightened around my hips. "Your happiness is my happiness, Lyov. I will try to be the best for you. I promise. Until my last breath."

Lyov pulled away and sighed before giving me the smallest smile. It was a rare one, and I liked that too. "Good. Now let me show this place. This is your home now. You are free to go anywhere as long as you stay in the estate, on our grounds. If you want to go outside the gates, you are allowed, but you will need to let me know so I can assign someone for your protection."

He waited for my response. I nodded and listened attentively. "Everything I do is for your safety, pretty Angel. Do not think I am chaining you down, because even though I want nothing but to tie you up and make sure you never leave my bed—I want your wings to spread open so you can fly."

My heart soared, as if my invisible wings really were spread out and I was flying...higher and higher into the bright sky. I soared toward Lyov.

BLOOD AND ROSES

He gripped my hand in his, our fingers entwining together as we continued inside. Our steps faltered as a woman stopped in front of us.

She raised her eyebrow at Lyov and then looked at me, her eyes searching my face. She then smiled. It was honest and sweet.

"I thought you were playing me," she muttered under her breath before pouting. "But it looks like you were telling the truth. You really brought someone home."

Lyov groaned in annoyance, but when I peeked up at him, he didn't look annoyed. Actually, he looked like he was fighting a smile.

The woman was wearing a black dress that came just above her knees. Her curves were outlined in the dress, and she towered a bit over me. Her black hair was tugged back in a ponytail, and her kind brown eyes were smiling down at me.

"Lena," she said after a second of silence.

I shook my head. "No. My name is Maria."

My eyes widened, and I moved closer to Lyov. *No. What have I done?*

My hand came up, and I clenched his arm, afraid he would pull away from me and be angry. I squeezed my eyes shut and fought back a sob that was threatening to break free from my throat.

"I'm sorry, Master," I whispered.

You don't speak unless I fucking command you, dirty slut. Keep that fucking mouth closed until it's time I shove my dick down your throat.

Slaves were never allowed to speak. It was the rule. An important one. If broken, we were punished—and the punishment would hurt. We would bleed. We would be starved—until our masters were satisfied we'd learned our lessons.

My legs weakened, and I started sinking down to my knees. *Always beg for forgiveness on your knees.*

I heard a growl. Low, dangerous, and angry. *Lyov.* It dragged me out of the darkness clouding my head.

I was jerked upright before my knees could touch the hard floor. "Open your fucking eyes, Maria."

He was angry. I made him angry.

I whimpered in response. I was supposed to make him happy. Not angry.

Lyov pulled me into his arms. I was pressed into his hard body, and his hand gripped the back of my neck. A firm command. A soft touch. "Open your eyes and look at me."

My eyes opened, and a single tear slipped down, leaving a wet trail on my cheek. His eyes were hard and angry, but his touch was soft and gentle.

Lyov's lips were pressed together in frustration. I could see him battling with his fury, but when his forehead dropped to mine, and he breathed out through his nose, as if my touch soothed him…I realized that he wasn't angry at *me*.

"Angel, tell me. What is my rule about you being on your knees?" he said to me.

I desperately hung on to him. My sniffles filled the vast room, and my chin wobbled with the effort to keep my tears at bay. "I should never kneel. Not unless…"

The words were stuck in my throat. Lyov nodded

BLOOD AND ROSES

and continued. "Not unless I ask you to. And all the reasons why you will kneel for me—they will never cause you tears, pain, or fear. It will be because you *want* to kneel for me. Because you *need* it as much as me. It will be for both of *us*. Not because you *think* you need to do it so I won't be angry with you."

I remained silent. "Do you understand?" he asked. Lyov's thumb was brushing up and down on the back of my neck now, while he still held me in place.

I nodded. But Lyov pushed the slightest bit. He knew my limits, and he never crossed them. "Your words, Angel. I need your words."

"I understand, Lyov."

"Good girl."

My lips parted, and I sucked in a deep breath. My heart raced. Those words made my body tingle. It liked the way Lyov said it. The clenching feeling in my stomach didn't ease. Actually, it tightened, and I found myself wanting to hear those words again.

Oh, how I wanted to please him.

I had to forget my past...the other rules. The other masters. I had to remember Lyov's rules because I belonged to him now.

His hand wrapped around mine again, and the back of his thumb grazed my knuckles. The touch was so tender that my heart ached. I never thought a man like him could hold so much gentleness.

There was so much more behind the cold, hard exterior he showed everyone.

We faced the woman again, but I couldn't meet

her eyes. I almost felt embarrassed. Ashamed.

"Maria, this is Lena. Lena, as you already know, this is Maria." Lyov's smooth voice calmed me, and I finally found the courage to look up.

Lena didn't stare at me weirdly. Instead, her kind eyes were glassy, and she gave me a wobbly smile. Her eyes met Lyov, and I saw her give him a brief nod before turning to me again.

"It is nice to finally meet you, Maria," she said sweetly. "I can't say I have heard a lot about you, but it doesn't matter. We'll be hanging out a lot, so we'll get to know each other then."

I guessed she was a friend of Lyov. Her shoulders were straight, and the way she stared at Lyov, without any fear, it told me she had some kind of power. She was respected. She would never cower underneath someone's feet.

Swallowing nervously, I gave her a smile of my own. "Thank you."

I didn't know what else to say or how much I could say. Lyov gave me freedom, but I was scared to venture too far.

Lyov cleared his throat, and he tugged me more into his body. This time, I couldn't help the smile that spread across my cheeks. Every other worry…all the fear that consumed me moments ago, everything disappeared.

It seemed Lyov liked me close to him. And my attention on him.

I peeked up at him, suddenly feeling shy. He glanced down, as if he knew I was looking at him. We stared at each other, and I forgot everyone else. The world ceased to exist, and it was just us.

BLOOD AND ROSES

Eventually, he broke our connection and looked back at Lena, who was grinning from ear to ear and practically bouncing on her toes with excitement.

"I will be showing Maria around. She's had a long night and will be resting today. You can have her tomorrow," Lyov spoke. His voice was hard and held no place for arguments.

Lena rolled her eyes in an act of exasperation but nodded in agreement. Lyov pulled me away, and she waved.

I found myself lifting my hand up and waving back, feeling strangely happy at her excitement. It was contagious.

Lyov and I climbed up the majestic staircase, our steps unhurried, as if we had all the time in the world. As if we owned everything.

"It's time to show you around. I hope you like it. My father built this when he started his business. And then it was handed over to me when he passed away. Everything that was his, I own now. You are *mine*. So this is your home. *Our* home," Lyov explained in his rough, deep voice.

Lyov wasn't really a man of words. He spoke a few, but each time, it held so many unsaid words. Every word spoken, they meant something. They held something deep within them.

You are mine.
This is your home.
Our home.

Our. Me and him. Us. We were one.

I was his. And he was mine.

I guessed it was as simple as that. Until one of us stopped breathing.

Chapter 10

Lyov

Her breathing was soft and even, a breathy sigh against the skin of my neck. Maria's head was buried in the curve of my shoulder, her legs thrown over mine as she burrowed deeper into my warmth.

I didn't have to see it…I could just feel it. Sense it, that my little pretty Angel was happy and smiling.

"Good morning," I muttered. My fingers traced random patterns on her bare arms, and I felt the goosebumps rising at my whispered touch. Maria shivered the slightest bit, clearly affected and loving my hands on her.

She hummed and then looked up. Her doe eyes, framed with thick long lashes, were laced with sleep. "Good morning."

A soft whisper with simple words, yet my cock woke up instantly, as if this little Angel had turned in a seductress with sultry words. My morning wood was now raging and desperate for some

BLOOD AND ROSES

attention.

Little fucker had a mind of his own. Fuck my whole fucking life.

Holding back a groan, I slightly shifted away from Maria. "So what do you want to do today? The estate is yours. You can roam around, do whatever you want. There are plenty of things to see and do," I said, diverting my mind somewhere else. Anything else except the thought of her wet virgin pu—

Maria smiled and shrugged. "You showed me around yesterday. This place is so big. If I explore alone, I will get lost."

"You won't be exploring alone. Lena will be with you. I had you for myself yesterday. Today, she will steal you." I chuckled at the thought. She was probably getting impatient downstairs, waiting for Maria to wake up.

"She's sweet." I rolled over to my side, so we were facing each other.

"She is. I think she's just excited that I have finally brought a woman home," I agreed.

Maria's cheeks tinted with a hint of color, and she bit on her lips unconsciously. She fluttered her eyelashes up at me, in the most innocent way that had me wanting to corrupt her in the most dangerous way.

"I am your first?" she asked, her voice small and childlike. It was the sweetness in my Angel that had drawn me to her. The idea of devouring her in the most savage way, tasting and taking that sweetness for my own, had me maniac.

"You are the only woman I have brought home

with me," I explained. *And probably the last, Angel.*

Maria's eyes lit up like a fucking Christmas tree. "I like it. I like being the only one."

She bit on her lips harder, and I could see Maria struggling not to smile at my words. My fingers touched her soft lips, and they parted in surprise, her teeth releasing their tight hold.

"Don't bite on your lips like that," I mumbled, thumbing the plump softness. I wanted to be the one biting on them.

Maria stared at me silently but with so much adoration that it took my breath away. I liked this look on her. The lazy, happy look, and the way she was staring at me. Adoring. Loving. As if I were the center of her whole universe.

I didn't think she realized she was giving me everything I needed. My Angel was feeding my fucked-up soul, and I wanted more of what she could give.

"I should get up." Maria's voice snapped me out of my thoughts, and I nodded.

Her fingers wrapped around my wrist, and she gently brought my hand up. Her lips grazed the inside of my palm in the softest kiss. A kiss of devotion.

So fucking beautiful in the middle of all the ugliness surrounding us. A strange lightness traveled its way into my body. My heart thudded with a strange beat. It was weird, but I liked it.

Maria smiled and then went to get up. The distance between us grew, and I instantly hated it. My hand snaked out fast, catching her wrist and pulling her back. She tumbled on the bed, her head

BLOOD AND ROSES

hitting my chest.

My eyes went to our clasped hands. I watched as my fingers entwined with hers. When ours eyes met, I found myself speechless, like a lovesick puppy.

Fuck me. I was falling down the rabbit hole. There was no way out. And stupidly, I was inviting it with open arms.

"Tell me something…" I started, my voice a little rough to my own ears. Maria shivered at my voice, but she waited.

I cleared my throat and started again. "Tell me something you like. Something you want."

She grew confused, and her eyebrows furrowed in question. "What do you mean?"

"What is something that you really want…something that you love but you don't have?" I explained.

I didn't even make any fucking sense to my own ears. I just wanted to give her something…something I knew she would love and appreciate. But I knew nothing about my sweet Angel.

Maria was silent for a second. I could see her brain running a mile a minute. Her lips twisted thoughtfully, and she cocked her head to the side, staring at me—debating if I were worthy enough to know her deepest secrets and desires.

She blinked and then looked down at my chest, breaking our eye contact. Her cheeks blushed beautifully. "I like to play…the piano."

"The piano?" I questioned, completely surprised that out of everything she could ask for…she asked to play the piano. Something so simple.

But if a piano she wanted...then my Angel was going to get her fucking piano.

Maria nodded almost excitedly. "I used to play it a lot at the abbey. Everyone liked it when I played the piano. They said I played it best. Sister Grace was the one who taught me."

Her words caused me to freeze. Maria must have noticed the change because her lips snapped closed and she stopped talking. I saw worry clouding her eyes, and she chewed on her lips nervously again.

"Did I say something wrong?" she whispered.

"The abbey? You mean a convent?" I asked slowly. My lungs squeezed, and I found it hard to breathe.

Maria nodded. "Yes. My aunt took me there after my parents died when I was fifteen. She brought me to Russia with her, where she was one of the respected sisters at the convent. I was in training to become one."

Fate had a nice way to play us all in the most fucked-up ways.

Well, fuck me. Like I had told Maria, I was the Devil in a pretty expensive suit, charming his way around to get what he wanted. And Maria...she was white purity wrapped in innocence.

Little did I know...she was more than that. I coughed back the laughter rising in the back of my throat.

My pretty Angel turned out to be a practicing nun. And little did she know, I was going to defile her in the most devilish way.

The idea of taking something that was *mine*

alone, something she considered *forbidden*. A fruit that was perfectly preserved for many years...it made me want to beat my chest like a caveman. And just like a fucking wild beast, I wanted to spread those creamy thighs open and show her exactly what I could do to her sweet little pussy.

I was a lucky bastard.

"Is that bad? That I am from a convent?" Her voice snapped me out of my thoughts, and I stared into her worried eyes. I shook my head, but she didn't look convinced.

"You fell silent," Maria pointed out. Her fingers now clenched mine tightly, as if she were scared I would disappear in thin air.

With my other hand, I gripped her chin and brought her head up while slowly lowering mine. Our lips were inches apart, and I felt her suck in a deep breath before she swallowed hard.

"Do you know what I'm going to do right now?" I asked softly. My thumb caressed her jaw and slowly moved to the thrumming vein in her neck.

She was nervous. Self-conscious. Worried. Maybe slightly scared. But she didn't pull away.

Instead her body moved more into mine, a puzzle molding together perfectly. I wove my fingers into her long hair that hung down her back. The soft black strands were soothing. When my hand touched her neck again, Maria shivered.

My fingers grazed her, testing the satiny skin at the base of her nape. Her lips parted at the touch, and her eyes fluttered closed when I continued with my gentle caress. A slow dance of seduction.

Maria nodded. The redness on her cheeks had me

smirking. "Tell me," I demanded, needing her words.

"You are going to…kiss me," she whispered. I felt the vibration of her sweetened voice all the way down to my toes. Fuck me. My Angel was going to kill me, and I would gladly hand her the knife to do the deed.

I responded, "Do you want me to?"

She bit on her lips, blushing even harder before answering. "Yes."

Her word was all the affirmation I needed. The moment that *yes* slipped past those ripe, pink lips, my head was already descending toward her.

Our lips whispered against each other, a feathered touch. Her lips moved against mine, revealing her inexperience, and I let her explore. I stayed still, caught in her magical trap.

I liked the feel of her kiss. I liked the way she was testing her boundaries and trying more…wanting more…needing more.

I felt that strange fluttery feeling in my chest again and sighed. My lips pressed harder into hers, deepening our sweet kiss. My tongue demanded access, parting the seams of her lips before her tongue met mine shyly.

I took her breath away, until she was breathless.

She took my breath away, until I was breathless.

Our kiss was a breathy sigh of sweetness, with a mix of wild.

Maria let out a small moan, and when I pulled away, her eyes were closed, her breathing accelerated.

She was so fucking beautiful.

BLOOD AND ROSES

I cupped the back of her head and urged her to look at me. When she opened her eyes, her blue ones so bright in the sunlight...my heart stuttered.

I didn't know that souls could catch on fire with only eye contact. Because right now, mine was burning with bright flames around my darkened soul.

"You are perfect, Angel. There's nothing wrong with you," I assured her when sensing her previous question still lingering in her mind.

Maria blushed harder, and she brought her hand up, her fingers touching her swollen lips. "Do you like kissing? You like being kissed?" I asked, already knowing the answer, yet I wanted to hear her to say it.

"I didn't like it before," she said. At her words, my hold tightened around her.

"When they would kiss me, I hated it. But with you, I like it very much. I want...more," she finished quietly, as if whispering a secret for my ears only.

A small, serene smile was on her lips, and I let go of the rage rolling furiously inside of me.

"A vast array of pleasure awaits us, Angel. That I can assure you."

I heard her hum in response, and I couldn't help but smile too. There was just something about her, something I couldn't wrap my finger around, but something that made me almost feel...*human*. She made me *feel* something deep within the vast emptiness of my heart.

Maria laid her head on my shoulder again. The thought of leaving to see Lena was long gone as she settled against me. Her hand laid on my chest, right over my beating heart.

She liked touching me…holding me, knowing I was there. Not just a fragment of her imagination. I was the piece that held her feet to the ground, the missing piece that she was searching for yet didn't know.

Those few months as a slave had done a number on her. They took her fucking heart, driven a blade through it, and watched it bleed red. But her soul was intact. I could see it.

Maria just needed a little push for her to realize that her wings hadn't been clipped. Just wounded. But with enough care, she could fly again.

But I was the devil incarnated. I was fucked in the head because I wanted to both watch her fly and tie her down.

I wanted her to see there was freedom in having ropes tied around her body. I wanted to show her that pain could turn into pleasure. Pain could both break and mend your soul.

The fucked-up part was that I wanted my Angel to cry. I needed…craved her tears. But I needed her to know that those tears I would cause, they would soothe her. They would liberate her trapped soul. Her body would sing for those tears to be cried.

Tears of pain. Tears of pleasure. Tears of love.

She would learn how to crave it…everything…*me*.

Every part of her screamed submissive. Maria needed a firm hand. Her submission rewarded by a dominance that would free her and show her the true beauty of this power exchange. She needed

BLOOD AND ROSES

someone to teach her how to love her true self, not hate it because of what those assholes did to her fragile soul.

But I needed to earn that right. I needed to be worthy enough for her to kneel for me.

I was going to be what she needed.

I was going to be her salvation.

And she was going to be my redemption.

Chapter 11

Maria

I was elsewhere as Lena talked mindlessly. My gaze focused on Lyov's back, and I found myself biting on my lips at the sight of him. I couldn't see his whole body, only his profile as he stood by the partially opened door.

He was talking with Isaak. His voice hushed, but I saw the frustration in their expressions. It told me it was something serious…something bad that Lyov didn't like. His back was straight and tensed, with his clenched fists at this sides.

The fury vibrating off him was new to me. Lyov was always sweet and gentle…with me, at least. But right now, the vicious aura coming off him was something entirely different. I wasn't sure how to feel about this. About *him.*

I wasn't foolish or as naïve as they thought. I knew Lyov was a dangerous man. He was *there*, at the Royalist. He bought me. He was just as bad as

BLOOD AND ROSES

those men. Lyov was a wealthy man, and his money was most likely dirty.

His life was a black hole. Dirty. Filthy. Rich. And deadly.

He was everything I shouldn't want, yet the fiery need for him inside of me surpassed all my morals. He had wrapped me in the cocoon of his sweetened words, his embrace so warm and safe that I had forgotten who he really was.

A touch on my arm brought me back to the present. My thoughts came to a screeching halt, and I looked at Lena.

"You didn't hear a word I said, did you?" she asked, her voice both sweet and firm. There was a slight accent in her voice. It was small but definitely there. It told me she was Russian, but years of living in America had taken away her native accent.

Lena stared at me with a raised eyebrow, the corner of her lips turned up in a knowing smile.

When I didn't reply, she let out a small laugh. "We were walking and then you stopped suddenly. We've been standing in this spot for about ten minutes, and all your attention was on that hot piece of man in there."

At her words, I felt myself straightening up. The way she spoke of Lyov, it seemed like they were both very close and familiar with each other. My chest burned and my stomach twisted in a way I didn't like.

Lena must have noticed the change because her eyebrows furrowed and she wrinkled her nose in disgust. "Oh no, I know what you're thinking, and that answer is a big *no*. I don't see Lyov like that.

He is my boss and a very close friend of mine. Family almost. I respect him." She paused and lifted her chin with a small smirk.

"It doesn't mean I can't appreciate all that hotness, though. But then again, Isaak is mouth-watering too. But love, I'm not interested in either of them. If you look closely, you will find someone else standing with them. *He* has my attention. All of it."

I leaned in closer to the door, still staying hidden for their sight and peered inside. She was right. There was another man standing there, listening attentively to every word Lyov spoke.

He was big, bulky, with a mean face. The man towered a little bit over Isaak and Lyov. His lips were pressed in a firm line, and his eyes were pits of darkness. He also wore a very similar suit. The guns attached to his holsters were the only difference.

He was a guard. But the way Lyov listened to him intently told me he was important.

"That's my man there. Boris Ivanshov. Lyov's most trusted bodyguard. He's the chief of security and handles this estate and every other place owned by Lyov."

Oh.

"You are married?" I asked incredulously. She didn't mention anything like that.

Lena laughed and shook her head. Her smile was bright, and I could see the love glowing on her face. "Not yet. He still hasn't properly asked. A few weeks ago, he said, *Buy a dress. We're getting married. I will speak to Boss and make sure it's official.* My response? I kicked him out of our room

BLOOD AND ROSES

and he wasn't allowed back for three days. We are not getting married until he asks me properly. All that alpha male, macho thing doesn't always work, you know."

She huffed in frustration, but there was nothing bitter in her words or the way she said them. Lena was very much swooning and irrevocably in love with that man. It was endearing to see her like this.

She was a small woman, yet her presence was anything but small. The thought of sweet Lena being with a man like the one behind those doors made me respect her even more.

Warmth caressed my skin. The pit of my stomach fluttered, and my body tingled in awareness. Our gazes met, and his grey eyes were intensely focused on mine. So deep that I could easily fall and drown in them. I wanted so badly to reach the depth of those eyes and sink into the marrow of Lyov's soul.

His eyes pierced mine without any veil to cover his unadulterated lust for me, and I found myself breathless for him

For the briefest moment, everyone else disappeared and it was just us.

Only me. Only him. Only this beautiful moment. Right here and now. The rest was forgotten as we drowned in each other. I craved this. I craved him with such intense need that it had me wanting to get on my knees for him and beg. Just a simple touch. Just a simple feel of Lyov's soul making love to mine.

When they noticed their boss's focus no longer with them, their attention quickly diverted to me too. I looked away from Lyov to find both Isaak and Boris staring at me with keen interest.

"I see we have a little stalker of our own, Lyov," Isaak pointed out with a raised eyebrow. He crossed his arms across his chest, as if waiting for me to explain why I was intruding.

A slice of fear slithered its way into my body. They didn't look threatening, but I was still caught, watching them behind the doors.

I took a step back, bumping into Lena. She held on to my shoulders, and I watched as Lyov stepped in front of the men. His huge body protectively blocked the path between us.

He growled something incorrigible under his breath, and both men snapped their gazes away from me and stood up straighter.

"You have him wrapped around your little finger," Lena whispered as she pulled me away from the door.

"I do?" I breathed in both astonishment and confusion. My heart was in knots, and my palms were suddenly sweaty. I clenched Lena's hand in mine, and she grinned in response.

"You do. It's about time," she said simply. "I have been waiting for this day."

More confused than ever now, I just followed Lena wherever she was taking me. But I couldn't stop the question from slipping past my lips. "You have been waiting…for me?"

Lena winked in response, and we continued our way down the stairs. "Lyov said you like gardening," she muttered absently.

My steps halted, and my breath was suddenly

BLOOD AND ROSES

stuck in my throat. "He did?"

Lyov and I spent last night and most of today in bed. He made me talk. He wanted my voice and my words. He said he wanted to know me. Not Rose. Or the slave.

He wanted to know Maria. The girl from the abbey, before she was taken away from the home she had come to love as she watched it burn to the ground.

For months, I was forbidden from talking. Only my screams of pain were demanded, but with Lyov—he wanted to learn the depths of me.

It was a dream come true. Stolen kisses here and there. Lyov's smile and laughter, that I was quickly finding out were only reserved for me.

It was the first time I had been in bed with a man—a man like Lyov Ivanshov—and he didn't make a move to demand more.

He didn't demand my body.

His desires for me were kept under wraps as he showed me the gentle side of the monster hidden underneath the layer of harshness and evil.

And in return, he stole my heart. He now held it in the palms of his hand, bleeding and raw for him to study.

He didn't want me to call him *Master*—but he had become the owner of my heart and soul. If that wasn't the meaning of Lyov Ivanshov *owning* me, then I didn't know what was.

No collars were needed. His firm presence, his gentle kisses, his full lips kissing me with a touch of possessiveness—they made me *his*.

"He learned a lot about me this morning. I wish I

could say the same about him. He was rather…silent," I finally shared with a mournful whisper.

She smiled and then shrugged. "That's Lyov for you. Just observing. I'm sure when the time comes, you will know everything about him."

"I want that," I admitted, my heart thumping about the idea of discovering all the hidden layers of Lyov Ivanshov.

I was sure to find dark things—but maybe I could turn them into roses. Maybe I could make his life…beautiful.

Blood and roses. I would make us fit in the most perfect way.

He called me his Angel. If that was truly the case, I would wrap my wings around him and show him a piece of heaven in the midst of hell.

"So Lyov told me to take you to our gardens and let you have fun," Lena continued, breaking through my thoughts. "Do you want that?" she pushed when I didn't answer fast enough.

When I nodded, her smile widened, and she clapped her hands. "Perfect."

We stopped by the door, and I noticed that we were at the back of the mansion, where the kitchen was situated. I had paid careful attention when Lyov and Lena had showed me around. It was a big house, and it was hauntingly beautiful.

Lyov said it was where I would live from now on…and I could make it my *home*.

Lena opened the large door, and we walked into the back garden. It was enormous, breathtaking, and a dream. I could spend hours outside here.

BLOOD AND ROSES

Free. Not trapped in a cage.

"We usually have someone come in once a week to take care of the garden. But if you want—"

"I will do it!" I quickly cut in before she could continue.

Lena smiled, her eyes flashing with delight. "I'll help if you need me. There's nothing much to do. You could pick flowers you want. I'll have them ordered, and you can plant them."

"Lilies. Back at the abbey, we had them. I was the one in charge of the garden, and I always paid careful attention to the flowers. I made sure they bloomed perfectly," I shared with a smile. The memories were bittersweet, and tears pricked my eyes.

I missed the sisters and the friends I made there, and now they were all…gone.

"I'll get them for you."

I watched as Lena walked away. Before going inside, she turned around. Her brown hair was shining in the sunlight, and her eyes were so clear with love.

"I'm happy you're here. If Lyov brought you home, then you're here to stay forever. I think we're going to be good friends, Maria."

She gave me a soft smile and left me with a clenching heart.

I liked that idea. Me and her…friends. I liked it even more that Lena was so accepting. Sometimes it was hard to tell whose soul was pure or not. Sometimes, deceit was veiled behind a pretty smile.

But I liked to believe that Lena was a pure soul. I had found a friend.

Walking into the sunlight and further into the gardens, I enjoyed all the beautiful flowers surrounding me. Their scent touched my nose, and I smiled. I loved it here. It was everything I had ever dreamed of.

My own little fantasy.

My knight in shining armor on his white horse. Our little castle. And we would live happily ever after.

Although, Lyov was no knight in shining armor. He saved me, but in this fairy tale—he was the beast.

After all, I didn't want a knight, for their armor would eventually grow rusty. No, I preferred the beast. For he would always protect me with his sharp claws.

"You're smiling." A voice snapped me out of my happy thoughts, and my stomach fluttered when I recognized who it belonged to. I was elbow deep into planting the seeds and lilies that Lena brought me. A few hours must have passed.

I didn't want to move…never wanted to leave this paradise.

But Lyov's voice was almost like a siren call. It was impossible to fight the effect it had on me. With his attention, warmth spread through me. I could feel his piercing gaze on my back, scorching my skin and making the butterflies in the pit of my stomach wild.

Standing up, I turned around to face him. I buried my dirty hands in my dress, as if I were caught doing something wrong.

Lyov's eyes traveled up my body, and I noticed I

BLOOD AND ROSES

had dirt all over me. When his smoldering gaze landed on mine, I tried to breathe. A hint of a smile appeared on his lips. He knew he had me caught in his webs.

I only wished I had the same effect on him. Did I make him breathless? Was his need for me the same as mine for him?

The feeling of wanting to please him…did he feel the same for me?

Lyov moved closer. His height was impressive, and I was forced to look up. He cupped my cheek, his thumb brushing the skin over my cheekbone.

"You had dirt here," he explained, yet he didn't stop caressing me.

My lips twitched with another smile, and he caught it. "You're happy," he remarked with confidence. It wasn't a question, more like a statement.

I nodded because he had the power to make me speechless. In his presence, my mind scrambled, trying to find coherent thoughts.

"Your words, sweet Angel. Give me your words." He pushed the slightest bit but never too much.

The firmness in his voice, with a touch of dominance, had a way of making my knees weak. I wanted to burrow into his embrace.

His other arm curled around my waist, and he pulled us closer, until our chests were touching. My eyes fluttered closed, and I leaned more into his palm, never wanting him to stop touching me.

"I am happy," I finally admitted, giving him the words he wanted.

"Does the garden make you happy...or is it something else?" The roughness in his voice caused a shiver to run through my body. There were raw emotions in his words.

My eyes opened, and I held his gaze. "*You* make me happy, Master."

His grip tightened around my hips. His eyes turned molten lava, and his chest vibrated with a low growl.

"*Maria*." He said my name like a whispered prayer—filled with warning and unsaid needs. "I don't think you understand what you do to me."

I was quick to reply this time. "Then tell me. I want to know."

He leaned down, until his lips feathered over mine. His voice was barely above a whisper now. "Oh, Angel. The things I want to do to you. So innocent yet so ready to be corrupted."

My lips parted with a little gasp, and he took the opportunity to kiss me, slipping his tongue past my lips and stealing my breath away.

My body trembled against his, and I gripped his arms for support, scared that my knees would buckle under the force of his needy kiss.

The reaction was instant. My body shuddered, and I sunk into his kiss. My back arched, and I leaned on my toes, silently demanding more. Our pull was magnetic.

I didn't know that souls had lips. For right now, just like his lips were kissing mine—our souls met, and they kissed so beautifully.

"If we don't stop now," he said, tearing his lips from mine for us to catch our breath, "I'm going to

BLOOD AND ROSES

fuck you right here."

He kissed a line down, sucking my plump lips before continuing a path over my chin and then my neck. His teeth grazed my skin, and I threw my head back, soaking it all in and still wanting more.

His words barely registered in my mind...I was lost in him.

Lyov pressed his forehead against my shoulder, and his body shuddered with each deep, rough breath he took. I put my arms around him and gripped his shoulders. I caressed the back of his neck, the way I noticed he liked.

The tension left his body, and we both finally breathed normally. My lips still tingled from his kisses, and I licked them, wanting to savor his lasting taste.

He eventually pulled away and grabbed my hands in his. "Let's go. I want to show you something."

I followed Lyov without any question. Our first stop was his bedroom. He waited for me to wash up quickly—standing in the bathroom and watching me with heated grey eyes.

I felt shy, a little nervous, but it seemed as if he didn't want to take his gaze off me for even a second. Only the shower doors separated us, and I wondered if he would take a step forward and open the doors.

I was his to take. He didn't have to wait...yet...he didn't touch me more than those kisses.

When I was done, I got into a clean dress. Lyov's hand was holding mine again, and we walked down the hall. A few doors away from the room.

We stopped in front a white double door, very similar to the others. I glanced up at him, waiting. Lyov brought his hand up, and in his palm was a key.

"Open the door," he ordered.

Doing as I was told, I took the key and opened the door. The lights were off, and the thick curtains were drawn together, stopping the sunlight from pouring in.

Lyov allowed me to walk into the dark room first. He went to the windows, and I watched speechlessly as he opened the curtains, letting some light in.

Finally, my eyes found his surprise.

My lips parted with a silent, trembling exhale. My heart skittered, and my chest tightened. Those crazy butterflies were back again.

Lyov stayed by the windows, gauging my reaction.

"A piano," I whispered.

I remembered telling him that a piano was what I dreamed of—something I wanted but couldn't have. But this man…this man who had everyone dancing to his tunes, had given me something so precious.

"It's yours," he whispered.

Walking closer, I finally laid a palm over the piano keys. "Thank you," I cried softly.

And then he asked me something. With those words, he stole my heart forever.

"Will you play for me, Angel?"

Chapter 12

Lyov

I had never seen a more beautiful sight. Watching Maria play the piano had become my favorite past-time. Just like it was her passion to play, it became my obsession to *watch* her.

I could spend every minute of the day in her presence, soaking it all in. The attraction was there. But it was more than that. It was more than me wanting to stick my cock into the depth of her, feeling her clench around me.

There was a pull between us. A magnetic connection, undeniable and growing stronger with each passing day we spent together. I wanted to understand what it was, but the feeling of confusion crowded my thoughts. I couldn't quite figure out what *this* was.

Over the days, the more I learned about her, the more I craved to know. Little by little, I started to show her...*me*. I couldn't refuse her when she looked up at me with those begging blue eyes.

So we exchanged our life stories. Hers were filled with roses. Mine were filled with blood. Yet we had somehow found a balance between us. I thought Maria would cower and run away. But every morning when I woke up, she was there sleeping peacefully in my arms.

She was the epitome of beauty. A soft tune to my raging rhythm. An elixir to my dark savageness.

Maria stopped playing, and she looked up, our eyes locking together. I remembered the first time she played the piano, two weeks ago. She had the same look in her eyes. The same look of wonder and happiness…and *something else*. As if I were the center of her universe. The only thing that mattered to her.

"Will you play for me, Angel?"

Maria nodded eagerly, tears still streaming down her cheeks. My chest tightened, and I couldn't figure out if they were happy tears or I had caused her pain—memories of her past resurfacing.

I crowded into her space, towering over her petite frame. Her body trembled with her choked cries, and before I could move, she leaned into me. Her back pressed against my front as she burrowed deeper into my embrace.

I couldn't help myself. In this moment, she looked so vulnerable…so innocent…so sweet, that all I wanted to do was hold her. Wrapping my arms around her, I did just that. I held her to me.

Breathing in her sweet lavender smell, I almost closed my eyes at the undeniable pleasure

BLOOD AND ROSES

overtaking my body. It wasn't desire. Yes, lust was there—but I felt something else while holding her in my arms.

She unexpectedly brought me warmth, and I never wanted to let go.

"I would love to play for you, Master." *Her sweetened words reached my ears, and I hardened at her words.*

Maria calling me Master was my undoing.

I almost reprimanded her, wanting to remind her of the rules, but I couldn't bring myself to do so.

The rules were broken a long time ago...after all, rules are made to be broken...even though I wanted to take her over my knees and turn her perfect ass cheeks red.

"You're not supposed to call me Master, Angel," *I finally said, my voice sounding too rough to my own ears.*

Maria turned around in my arms, and she faced me, giving me a strange look. She studied me for a second and then nodded.

"I know. But it seems that you like it when I call you Master," *she explained.*

So the little Angel caught that.

Of course, she did. My dick was currently waving for attention between our pressed bodies.

"I want to please you, Lyov. And it brings me great happiness to see you pleased," *Maria continued with a whispered smile on her plump lips. I wanted to devour that pink lush perfection.*

I palmed her cheeks. She leaned into my touch, and my thumb brushed her tears away.

"Tell me those were happy tears," *I breathed,*

my chest clenching again. I was sinking in a deep vortex, the world was shifting and aligning, and fuck me, this woman was going to be the death of me.

Maria smiled, and I wanted to kiss her. Just because. Plain and simple.

She grabbed my hand and brought it to her lips, placing a kiss in the middle of my palm. Her blue eyes shone with unshed tears as she stared up at me. Beautiful.

"They are happy tears. You made me happy. Thank you for this gift. I shall treasure it for the rest of my life," Maria said with conviction.

"Then you should make me happy now. I want you to play for me." I had asked her before, but this time the words came out as a command.

Maria didn't seem to mind. Actually, her smile widened, and she gave me a silent laugh before turning back to the piano. Not before I saw the twinkle in her eyes.

My heart jumped a little at the thought of me making her happy.

I sat on the couch in front of the piano...and waited.

Our gazes locked for the briefest second before she looked down again. The color in her cheeks rose as she blushed. Maria chewed on her lips shyly, her teeth pulling at her bottom lip.

I bought her. I had her suck my cock, had her swallow my cum in front of people. I had her legs spread open as I devoured her cunt, drinking in her sweet taste.

And here she was. Shy. Innocent. Nervous. And I

found it all endearing.

Maria took a deep breath, and I eagerly waited. My body was strung tight. I leaned forward, my feet planted firmly on the ground, my elbows on my knees, and my fingers laced together. She had my avid attention.

Finally, she played.

And this sweet little Angel had me ensnared in her trap.

What a beautiful trap it was.

With the first tune, when our eyes met again, I knew in that exact moment I was never letting Maria go.

My thoughts disappeared when Maria stood up from behind the piano. Two weeks since all of this started. And now...a deep yearning inside of me was taking root.

She walked forward and stopped in front of me, her shadow falling over my seated position. Maria licked her lips nervously, and she chewed on them.

She was clearly unaware how goddamn vulnerable she was and how much more tempting that made her. She drew me in like a moth to a flame at night.

So fucking tempting that she had ignited something inside of me. It was visceral, and the beast clawed at me, wanting to be let out so he could have his fun with *his* sweet Angel.

Maria played with the hem of her dress, and I watched as her brow furrowed in concentration. We had gotten close over the last few days, and she had started to speak her mind without having me to push for it or ask.

She was slowly easing into this lifestyle…into being my woman. Ah fuck. That thought did it. My dick hardened, and I almost cursed at the bastard.

Two weeks of being celibate was taking a toll on both of us. My dick. And me. My hands were doing most of the job, but it wasn't enough anymore.

"Lyov," she whispered, breaking through my lust-filled thoughts.

"Yes, Maria?" I questioned, looking up.

"Umm…" she stammered at first and then snapped her mouth shut.

"Is something wrong?"

She shook her head, and I saw the frustration lines on her forehead. My Angel wanted something, yet she couldn't bring herself to ask me.

My head cocked to the side as I waited. Taking her wrist in my hand, my fingers traced the beating pulse there. It must have soothed her because her shoulder slumped and her lips quivered into a small smile.

Her lips parted, and her next words were my undoing.

"Will you kiss me?"

I pulled her onto my lap, trying to restrain myself because I was treading on a thin line. Maria had to step carefully or else this was going to end with my cock being a happy little bastard.

My Angel tumbled into my embrace and melted into me. "Please," she breathed.

Our lips feathered against each other, our breaths mingling in the tight space between us. Our kiss was slow, a sweet making of love. I licked the seam

BLOOD AND ROSES

of her lips, and Maria gave me a silent gasp, opening herself for me.

I dove forward, pushing my tongue past her parted lips, and I fucking *kissed* her. I kissed her the way I wanted. I devoured her with my lips, and she surrendered into it. I fucked her mouth with my tongue, and she took it, moaning and silently begging for me.

It had been a slow seduction till now. But I didn't think I could go slow now.

Her hands gripped my shoulders, and her nails dug into my crisp white shirt, leaving their imprint underneath, on my skin. Maria trembled in my embrace, and I shifted her over my lap until she was straddling me.

My cock pressed against the juncture of her thighs, and she pulled away, another moan escaping past her lips.

My lips never left her skin as I continued to place open kisses down the path of her neck, sucking on the flesh and biting down. She quivered and cried out when my hand cupped her breast.

"Too fast?" I asked, already knowing this answer.

She was a fucking virgin, for fuck's sake. Although she was very accustomed to giving pleasure, she wasn't used to receiving it. I made it my mission to rectify that.

Maria shook her head silently. Her fingers went to my hand, and she pulled at my hair, demanding me to kiss her again. "No. Please. *More*," she breathed before my lips slammed on hers again.

My fingers tweaked her nipple until I could feel

the hardened point through her dress. Her lips moved against mine, and I had to suck in a deep breath. Her dress had ridden up.

The bulge was now rubbing against her panties through multiple layers of clothing. I bet she was soaked down there. My other hand went between our bodies, my fingers inching their way up until I found what I was looking for.

Drenched.

The sweet little Angel was dripping wet for me, and I had only kissed her.

"Room. I. Am. Taking. You. To. Our. Room," I said between each kiss. Maria nodded in response, and I stood up.

Her legs wrapped around my waist, and I held her ass in the palms of my hands as I strode out of the piano room and into our bedroom.

I kicked the door closed and locked it behind us before walking further into the room. Placing her in the middle of the bed, I knelt between her spread thighs.

Her black hair was splayed across our white pillows, and Maria smiled serenely up at me. Her lips were red and swollen, and they appeared thoroughly kissed.

Her chest rose up and down with each panting breath. My heart thundered in my chest.

I laid my body on top of hers, covering every inch. Our chests were pressed tight, and I could feel her puckered nipples through her dress.

"Maria, do you want this? Do you *really* want this?" I groaned in her ears.

In response, her legs spread open for me, and I

sunk between her thighs. *Fuck.* There was no going back.

I pulled back enough to look into her eyes. "I am going to be your *first*."

Maria smiled and nodded. "My first. I want that, Lyov. Please."

"Your fucking only, Angel."

When she nodded again, my cock hardened further between us, and I had to hold back the urge to grind against the fucking bed like a horny teen.

"I like you being my only." After her words, a shadow fell over her expression, and her lips tightened. I knew exactly what she was thinking…and it fucking *hurt*.

She wasn't my only…

My lips pressed against hers, and I hoped to kiss the pain away. "If I had found you sooner, I would have made you mine…and I would have been yours. But right now, all I can give you is this promise. As long as you are mine, I am yours."

Her eyes flashed, and she let out a quivering exhale. "I know, Lyov. Make me yours."

"Gladly."

Pulling away, I quickly shed my clothes until I was naked. Her eyes drank me in greedily, and when they landed on my hardened length, she swallowed nervously.

I huffed back a laugh. She was very acquainted with my dick and its size, yet she was shy every time.

Maria sat up, and I helped her take her dress off. She wasn't wearing any bra underneath, and my gaze zoned in on her wet cotton-clad pussy. With my body pressing against her, she sunk onto her back again. She stared at me with wide, lustful eyes, with a hint of nervousness.

But no fear. None at all.

She trusted me.

Maria moaned when I brought my hand between us, moving between her legs to feel how wet she was. As soon as my fingers made contact with the fabric of her panties, her hips bucked upward and she hissed out a breath.

My lips dipped to her nipples, and I took one peak point between my teeth. My hands slid behind her back, and I arched her toward me. Maria cried out when I sucked hard and fast, teasing her. Her skin flushed, and I continued sucking, biting, and licking every inch of her.

I was throbbing hard against her pussy, and I was tempted to just push her panties aside and thrust into the tight heat waiting for me.

But I forced myself to take it slow. As slow as I could.

Maria whimpered when my fingers found their way into her panties. I traced the wet slit, and when I found her clit, her back bowed off the bed and she moaned out loud.

The taste of her skin was fresh on my lips as I dove in. I kissed down a path, between the valley of her tits and down her stomach until I was exactly where I wanted.

Taking a deep breath, her scent was all I could smell, and it drove me fucking *wild*. I pulled her panties away from her body and pressed the fabric into my nose. Maria gasped and started to protest.

BLOOD AND ROSES

I leveled her with a hard look. The protest died on her lips, and her eyes flashed with molten desire.

"You will never refuse me your sweetness," I growled.

Throwing the panties over my pile of clothes on the ground, I turned back to Maria. "I'll keep this as a souvenir. It's mine now."

My sweet Angel clenched at my words, and she tried to close her legs. Pushing my wide shoulders between her thighs, I spread them open for me. My hands cupped her ass, and I lifted her up. Her pussy was right in front of me, taunting and tempting me with its intoxicating sweet scent.

I was a starved beast, and my mouth watered at the thought of tasting her dripping essence. I lowered myself between her legs, and Maria wrapped her fingers around my hair.

She couldn't decide if she wanted me closer or she wanted to push me away.

I made the decision for her.

My tongue peeked out, and I dragged it against the pink slit. One long lick and I almost came right then and there at the taste of her.

Fucking heaven.

Eating Maria's pussy was now my new favorite past time.

"Lyov," she begged.

I smirked against her core. "Tell me. Beg me to lick you. Beg me to suck your sweet dripping cunt, Maria."

She cried out in frustration when I licked her again, but not enough to satisfy her. "*Please*," she begged. "I...I...taste me...please...I want..."

I hummed against her pussy before I fucking *pounced*.

I buried my face between her thighs and did exactly just that…I fucked her cunt with my mouth. She tasted divine, fucking heaven on earth. I suckled on her clit before my teeth grazed over the sensitive nub. Placing my lips exactly where Maria wanted me, I sucked at her wetness. Licking and diving right through my fucking dessert.

Her hips bucked upward, and she cried out again. "Lyov!" Her voice was hoarse and needy.

She desperately pushed into my mouth, wanting more. I kept bringing her right over the edge before pulling away and not letting her fall. I knew she needed to come; her body was strung tight—telling me she was very close.

My cock throbbed, and fuck, I never wanted to stop. She was my favorite candy flavor.

I dragged out her pleasure before pushing a finger inside her tight heat. Maria clenched, and she gasped for breath. I pulled out and then pushed back in, crooking my finger inside of her. When she bucked and grinded her hips into my face, I knew I found her sweetest spot.

Like honey dew, she dripped with my favorite sugary syrup. She was so drenched that my chin was dripping with her wetness as I dove in for more.

I pushed her legs, bending her knees up and back toward her chest. I had the perfect view of her tight little asshole. Long licks, my tongue tracing those swollen lips, her clit, and down to her puckered hole between her gorgeous ass cheeks.

BLOOD AND ROSES

I was a man possessed. My finger continued to thrust into her clenching core, forcing her to take me deep as I continued to drink her honey.

Maria sobbed, her body shuddering with pleasure. I dragged out her moans and whimpers. My dick wept and begged for relief. Pressing my hips against the mattress, I tried to relieve the pain, but fuck, it needed inside her heat. Now.

My teeth grazed her clit, and I thrust inside at the same time, two fingers pressing inside her tightness.

Finally…fucking finally…I got what I wanted and felt the gush I was working toward. Maria screamed as hot liquid soaked my hand. I pulled away just in time to see her squirt from deep inside.

"Lyov!"

Her knees tried to close, but I stopped her with a low growl. She cried out, her body quivering so hard, I was almost scared she would hurt herself.

I brought my fingers to my mouth and sucked on her sweet juices. Maria stared at me through hooded eyes, her lips parted as she continued to gasp for breath.

I grinned to myself as I lowered onto her body again. Maria laid limp underneath me. My lips feathered over the beating pulse on the column of her neck.

"I am going to make sweet love to you now, Angel."

My mouth found hers, and we kissed feverishly. So fucking needy for each other. In that moment, I needed her more than I needed air. And when Maria continued to kiss me, I knew she felt the same.

Maria whimpered and moved underneath me.

"Wrap your legs around me," I ordered.

She did as commanded, her ankles locking around my legs. The head of my cock slowly pushed inside, and Maria stilled.

"It will hurt a little. But please know, I will make it a sweet pain," I growled into her lips.

Maria nodded. I felt her pussy clench as I continued to push inside. Maria gripped my shoulders, her nails digging almost painfully into my skin.

I slowly stretched her, our hips working against each other before I finally drove all the way inside. Every inch of me was buried deep inside her tight cunt, and I could hardly fucking breathe.

Maria cried out, and I kissed her, hoping to take the pain away. I didn't move, waiting for her to grow accustomed to my thickness.

But she was so fucking tight. Her virgin pussy was making it hard not to come within seconds of being inside her. I grabbed her ass and held her up to me.

With one hand, I pushed between our joined bodies. My thumb circled her clit, and Maria let out a small, pained moan.

Finally, I started moving.

"Slowly," I whispered to Maria. "Just like this, Angel."

I pulled back and eased right back in. My cock slid inside so easily, her pussy taking me in. Her tight muscles protested for the slightest bit, but she was so wet it made it easy.

Maria gasped, and her hips slowly started to move against mine. My breath caught in my throat,

BLOOD AND ROSES

and I squeezed her to me. I fucked her sweetly.

I guess…I made love to her.

I made love to my Angel.

And this moment was raw and beautiful.

While I loved frantic fucking…rough and wild, this was…amazing. This was everything. A slow burn as I thrust back into her pussy. A pleasure from deep within as I pulled out and pumped back in, my hips rocking against hers.

With my hands on either side of her face, I propped up over Maria. I watched her face as I drove in and out of her waiting cunt. Her core clenched and unclenched. I throbbed inside her.

Her eyes met mine, and my muscles rippled with awareness, with the feel that this was so much more.

Her back arched, and she pulsed around me. I felt her coming, and I thrust inside, resting deep before I came too. I sunk into her body and buried my face in her neck.

Maria held me. And I returned the embrace as I emptied myself inside of her.

Point of no return.

This was it.

Fuck. Maria was hooked deep inside my heart, buried far within reach, in a place I'd never felt before. Not in all the years I had spent with countless other women.

It fucking terrified me, yet here I was—playing the wild card. Playing with fate. This sweet Angel was shaking the grounds, the firm, iron-fisted control I had over everything. My life. My business. My fucking empire.

There was no going back.

Chapter 13

Maria

My eyes fluttered open and closed, the bright sunlight affecting my sight. I eventually decided to keep my eyes closed and just burrow deeper into the warmth penetrating my naked back.

The band of steel around my hips made me smile, and I placed a hand over it. Lyov's hold was firm yet gentle. Strong and protective. In his sleep, his grip tightened around my waist, and I felt him pulling me closer.

I melted into his embrace and stayed quiet. It was early in the morning. Usually Lyov would always wake up before me and leave our bed, but never before feeling my lips against his. I would wake up, my lips tingling from his morning kiss, and I would watch him leave. Then, I would fall back asleep in my small, little happy cocoon.

But today was different. Today, I had a chance to admire Lyov in the morning light.

Turning around in his embrace without waking

him up, I wrapped an arm around his waist and cuddled into him. My head rested on his chest, and I listened to his heartbeat.

Slow. Calm. Steady.

Everything it wasn't when he made love to me. Every time.

Three weeks ago, I had seen another side of Lyov, when he first made love to me. He was always in control. Commanding. The aura around him was always dark, something akin to menace. There was nothing sweet about Lyov Ivanshov.

But with his body against mine, his icy grey eyes had softened and his expression had held something of wonder. The liquid fear in the pit of my belly had melted away, turning into something else. A sensation that had my body respond to him.

It had been a sweet ache between my legs as I welcomed him into my body and allowed him to take my virginity.

He laid on top of me. Our chests pressed together. And with our bodies connected, in the aftermath of our lovemaking, I had felt his heartbeat.

Strong. Hard. Fast. There was nothing steady or controlled about his reaction. His heart pounded against mine, and his chest rose and fell fast. He held me tightly as if he never wanted to let me go.

And I held him back. Because I never wanted to let him go either.

We had been breathless, and our heartbeats had created a song.

My hands traveled up his arms, and I could feel his muscles underneath. His bicep bunched under

BLOOD AND ROSES

my wandering touch, and a smile tugged at my lips. Every inch of him was hard and defined.

I looked up and up until my eyes were on his perfectly sculptured face. He hadn't shaved for a few days, so his jaw was covered with some rough stubble. I liked it.

I liked it even more when he would purposely rub his face against my naked skin to tickle me. His eyes would light up at the sound of my laughter; that was how I knew he loved it.

"Good morning."

My eyes widened, and I automatically hid my face in Lyov's chest. His chest vibrated with his chuckle, and my cheeks heated in slight embarrassment.

"There's nothing wrong with you checking me out, Angel," he rasped, his voice gravelly with sleep.

His fingers were in my hair, and he tugged until I was forced to look up into his teasing eyes.

I cleared my throat and pouted. "You're teasing me now."

He leaned his head and gave me a loud, smacking kiss on my pouty lips. "And I love this pout. So freaking cute."

I stuck my tongue out, and he laughed even harder. "See? Cute," he tried to convince me.

He took my palm and placed it flat on his cheek. "Explore all you want, baby. It's all yours, and you know it."

I couldn't hide the smile. My fingers explored, and when they reached his lips, he kissed them. My heart warmed, and my stomach did somersaults.

Could he be any more perfect than this?

His fingers traced some patterns over my lips where the bedsheet had ridden low. We were both naked from last night's activities. It was how every night ended.

I spent the morning with Lyov in bed. The rest of the day with Lena. Oh, bless her sweet soul. I was absolutely in love with this tiny woman whose heart was a gigantic place of warmth and love. Lyov and I would have all our meals together.

And after dinner—Lyov and I were inseparable. Sometimes, I would play the piano. Other times, I would read him a story, a book I found in his library. He would be quiet, just listening to me read to him.

Then in the dark, our sweat-slicked bodies tangled together, exchanging breaths and moans of pleasure until we would slip into unconsciousness.

It was perfect. I didn't want anything more than this beautiful life Lyov had granted me.

"…Maria."

I looked up in surprise and met Lyov's questioning gaze. "You were lost in your thoughts again," he told me.

I bit on my lips nervously, and he tugged them from between my teeth. "I don't like it when I don't have your full attention, Angel," he joked with a raised eyebrow.

I knew he was teasing me, but his words were somewhat laced with seriousness. Leaning upward, my lips feathered against his.

With my head buried into his neck, I placed a kiss on his beating pulse before speaking. "You are

BLOOD AND ROSES

all I think about, Lyov. Even when I am lost in my thoughts, it is *you* I am thinking of. There is no one else."

He gripped my hips hard, almost possessively. "Good."

I smiled and held him closer. We stayed like this, our legs entwined together—in a safe cocoon. In this moment, with Lyov's strong arms around me, I knew that nobody could ever hurt me.

He would be my shield.

And I realized that I wanted to be his protector.

It was my silent vow.

He was a bad man, leading me into his darkness, and I was gladly welcoming it. Every day, for the rest of my life, I would be waiting for Lyov to come home. If he was sad, I would make him happy.

If he was angry, I would hold him until he was no longer fuming. If he needed someone to hold him, my arms would be there to embrace him.

From this day on, Lyov was mine as much as I was his. Leaning up, I placed a quick kiss on his lips, sealing my vow. Lyov looked surprised, but he grinned happily, shaking his head and hugging me to him.

I think I love you, Master.

The words were trapped in my throat, but I smiled, knowing we had the rest of our lives to whisper those words to each other.

Minutes blended together, and Lyov finally spoke up. "We need to talk, Maria."

Confused, I looked up and waited for him to continue. He leveled me with a look that told me he was serious.

My heart pounded in my ribcage at the sudden change. He tucked a strand of my hair behind my ear, his touch lingering right over my pulse point. "Don't be scared, sweet Angel. I didn't want to ask you before, fearing it would upset you, and that's the last thing I want to do. To make you sad. But now it's time. I need to know, Maria."

I clenched his fingers in an act to soothe my worry. Our entwined hands laid over his heart, and my gaze was drawn over the rise and fall of his chest.

"What happened to the abbey, Maria?"

At his question, my head snapped up and my heart stuttered. The pit of my stomach twisted in pain, and my body trembled at the horrible reminder.

"How were you taken?" Lyov pushed.

My eyes blurred with unshed tears as the past came back, drowning and pulling me under in the suffocating darkness.

These were memories I never wanted to revisit. I had them locked away, but now…I couldn't hide anymore.

A loud crash disturbed my sleep. More noise came from downstairs, and I raised my head to listen.

There were screams. And then another bang.

I felt a cold hand on my arm, and I almost screamed before I realized that it was Sophia. "I'm scared, Maria," she whispered. I could hear the tears in her voice.

Gripping her hand in mine, I shushed her. "It's

BLOOD AND ROSES

going to be okay," I tried to soothe the little girl.

We both sat up in the bed and stared at the door of the room we shared together. We were the youngest. Sophia was only five, an orphan the sisters found in the cold streets of Russia. We had become fast friends, and she was always attached to my hip.

Another loud bang echoed in the building that was once filled with only peace and laughter. Gunshots.

My body trembled, and I held Sophia closer, trying to muffle her fearful cries. When I heard Sister Grace's voice, screaming in pain, my body acted of its own accord.

I lost my family once.

And these women...they were all I had left.

I lurched forward, getting off the bed. In my haste, I tripped over my long white nightgown and went down in a heap. Sophie cried out and rushed to me. I shook my head and pushed her toward the bathroom.

"Go hide. Now!" I hissed.

"But...but..."

"Sophia. Please."

Her little body quaked, and her shoulders drew in. With her tiny, skinny arms wrapped around her body, she looked so fragile and vulnerable. It was my job to protect this innocent soul.

"Don't come out until I come for you. Open the bottom cabinet and crawl in. Close the doors and stay there," I ordered, my voice surprisingly strong even though I felt the opposite.

The screams grew louder as I watched Sophia do

as she was told. Tears dripped down my cheeks, and I swiped away the wetness.

Sister Grace's anguished cries continued, and I quickly got to my feet. The door opened before I could reach it.

In the darkness of the room, a man loomed at the doorstep. He was big. Tall. Vicious. And when he saw me...he smirked.

I tried to scramble away, but his arms snaked out so quickly that all I could do was scream when he grabbed hold of me.

I kicked and fought as he dragged me out of the safety of my room by my hair. Scratching at his arm, I drew blood, but it didn't faze him. He only laughed mockingly.

My legs gave out underneath me as we reached the stairs. He continued to drag me down, my body hitting each step painfully.

He threw me on the ground like a ragdoll, and I rolled over, my ribs hurting, and I found it hard to take each breath.

Then my eyes made contact with hazel ones—the same ones I had grown to love too dearly. Once they were filled with warmth...now they were filled with agony.

"Sister Grace." My lips formed the word, but it was only a whisper that came out.

Tears ran down her cheeks, and when I finally saw the whole thing, I let out a loud sob. No. Oh no. Jesus. No. Lord, please have mercy.

Her usual nightgown was in shreds, her body naked for all to see. The man mounted her weak body, and I saw him thrust inside her.

She closed her eyes, and he laughed. He slapped her, demanding that she look at him. Her eyes stayed stubbornly closed, and she bit on her lips too hard; it was bleeding.

I tried to move, but the man who had dragged me down pushed his booted foot into my hips, holding me down. A scream tore out from my throat as he pressed down on my bruised ribs.

"Look, little girl. This is what's going to happen to you."

He spat in my face, and I could only watch helplessly as the man stood up over Sister Grace's body. He held onto his hardened length, and I watched as he jerked off, pearly white substance coating her face.

He continued to mock her, and I silently prayed to the higher powers. Prayed that He would bring an end to this pain and humiliation.

"I'll be next," another man announced, lifting himself from Sister Anna's limp...lifeless body. He kicked her dead body away. She had been used too.

The man sauntered over to Sister Grace. I grappled, but it was no use. More men filtered into the building, turning the abbey into a bloodbath.

I watched as all the sisters, one by one, were used...and then killed.

"She is young, this one," another voice joined, pointing at me.

"Yeah. We will bring her for Boss."

"Aww, c'mon. Let us have some fun with her first."

"No. Boss said he wanted a young virgin pussy."

"How do you know she is virgin?"

"Because they all are. It's a fucking convent. Women with pure bodies, whose pussies have never even been touched. This one is the only youngest. From my best bet, she isn't even legal yet."

One of the men knelt beside my shaking body. He smirked, his yellow teeth and horrid breath making me want to retch.

"Can I at least taste her? C'mon. One lick. I won't take her precious virginity. I just want one taste of this pussy."

"Okay. One taste, asshole."

He smirked and dragged my legs apart. I kicked at him, but he punched my stomach in response. My eyes widened at the assault, and my body tightened in agony.

I felt him rip away my panties, and I watched as his head dipped between my legs. Sister Grace screamed in rage. My eyes went to hers, and her face turned red as she stared at the man between my legs.

"Let her go!"

This time she fought, but her body was too weak against those men. The one taking his turn now rolled her over on her stomach and pulled her up on her knees until her ass was in the air.

"I don't want leftovers, you know." *He laughed horridly as he kicked her legs wider apart.* *"They used your pussy. I'll take your ass instead. I bet it's tight. Never had a dick in this hole, have you?"*

I felt the man between my legs move closer to my crotch, and then I felt his tongue on me.

He hummed against my flesh as he licked me again. My stomach twisted in disgust, and bile rose

BLOOD AND ROSES

in my throat. Not able to bear it any longer, I closed my eyes and welcomed the darkness.

Howls of agony came from the sisters.

And when I heard that little voice, my eyes snapped open.

"Mariaaaa!"

Little Sophia.

Oh my God. NO!

The man between my legs was long finished, but I was still held down by the one who had dragged me out of my room. This time his boot was right between my legs, pressing down hard where the other man had just licked me before.

He smirked, daring me to fight him. His hard face was my worst nightmare. He could have been a beautiful man...but now he was just ugly.

My eyes moved to the left, toward the stairs. I watched as another bulky man dragged Sophia down. She was crying so hard, her little body shaking so badly that I was scared she would hurt herself.

She tried to reach for me, but the man slapped her into silence. "I found another young one."

"There are only two here. This one—" He kicked me between my legs. "And that little girl."

Another voice joined in. "Nothing left here. We should get going. Bring these two to Boss and he will decide their fate."

I was pulled up by my hair. From the corner of my eyes, I saw the man assaulting Sister Grace from behind pull out from her body. She was bleeding profusely, and his male part, now soft, was covered in blood. She sunk to the ground, and I watched in horror as the man pulled out a gun and pointed it at her head.

The gunshot was louder than anything I'd ever heard. It went straight through my broken heart, and I heard Sophia screaming.

Everything that I knew...was now gone.

The floor of the abbey was covered in blood.

All the sisters now laid on the ground...used...broken...bleeding...dead.

They...who devoted their lives to the goodness of others, they died such a painful death. Every teaching the sisters had preached to me was wrong.

Even good people suffered sometimes. And sometimes, it was the good people who suffered the most, while the bad ones continued to live their lives. There were no retributions.

Innocence was taken in the cruelest way. They took the heart of two young girls and smashed them to the ground.

The one holding onto Sophia wrapped his fist around her hair and pulled her feet off the floor. "Let's go."

She tried to reach for me again, her little arms begging for me to hold her. Protect her. I staggered onto my feet as I was pulled by the hair too. My scalp burned, and I could only imagine what little Sophia was going through.

A gun was pressed into my neck. The cold barrel caused me to tremble, and I limped forward.

We walked out of the building, and I could only watch as the man continued to mockingly slap Sophia. He could tell I was angry, fuming at his actions.

BLOOD AND ROSES

He did it purposely to tease me, knowing that I was completely helpless to save the little girl who had woven her way into my heart. My little princess.

A small growl escaped past my lips when he slapped her again before letting her go. Her knees hit the ground hard, and she cried out, curling her body into a ball.

He grabbed her arms, shaking and pulling her back up. His leg moved, and I knew he was going to kick her.

I saw red.

Ignoring the agony going through my broken body, I twisted around and grabbed the gun. His shock was short-lived as I kneed him hard between his legs and tore the gun from his hand.

He sunk to the ground and screamed like a little girl. I took satisfaction in his pain and kicked him again. There were screams, but before anyone could grab me, I pointed the gun at the one holding Sophia.

When everyone froze, I knew instantly he was the leader of this group.

My vision blurred, and I shook my head, trying to keep myself straight. I could barely stand up. My knees weakened, and I locked them together.

Taking a step forward, I tried to hide my wincing. "Let her go," I hissed through gritted teeth.

He smiled in the dark, his teeth flashing sinisterly. "Or what?"

"I will shoot you."

"Go ahead, doll."

165

"Let. Her. Go!" I screamed, taking another step into his direction. The gun was right over his chest. I didn't want to miss his heart.

"Maria," she whimpered, her sniffles breaking my heart further.

"Make me let her go, Maria," he taunted, his lips curling up when he said my name.

When I didn't move, my heart pounding too hard in my chest, he laughed. "You know what she's going to be turned into?"

When I didn't answer, he grabbed her jaw and bent down, licking a dirty path up her cheek. "A little fuck toy for us. Just like you're going to be."

I raged, my fingers feathering over the trigger.

"Maybe we will fill you up so many times that you might even pop out a baby or two for us. Perfect. We will train them just like we're gonna train you to be the perfect little slave."

He raised an eyebrow. "And this one, she's going to be the perfect slave," he continued, now referring to Sophia.

That was the line.

I pulled the trigger. The gunshot rung through my ears. The force of the gun going off pushed my body back, and I fell to the ground. My eyes squeezed shut as another wave of agony went through my body.

I breathed through the pain. There was silence, and then I heard laughter.

My eyes snapped open, and I wish in that moment...I was blind.

Sophia laid on the ground. Lifeless. Bloodied. Her neck was torn open.

The man who once was holding onto her held his stomach and continued to howl with laughter. The others joined.

My bullet missed him.
My bullet went through Sophia's neck.
I killed Sophia.
I killed my little princess.

I couldn't tear my eyes away from the scene in front of me. My lips parted, and I screamed a soundless scream. My fingers dug into the dirt, and I sobbed to the moon.

My whole body quaked viciously, and I was cold...so cold...so, so cold.

The man walked toward me, but still I couldn't stop looking at Sophia. Her tiny body was broken. I broke her.

He took the gun from my hand and hit the barrel of it into my temple. Another searing pain hit me. Blood seeped from my brow, and it dripped down the bridge of my nose and the coldness of it lingered over my dried lips. I could taste the metallic essence of it. I was soggy and shivering. My breath came out in harsh, broken panting.

Darkness clouded my vision. And from the corner of my eyes, I saw the abbey on fire. The building burned in bright red flames. Someone dragged Sophia's limp body and threw her into the raging fires.

I could only watch.
I fell...I fell hard into the pit of darkness.
Everything hurt.
Until nothing hurt.
Silence.

"Angel."

I was being rocked back and forth. "Shhh, Angel. I got you. You're safe. I have you, sweet Angel."

Lyov's strong voice broke through my memories. I was on his lap, and he cradled me like a baby. He kissed my forehead and continued to whisper soothing words into my ears.

My whole body was shaking, and my teeth chattered together, as if I were still cold from *that* day.

Lyov's arm tightened around me. He wrapped the bedsheet around us, trying to warm my shivering body. He continued to hold me like a baby, and I curled more into his embrace.

"It…was…a massacre. They came…to…destroy…us. I lost…everything. I…killed…her."

Chapter 14

Lyov

I never knew the meaning of true horror until the moment I listened to my Angel relive her memories. The faraway look in her eyes, those silent tears running down her rosy velvet cheeks…they were my undoing.

In this moment, Maria wore her broken heart on her sleeve. My chest ached, and I felt anger, a deathly fury at the men who had a hand in destroying my Angel's life—her innocence taken in the blink of an eye. I felt a deep, surprising need to avenge the women whose honor were taken from them before losing their lives in such a cruel way.

But the anger was only a shield of pain at Maria's words. I felt everything she felt, and my heart clenched when she released the first agonized sob, her body shaking with each assaulting memory. My emotions turned jagged, and my insides were tight in knots.

I curled my arms around her body and pulled her

into my lap, listening to the horrifying tale of how she went from a happy young lady to being kidnapped and thrown into a cage, where *monsters* were sneering from the outside, watching the show.

The story of beauty…to ugliness.

The world isn't exactly beautiful. But there are some people who don't deserve to be touched by the ugliness of it. Maria was one of those. She didn't deserve this.

And I somewhat had a hand in her undoing.

I was the fucking Master behind it all. I owned The Royalist. Those men were doing what needed to be done to put money into our pockets.

I never cared where these women came from. I never cared what was being done…all I cared was that my *business* flourished. All I cared about was by the end of a night, I was a richer man by a few million.

I never realized that *this* was the nightmare. That I was unknowingly breaking so many innocent souls.

My arms tightened around my Angel, and I closed my burning eyes. The Devil perched on my shoulders, whispering in my ears, trying to drag me down to hell again. But I shook my head. Not anymore.

This ended here. Tonight.

This fucked-up arena, the place where the Masters sat…everything was about to be burned to the ground. Only the ashes would be left, scattered to the open air.

Maria and I sat there for the longest time. Her tears eventually stopped, and her sobs turned into tiny hiccups. Her breathing was harsh against my neck. Her arms were curled around me, holding so tight.

She thought of me as her shield. Her protector. Her savior. Yet I was none of that. It made me sick. What a cruel fate.

"...Maria," I said, my voice coming out in a hoarse whisper. I cleared my throat, the emotions heavy there.

Her hold grew tighter on me before she eventually pulled away to look into my face. Her eyes were red and puffy. Her expression was hollow—I hated this look...this look of utter brokenness on her face. I wanted nothing more than to erase it all.

She moved in my arms until her thighs were straddling me on either side. Maria cupped my cheeks in her hands, and her lips twitched with a sad smile. "Why do you look like this, Lyov?"

Bringing my hand up, I held her touch there. "Look like what?"

"As if you are in pain. I don't like it," she expressed with a small whisper. The tip of her fingers caressed my rough stubble. "I don't like this look on your face. It hurts me more than I am already hurting."

Fuck. She was going to be the death of me.

My Angel was going to kill me one day. Slowly. With a fucking dagger slowly cutting through my open heart and I would be powerless to stop her.

"The Lyov I am used to, he is strong. He is powerful. He is not broken. Not *this* Lyov in front of me."

"I am a bad man, Angel," I finally said.

"A bad man with a big heart," she cut off before I could continue.

I laughed humorlessly. What a fucking joke.

"Sweet Angel, how wrong you are."

Maria moved closer, until our chests were touching. She laid her forehead against mine, and I took in a slow breath, my body shuddering with the effort to keep the swirling emotions at bay.

"If you were truly a bad man…your eyes would not be filled with tears right now, *Master.*"

I blinked, shock coursing through me. And that was when I felt it. A single fucking tear sliding down my cheek.

Maria quickly kissed it away, her lips lingering on my cheek for what felt like the longest time.

One of her hands released my cheek, and it came down to rest over her naked chest. Her fingers splayed out. Her words were whispered against my cheek, her lips caressing my skin. "Your heart is pounding. Just like mine. I am in pain. So are you. A bad man with bad intentions would not be feeling that."

I gripped her hips, my fingers digging into her skin. She didn't flinch. No, she moved more into my body, plastering herself against my embrace. Maria sunk into me, and I held her there.

My jaw clenched and my teeth grinded together. I was angry at myself. "I see you're trying to find goodness in everyone. But some people are just plain ugly in the inside."

"Lyov," Maria breathed. Her lips met mine in a feather kiss. "People are not born bad. It is the

BLOOD AND ROSES

world that turns us ugly, but somehow in a deep corner...there is something beautiful hidden. Not everyone has that corner. But sometimes, even the ugliest soul has it."

I am the Devil from hell, Angel.

She kissed me again, and I tasted her tears. My Angel was still hurting. And it fucking gutted me from deep inside.

"Angel, I am not a man who just happened to be there that night," I started.

She pulled away, her brows furrowed in confusion. "What do you mean?"

Her eyes focused on me as she waited for me to continue. "I own the Royalist. I own that damn place, Maria."

I waited for a reaction, but I got none. Maria cocked her head to the side, and a moment later, she nodded. "I know."

I reared back in surprise. There were dark parts of my life that I had been trying to hide from her. I had been trying to be her Prince Charming...yet all along she knew I was the monster.

"I heard the people talking that night. Valentin too. I knew who you were since the beginning. I am not as gullible or naïve as you think, Lyov. I am well aware of who and what type of man you are."

I opened my mouth to protest, but I couldn't really form any words. Maria placed a finger on my lips, silencing me. "I know I should hate you. But I can't bring myself to do so when you have saved me from that place. You gave me something beautiful, *Master*. And I can't hate you for that."

My hands shook, and I fisted them against her

sides. Before I could stop myself, I slammed my lips against hers. She kissed me back without hesitation. When I demanded control, she gave it to me. Her lips were plump under mine, and they parted as my tongue traced their seams.

"Maria. I'm going to end this," I growled into our kiss.

"How?" she asked when we pulled apart. "How will you end this *game*?"

"I own it. I can take it down whenever I fucking want," I hissed through clenched teeth.

Maria looked sad at my confession. Her shoulders slumped. "Is it that easy?"

No. It wasn't. And she knew it wouldn't be. The realization sat heavily on us. But then again, I was the fucking King. My words were law. I would find one way or another to bring it all down. Whether I had to create more enemies along the way, I didn't care.

Maria's gentle touch on my cheeks brought my attention back to her. "Lyov. I don't want you to end this because you *think* it will bring me peace or make me happy…because you think this is what I want. I *need* you to stop this because it is right to do so. Because you truly believe in giving freedom to all those trapped souls and saving any other future victims of this cruel game."

I cupped her jaw firmly. "I am a selfish man, Maria. I think about myself, without considering the consequences of my actions. I do things for my benefit. And The Royalist is the outcome of that. I never thought of what happened behind the scenes. Fuck, I barely attend the auctions or any of the

BLOOD AND ROSES

events. It is run by Valentin, and I only know about the money that ends up in my bank account. To me, nothing else mattered. I chose to stay blind to everything else. But Angel, I can't stay blind anymore. Not now, when you are in my life. And especially not when I am hoping to keep you with me, by my side...for the rest of my fucking existence."

Her lips parted, and she breathed, a silent gasp escaping past her throat. "But..."

"You are right. I'm doing this so I can give you peace. But I am also doing this because there should never be another Maria or Sophia affiliated with the name of my Empire."

At the mention of Sophia, Maria flinched, and her expression became pained. Her nails dug into my shoulders, and she looked down. The crestfallen look on her face had me shaking her slightly. I nudged her face up and held her there.

"Don't look away from me. Don't hide."

"I killed her..." she whispered. A fragile soul. A vulnerable heart. A broken Angel.

"You liberated her."

Her eyes widened, and she choked back a sob, shaking her head—refusing to accept my words. "No. I killed her. She would have been alive if I didn't..."

"She would have been a slave. She would have been...*dead*. Not *living*. Maria, think about it. Really think of what would have become of her if she were alive. If those men had thrown her into that cage, just like you were. You saved her, goddamn it!" I snapped when she kept shaking her head.

"Stop thinking of it from your perspective. Think of it from hers. Damn it. She is probably thanking you from the fucking heavens above."

Maria lurched forward and wrapped her arms around my neck, burying her face there. She sobbed loudly, without any care. "It hurts, Lyov. It hurts so much. I miss her. I miss my little princess. All I can see is her blood. Her neck…oh my God. I can't stop seeing it. Over…and over again in my head."

I held her while shaking with fury again. But Maria didn't need me to think of a bloodbath right now. She didn't need me to think of how to turn the soils of the abbey a deep red with those men's insides wrenched open and laid on the ground, right where Sophia took her last breath. I was going to hang each and every one of them by their fucking intestines.

That would come later.

When her sobs turned into exhausted hiccups and small, breathy sighs, she pulled away. Her eyes were glassy, and I saw the *look* in them. A desperate need. Not lust. No, not that. It was something deeper. Something so much more.

Right now, my Angel needed me to hold her and take her pain away. Erase every bad memory and replace them with new ones. *Our* memories. The good ones. The happy ones. Maria deserved nothing less.

"Make me forget, Master. Make it all go away. *Please*."

"Maria," I started, but she cut me off.

"Please."

BLOOD AND ROSES

Our lips found each other again, and she rocked against me. I could feel my length hardening, and she gasped against my lips before moaning when I pressed against the juncture of her thighs, right where she needed me.

My fingers wrapped around her neck, holding her in my grip. Her eyes fluttered closed, and she surrendered to my touch. My thumb stroked down the edge of her collarbone, and I explored the delicate lines of her throat. When my lips found their way to the throbbing vein there, she threw her head back and sighed in both pleasure and relief.

My other hand was ghosting over her bare arm, her back, caressing her. "Your skin is like silk. I can't stop touching you."

"Never stop. Don't stop. I want it all."

The pulse in her neck beat against my lips, and I continued to kiss down. When I reached the valley of her breasts, I sneaked a peek up at her. Maria's eyes opened, and she brought her hands to the back of my head, pressing me against her.

I took one nipple between my lips, and she arched her back for me. There was a fire burning in me. With every touch, it sparked the flint of desire. Over and over again.

Maria continued to move, rocking her hips back and forth. One of her hands went between us, and she gripped my hard cock in her hand. I let her guide me into her heated core. She sunk down onto me, taking every inch of me slowly. She savored this moment, and I did the same.

My hardness against her softness. We fit. Perfectly. Beautifully. Our bodies were pieces of puzzles, joining, fitting, and molding to create one perfect piece. *Us*.

I let her set the pace, but my hand around her throat told both of us *who* really was in control. Maria moved slowly, building her pleasure and mine. It was a slow, burning love. And in that moment, it was everything we needed.

We both found our release, and I felt her in place. She didn't let go, either. My heart accelerated when I heard her whisper my name like a prayer.

"Lyov."

If anyone heard it…they would have thought she was on her knees, in some Godly place, praying for some kind of salvation to the higher powers. But no…*I* was her salvation. *I* was her fucking prayer.

And I was going to make everything right again. My Angel deserved nothing less.

Chapter 15

Lyov

3 weeks later

"Yes?" I grunted when I answered the call. My eyes stayed on Maria as she walked out of my office. Her perfect round ass swayed beneath her dress, and I almost growled.

Before closing the door, she peeked over her shoulders and gave me sweet smile. Little minx knew exactly what she could do to my dick.

Isaak was silent for a moment before he spoke. "Lyov. Are you sure about this? You know I stand with you. You have Agron's and Gavrikov's support too. It's the right fucking thing to do. But shutting down The Royalist will come with a cost. You already have enough enemies."

"I know. I am ready for the aftermath."

"I don't think you are. None of us are, Lyov," he muttered.

"This might not affect us...our Empire, our

business. We have other revenues besides The Royalist. But what about the ones who depend on it? You are about to royally piss them off. Solonik won't go down without a fight. You know this is the only thing he truly put his money in and where he cashes out. Let's not forget the fucking Mexicans. Carlos will come for your throat. What about the Japanese?"

I stayed silent. All of those thoughts had already been running through my head already. I was playing a dangerous game. I was about to start a fire that wouldn't easily be put out.

"Can we afford having them all as our enemies?" Isaak continued.

"Yeah. It's worth it," I replied.

"If they refuse? Try to put up a fight?"

I grabbed my glass and poured the rest of the scotch down my throat. It burned, and I welcomed it. "Kill them. Let it be a warning."

Isaak sighed. "Okay. I'll call for a meeting then. Have all the associates in one place, and the announcement will be made. We will go from there."

"Hmm."

I looked down at the empty glass. Was this how Maria felt? When she was trapped in those cages? *Empty.*

"How is Maria?" Isaak asked, sounding both curious and slightly worried.

I thought of her waking up, laughing, and purposely rubbing her hair in my face this morning to wake me up. I thought of her kisses and the way she smiled up at me after breakfast.

BLOOD AND ROSES

Or the night before, how she ran straight into my arms when I came home. *I missed you,* she had whispered.

Her blue eyes no longer held darkness or a shadow. They were clear…they were beautiful. They lit up every morning when she woke up.

"She's happy," I replied.

"Good. And you?"

I closed my eyes, my heart thumping. "I think…I am happy too."

"I guess it is all worth it then."

"Isaak, is it done?" I asked, knowing this conversation was coming to an end.

"Yeah. I just checked. The money is in your account," he replied. I could tell he was smirking. That little shit. He was enjoying this as much as I was.

"It won't be traced back to us?" I questioned, leaning back against my chair and throwing my legs over the desk. I crossed my ankles and waited for his answer.

"Are you seriously questioning my abilities right now?"

"Well…yes. I am. You have a problem with that?"

"Bastard."

I smirked. "Want to say that to my face?"

"I will. When I get home. Fuck. I miss home."

A chuckle vibrated through my chest at his sad dilemma. "You'll survive."

We hung up, and I looked up the ceiling. My lips twitched with another smirk. Valentin just became a poorer man.

The money I paid for Maria as a slave...I just took it back. Almost twice as much. Isaak played with numbers. Just so Solonik wouldn't get suspicious.

I always meant to take that money back. I bought my Angel to get her out of that hellhole safely. But I would not have her worth be measured by how much I paid for her. She was worth so much more than a few million.

I had made so many mistakes in my life. I had taken things that weren't mine to take. I have done cruel things. I am a bad man.

But my Angel was the best thing that had ever happened to me. She would never be just another mistake.

That night was worth more than a thousand nights. And I wouldn't have it tainted.

My sweet Maria went way beyond the walls of my soul. She was day kissing night, that very first touch that happened every day...every time, that lingering beautiful touch of two opposites kissing each other. She was *that* to me. She was my beautiful starlight—an Angel—and I would continue to bask in the light of her halo for the rest of our lives.

She was worth more than money. She was worthy of the world at her feet.

Maria was meant to be my Queen all along.

Chapter 16

Maria

6 months later

When the car came to a stop, Lena and I stepped out with our shopping bags. She was practically sprinting for the doors, and I laughed, trying to catch up with her.

"Hurry," she yelled. "I want to change before Boris comes home."

I couldn't help but shake my head with excitement. Boris and Lena had been together for the longest time, yet they were still very much in love. The honeymoon stage, as Lena liked to put it, never passed away between them, even after almost four years of being together. I loved catching them during their little stolen moments, when they thought nobody was watching them. It was endearing to watch Boris change the moment Lena was in his presence. His hardened expression, the shield he had up every other time, would melt away, and in its place was soft eyes for his Lena.

I guess love like theirs was rare.

My smile widened, and my heart thumped. The butterflies in my stomach increased when I thought of Lyov and me. How similar we were and how much I had grown to crave Lyov more over the months we had been together.

Those brewing feelings inside of me continued to build up with each passing day. Every time I was in Lyov's presence, I was so utterly lost in him. He had me completely ensnared in his alluring trap. Lyov Ivanshov was dangerous. He was a killer. He was cold. He was your worst nightmare. Oh, but what a beautiful nightmare he was.

I had learned to love it, as much as I loved his good sides. It was impossible to only love half of someone's soul.

Lena pulled me into the house, bringing my attention back to her. She wiggled her hips and winked. "He is going to love this new lingerie. And red is his favorite color on me."

"I can tell. Because you bought three different sets. All in red."

Lena shrugged and then bit on her lips, almost shyly. But I knew differently. She was a little minx and loved to play games with Boris. She knew every button of his, and she was about to push them all tonight. Boris had proposed again, the night before. Properly this time. She said *yes*. Tonight was her way of celebration.

Lena and I were closing on the main staircase when we suddenly stopped short. Isaak appeared in front of us, blocking our path. Our laughter died

BLOOD AND ROSES

down at the expression on his face.

"Where were you both?" he snapped. "You went out alone."

Immediately, a sense of uneasiness creeped its way into my body. The harsh look he gave us said he was mad.

Oh God. I knew instantly what this was about. Like a click in my mind and I just *knew*. My stomach twisted, and I closed my eyes in dread.

When Lena sighed in exasperation, I opened my eyes again. She raised her arms and wiggled her shopping bags in front of him. "Shopping. Can't you see? Is there a problem?"

I wanted to pull at her arms and stop her from speaking, from making this worse. This was not the time to sass Isaak.

Lena cleared her throat before continuing. "Weren't you and Lyov coming home tomorrow?"

Isaak didn't answer. Instead, his dark eyes pinned me on the spot. "Lyov is waiting for you upstairs."

My throat was suddenly dry. I opened my mouth to speak, but my words didn't come out. Instead, I snapped it shut again and nodded. Isaak stalked away, and Lena finally realized something wasn't exactly right.

She looked back at me, and her brows furrowed in confusion. "Is Lyov mad?"

My fingers tightened around my shopping bags, and I shrugged. "I don't know. He's waiting for me. I'll go and talk to him."

Lena pulled me back when I took a trembling step toward the stairs. She looked very displeased about the thought of Lyov being mad at me. Her voice dropped an octave when she spoke.

"Is he angry because we left without any protection? I know he expects us to take bodyguards with us every time we leave, but I didn't think this would be an issue. If it is, I can talk to him and explain."

My throat was dry, and I swallowed a few times before answering. "Lyov wants to see *me*. It will be okay."

The frown on Lena's face didn't disappear. Instead, she looked aggravated and utterly saddened by the fact that Lyov and I could possibly have a problem between us. "But from Isaak's words, I can tell Lyov is mad. And I don't want you to face him like this, Maria. Lyov is a little…*uncontrollable* when he's pissed off. When he's like this, he's not the man you're accustomed to."

I quickly pulled my hand away from her grasp, shocked and appalled by the meaning of her words. My heart thumped with the need to defend the man I had grown to love. "I'm not scared of Lyov. He will never hurt me."

Her eyes widened, realizing her mistake, and she tried to reason with me. "I know. I didn't say he would hurt you. But…"

I stopped her tirade of words with a shake of my head. "I know *my* Lyov. I know I can handle him when he's like this."

I appreciated Lena wanting to help, but Lyov could be a wild beast, and only I knew how to tame the monster if it really came to it.

Placing a hand on Lena's shoulders, I gave her a

BLOOD AND ROSES

comforting pat. "Don't worry. Today was fun. Thank you for spending it with me." She gave me a tight smile and watched me walk away.

Each step I took was hard. Lyov had come home early. And I wasn't here. I wasn't here to hug him or kiss him or welcome him home like every other time. My smiles were not the first thing he saw as soon as he stepped inside *our* home.

He always told me how he couldn't wait to come back to me. How the only thing he cared about was to see me again...*His Angel*. He said I calmed him. Every time he was away from me, he said it was the hardest for him. And when I was in his embrace again, everything was right for him—for *us*.

But that wasn't the worst part. Me not being home was not the problem. Lyov wouldn't be angry about something like this. *No*. It was entirely something else that had me crippled with nervousness.

The rules. The rules that I had never once broken...but I did today.

Panic rose in my chest, and my breathing was ragged as I reached the door of our bedroom. I opened it with sweaty palms.

When I walked inside, my knees weakened. There was nothing warm or welcoming about our room. Not like always. This time, it was dark and brooding. A heavy air around us.

Darkness enveloped me, but I could still see him. My Lyov. My Master. He was standing by the large windows that overlooked the back garden, staring intently into the pitch-black night. The moon in the sky cast a small, soft glow on his hardened face.

Lyov looked vicious.

Cold sweat broke out across the skin of my neck, and my heart raced. I felt for the light switch across the wall beside the door. The room was finally illuminated, and I could see him better.

He was still dressed in his immaculate black suit. Lyov stood stoically, his arms behind his back, his fingers laced together. He looked in control and ready to take on the world.

"Lyov," I whispered, taking a step toward him. He didn't answer. He didn't even turn around or acknowledge me. The only reaction I got was his body tightening at the sound of my voice.

There was a lump in my throat when I tried to speak. I said his name again, taking another step further inside the room.

Finally, he spoke. My heart clenched and then soared. But the bittersweet relief that had flooded through me disappeared just as quickly as I felt it, when I acknowledged his words.

Realization dawned to me, and tears sprung to my eyes.

"Go to bed."

Three simple cold words.

"I..." I started but couldn't formulate a correct sentence. I could only say his name. It was the only thing that made sense to me. The only thing that felt *right*. "*Lyov.*"

"Will you please look at...me?" I whispered, my voice breaking.

He faced me, and I breathed in a painful breath. Dark grey eyes. Dark angry eyes. Filled with something akin to *hurt*.

BLOOD AND ROSES

His jaw clenched, and I saw him grit his teeth. The tired look on his face was masked with harshness. But underneath it all…I saw the one thing that had the power to break me.

I saw disappointment in his gaze.

A sense of emptiness filled my chest, and my stomach dropped. I felt hollow. My fingers twitched, and my arms were begging to wrap around Lyov and hold him.

I am sorry, Master, I wanted to say. But I couldn't speak.

"I don't like to repeat myself. Go to sleep, Maria."

He stared at me, waiting and watching my reaction. When I didn't move, he cocked his head to the side. He looked menacing. I wasn't scared, though. There was no fear. Not at all.

My gaze skittered to the bed before I looked at Lyov again. *Please hold me.*

Maybe he could tell something from my expression because he sighed and pinched his eyes closed. "*Please*, Maria."

That did it. His almost broken *please*. Him begging me.

"Okay," I agreed. Leaving my shopping bags in the corner of the room, I quickly changed my clothes and pulled on my nightgown. After turning off the lights, I climbed into bed.

Lyov still hadn't moved from his position. His back stayed straight, his body tight as he watched my every move. I pulled the bedsheet over my body and laid on my side, facing the window, where he was standing.

He sat down on the couch. We were still facing each other. We were still staring, our gaze never wavering from each other. The silence between us stretched.

I took in a deep breath. Even though he wasn't touching me, holding me…even though in this moment, Lyov was emotionally and physically withdrawn from me, his presence was still my safe haven.

Lyov *knew* that. Without as much as a touch, he brought me comfort.

My eyes started to droop, and a sense of something heavy settled over my shoulders. I forced myself to stay awake, not wanting to look away from my Lyov for even a second.

After a few more seconds of battling against my sleep, through hazy eyes, I watched Lyov stand up and walk away. *No. Come back.*

I didn't have the energy to call him back. I was cocooned in a smog of despair, and it hurt. It hurt so much, knowing that I had hurt Lyov. My heart broke a thousand times when I thought about how stupid I was. They were simple rules to follow. Lyov never asked much of me. I was given what I needed…or wanted. He gave me everything and asked so little in return. Yet…I messed up.

I was reckless. Selfish. It hurt even more when I realized that I *purposely* went against him, knowing full well of the consequences. I was literally silently begging for this mess.

Lyov. His name was just a whisper in my mind as sleep took over, and I went under, sinking into the darkness.

BLOOD AND ROSES

***

In the faraway world of my sleep, I felt the bed move. And then I felt his touch. I forced myself to open my eyes, to gaze upon Lyov's face, but sleep was lulling me hard into the darkness, and I couldn't fight the dense fog.

So I just let myself *feel* it. Him. His touch. His sweet gentle caress that I had desperately yearned for. He had refused to give it to me, leaving me cold and wanting. *Needing*.

Gently, he stroked his finger down my cheek, and I wanted to move into his touch. I wanted to weep with happiness. Master was touching me. He wasn't angry anymore. I hoped he wasn't.

Lyov tucked my hair behind my ears, and he continued to caress the round softness of my cheeks and then traced the edge my jaw. His warm plump lips feathered over my forehead in a sweet kiss. "Angel," he whispered, and I smiled. My soul was filled with warmth and contentment.

I wanted to lose myself in him, drown in him and his scent. *Don't stop touching me. Please. Don't be mad anymore.*

A sigh escaped past my lips, and his touch disappeared. I reached for him through my dreams, fighting against cloudy binds. Master was gone again. There was a dull ache in my chest again, but this time, I let the fogginess of sleep sweep me away.

The next time I woke up, the sense of despair had still not left me. I rolled over in bed, hoping to find Lyov. When I touched cold emptiness, tears stung my eyes. I looked around the room, searching for him, and I found nothing. Not even a glimpse of my hard, angry, yet gentle lover.

Getting out of bed, I left the room. I could tell it was still in the middle of the night. The house was dark and eerily silent. Everyone was asleep as I went in search for *Master*. My bare feet softly padded across the hall, and I stopped in front of the piano room.

I could feel him from the other side of the door. His presence was overwhelming even with a barrier between us. My heartbeat turned erratic, and I breathed through my nose, forcing a deep gulp of air. I softly opened the door and walked inside. Closing it behind me, my gaze instantly found Lyov.

Master was sitting on his usual couch, the seat that belonged to me. The same place he always sat to watch me play the piano.

His legs were spread out in front of him, and his hands were fisted on his lap. He had leaned his head back against the couch, and his eyes were closed. I walked closer, my gaze never leaving his sleeping form. Stopping in front of him, I drank in my fill, taking in every inch of this dark, beautiful man, whom I had the pleasure of calling *mine.*

My strong Lyov, my master, my King…he looked defeated in his sleep. A wounded animal. But even then, the angry lines on his forehead were still present. How did I mess up so bad?

I went down in front of him, between his legs. I tucked my ankle beneath me and sat back on my haunches, kneeling for my Master. With my body cradled between his legs, I pressed into him and placed my head over his right thigh.

A sigh of contentment and relief expelled from the most inner part of me. I was overwhelmed, and I closed my eyes. My soul was both calm and a stormy nest.

His thigh twitched underneath my cheek, and I knew he was awake. I felt his arm move, and a smile whispered against my lips, expecting him to touch me. But Lyov didn't.

Nervous apprehension fluttered deep inside my stomach, and I peeked up at him. His eyes were on me, focused intently. He was giving me a very mean look, and I swallowed, wetting my lips.

Lyov didn't touch me, but he spoke. One word. One simple question that I didn't truly have an answer for. "Why?"

Lifting my head from his lap, I stayed in my kneeling position. "I wasn't thinking properly. I didn't think it would be dangerous. I thought that maybe…"

My words were halted when Lyov lurched forward, and he gripped my throat. There was nothing rough about the way he manhandled me. *No*. His touch was surprisingly gentle. But I didn't miss the dominance in his hold. And I also didn't miss the possessive gleam in his grey eyes.

"You thought it wouldn't be dangerous?" he whispered, oh so quietly. *That* voice. It did things to me. Even with Lyov angry, my body tingled, and I pressed more into his touch. His fingers tightened the slightest bit around my neck.

I licked my lips again, and Master watched with

hungry attention. "I didn't mean to worry you. I am sorry."

"Worry me? You didn't mean to *worry* me? Is that all you have to say for yourself, Maria? I have those bodyguards there to protect you! They are not to leave your side the moment you step out of the estate. *Fuck*! Do you understand that I do *this*...I do everything to *protect* you? Do you understand that these men are there to keep you safe? It's the only fucking way I can bear to be away from you, for you to be out of my sight. Because I know you can be safe with them. Otherwise, I would lose my fucking mind."

My lips parted with a breathy sigh. I wanted to speak, but I was at a loss for words. I was so careless and insensitive. *God*. I really did mess up. When I went to apologize again, Lyov's lips curled back into a snarl, and my mouth snapped shut immediately.

"I have enemies, Maria. Too many to count. And in the last six months, I have made dozens more. Do you know that I am a target every single fucking day? Do you understand that to *kill* me, to fuck me up, to *destroy* me...they will *destroy* you? They will come at you, Maria. And they will be merciless. To hurt me...they will hurt you. Do you not see that every day, I live in fear? I wake up in fear. I go to sleep in fear. Because the mere thought of losing you drives me to the point of insanity."

Each word came out with a growl, his chest heaving, his eyes...*uncivilized*.

"I am a mad man, Maria. And you tested my patience today," he hissed, his face coming so close

BLOOD AND ROSES

to mine, and I shivered in his hold.

My hand came up and gripped his wrist, not to dislodge his hold from my throat but to keep it there. His eyes flared dangerously, and I knew I was playing with fire.

"I am sorry," I whispered.

"No. I don't think you are."

Shock coursed through my body at his words, and I flinched. The tears made another appearance. I tried to deny his claim, but the look on his face stopped me.

"Stand up," he ordered softly. But oh, it was every bit menacing.

My body was his, my mind was his…and I obeyed instantly. There was no hesitation. His grip released my throat, and I stood up on shaking legs in front of Master.

"You broke my rules, Maria. The rules are there to protect you, and you consciously went against me. I can't keep you safe like this."

My chin wobbled against the effort to keep my tears at bay. I was ashamed. Embarrassed. And wanted nothing more than for Lyov to just hold me.

But he was angry. I'd made him angry.

"You know what happens when you break one of my rules. You are aware of the consequences," he continued in the same harsh, rough voice.

I nodded silently.

"Your words," he demanded. Each word hit me like a harsh lash against my fragile skin. Lyov was brutal.

"Yes. I am aware of the consequences, Master."
Maybe…just maybe that was why I did it.

He stared me down, his grey eyes icy. "Good. Undress then."

Chapter 17

Maria

I went to quickly do as I was told, gripping my nightgown and starting to pull it over my head, but Lyov's voice stopped me.

"Slowly, Maria. Undress slowly for me."

His words sent a shiver down my body, all the way to my toes. My thighs clenched. Lyov sat back lazily and watched me intently. Without taking his eyes off me, he took a bottle of scotch from the small table beside him and poured some in a glass.

His head was cocked to the side as he brought the glass to his lips and sipped slowly. The darkness in his eyes didn't disappear. It was still there and more. Intense. Furious. Dangerous.

There was a fiery need inside of me. My hands trembled as I brought them up to unbutton my nightgown. My fingers fumbled with the buttons, and Lyov watched me with rapt attention, an eyebrow raised mockingly.

Finally, when all six buttons were open, I

breathed out a sigh. My hands paused, and my stomach clenched. Slowly, like Lyov wanted me to, I pushed the nightgown down my shoulders and then my arms before it pooled at my feet.

I was left with only my bra and panties. The cold air caressed me, and goosebumps rose on my skin. I shivered even though Lyov's heat was penetrating into my every pore.

His gaze was filled with danger, brutality...and *need.*

At the thought of Lyov being in complete control and seeing him exude dominance with just a mere glance, or just a simple word—it had my senses in override. My body was warm, too hot—and I could feel moist sweat dribble down between my ample breasts. My body responded to him, and I almost moaned. He hadn't even touched me yet.

Master leaned forward, and I stood still, my lungs squeezing and my breath trapped in my throat. His hand reached out, and oh so softly, he touched my stomach. One finger, with just his tip, his touch whispered downward, and I fought against the urge to shudder, fall to my knees, and beg him to touch me more.

Our eyes never wavered from each other as he continued. Down and down, traveling to my thighs and then into the inner part of me. My legs spread just a little wider to give him more space. Now, his finger trailed up, and my lips parted into a silent gasp. Lyov stopped against the edge of my panties, his hand still between my legs. He didn't touch me *there*, where I was dripping juices for him.

Master *tsked* darkly and almost mockingly. "I

have barely even touched you and your panties are soaked through, Maria. I guess you like the idea of me taking what I want…and what is about to happen."

He removed his hand from between my legs and sat up, taking away his warm touch.

My clothing seemed to tighten around my skin, making me itchy. My breasts swelled, and my bra was squeezing me, making it hard to breathe through my clenched lungs. My panties were pulled tight between my thighs, pressing and sticky against my aching pussy. I was becoming wetter, a pool of warmth gathering there. His eyes were dark and fierce, smoldering. His sharp jaw was steeled and intimidating.

Master snapped his fingers at me before speaking in that deep, cold voice of his. "Go on. Finish up your work, Maria. Take off your panties and bra. Show me what you're hiding underneath."

My hands traveled up my stomach to my bra. I unclipped it from the back and held the cups to my breasts for a few slow seconds before slowly peeling it away from my skin, watching Master's reaction. His jaw clenched, and his fingers tightened around his glass.

My nipples were hard and aching for his mouth, his tongue…his teeth. The bra slipped through my fingers and fell to my feet. Lyov swallowed, and I saw him watch the rise and fall of my heaving chest.

Slowly, leisurely, seductively, my fingers whispered over my skin. Down my stomach, below my navel, and I stopped at the edge of my panties.

He took a long drink from his glass. I felt like a vixen when I saw the big hardened bulge through his pants.

I slipped my panties down. My heart thumped, my stomach fluttered, and I bit on my lips when it made a small, wet, sticky sound as it pulled away from my clenching heated core. I let it fall at my feet.

Finally, I stood naked in front of Master.

He took in a deep breath, and I saw his bulge twitch. I knew he was taking in my smell that now saturated the air around us. He licked his lips, and I felt myself drip between my legs.

Lyov's eyes went there, and I saw them flare with hunger as he watched my wetness travel down, coating my inner thighs. He stretched his legs out, pushing his feet between mine, kicking them wider open.

My knees trembled, but I stood there, letting him inspect me with those eyes that promised pain and pleasure. He watched like a predator stalking his prey. His gaze stroked my body, and it felt like a paintbrush spreading liquid fire down every inch of my skin.

When Lyov finally spoke, I shuddered. "Turn around." I did as I was commanded, turning away from him. I almost whimpered in protest but knew it would get me nowhere.

"On your knees." I instantly dropped to my knees.

"Good girl," he whispered in slow appreciation. "Put your hands flat on the floor, a few inches away from your body. Lean over and push your ass in the

BLOOD AND ROSES

air. Spread your legs a little."

My body trembled, and the inside of me grew molten with desire. Taking a deep breath, I got into the position Master told me to. I placed my forehead on the back on my hands and waited.

Cold air feathered over my exposed ass and pussy. It was in that moment that I realized how open I was to Lyov in this position. *Oh God.*

If it was possible, I grew even wetter. I heard Lyov give out a low groan, and I couldn't help but smile. Knowing that I affected him the same way he did to me…well, it pleased me more than anything in this world.

"Maria," he started.

"Yes, Master?"

"Do you understand what is about to happen?" he asked, his voice hard and in control again.

"Yes, Master."

"Do you agree that you deserve to be punished?"

I clenched when he spoke again. Closing my eyes, I sucked in another deep breath. The scent of me filled my nose, and my legs shook. "Yes, Master. I agree."

"Why do you think you need to be punished?" he continued in the same cold tone.

This time, I tripped over my words. "Because…because I broke…your…rules, Master. You do everything to protect me, but I was selfish and reckless. I put myself in danger, and in doing so, I…worried you. I hurt you. I need to face the…consequences of breaking your rules."

"Good girl." My heart soared at those two words. "How do you think you should be punished?"

201

Shock jolted through my system at his question. *He* was asking *me* to choose my punishment?

"You can decide for me, Master. It is your right."

The small click of glass against the wood told me he had placed his drink down. "Turn around, Maria."

My eyes widened. I sat up and turned around, although still kneeling for Lyov. I felt the heat of him as he leaned over me. His fingers went under my chin, and he tipped my face up to his. Our eyes locked. His were still missing any sign of warmth. His stares could cut me and make me bleed. They were still dark and hard, but I could see that his anger had somewhat diminished.

"I am giving you a choice," he said in a low voice.

Completely enthralled into those deep grey eyes, I whispered, "I don't want to make a choice. Whatever you choose for me, I accept it, Master."

I could tell my answer satisfied him. He loved being in control, and my submission had fed his urge to dominate me. I could hardly breathe now. His touch was fire against my jaw, and my eyes almost fluttered close.

"You were gone for eight hours. Without protection. You will receive two spanks for each hour you were gone. That totals sixteen. Do you agree, Maria?"

I nodded without any reflection. I didn't have to. I trusted Lyov. He knew me, and he knew what I needed and how much I could take.

"Your words," he pushed with a small, breathy speech.

BLOOD AND ROSES

"Yes, Master. I agree."

He looked pleased. Oh, how pleased he looked. I made him proud of me.

Lyov released me and sat back against the couch. His hand came up to his neck, and I watched as he tugged at his tie, almost roughly. He pulled it over his head and dropped it on the floor. Slowly, he unbuttoned the first three buttons of his crisp white shirt, and then he rolled up his sleeves up to his elbows.

I watched his mouth take in the breath I was craving to steal from him. My body shuddered when his hands fell down to his lap again. My gaze went to his belt, and then it snapped up again, to look at Lyov's eyes.

He smirked coldly at my expression. "No. Not the belt. You aren't ready for that *yet*. It will be my palm turning your ass red until you can't sit down, Maria."

My lungs burned, and I almost passed out right there. Lyov motioned for me to stand up, and I did so on trembling legs. It was a wonder I could still stand up.

His arm reached out, and then I was being pulled into him. It happened fast. I was standing one second and the next, I was over his lap. My stomach pressed against his thighs and my head was hanging down. My ass was perched over and up in the air, right where he wanted me.

"You will count each time my palm comes down on your ass, Maria. Sixteen. If you miss one count, we start over again, and I will add one more for each time you miss a count. Is that understood?" he growled.

"Yes, Master," I breathed.

"If you want me to stop at any time, you just say the word *stop* and I will. But Maria, you will use that word *only* if you feel you can't take it anymore. You will *not* use the word just to get out of punishment. Is that understood?"

Everything was in knots as I responded, "Yes, Master."

His palm caressed my ass cheeks, and I closed my eyes, trying to breathe. I was nervous. I was a wreck with desire and anticipation. There was a touch of fear at the unexpected, but nothing to ruin my *need* for Lyov.

His wandering touch was gentle and exquisitely soft as he kneaded the softness of my ass. One of his hands came between us, and he cupped my breast. He gave me a small squeeze, and I clenched, more wetness dripping between my thighs. Lyov continued to caress me, and then he pulled my ass cheeks apart.

My cheeks heated in slight embarrassment, but when he hummed in appreciation, a sizzle of excitement went through me. I started to squirm when his fingers trailed between the crack and then down my wet lips.

His touch disappeared from my skin. My heart pounded in anxiety, and anticipation licked its way through my fevered body. I tried to look over my shoulder but stopped when his palm suddenly came down and made contact with my left cheek.

I flinched at the unexpected spank, and my back arched. It was a small sting, didn't hurt too much, but it was the unexpected that made me gasp.

His palm stayed there, waiting. "One," I gasped quickly.

He hummed again. Lyov slowly stroked my skin again before his touch disappeared. This time, I knew what was coming. The second spank, this time on my right cheek, wasn't too bad. The pain intensity was the same as the first.

"Two," I breathed.

"Such a pretty little ass, Maria. I would say it's a shame I have to turn it red, but that would be a lie."

He ran his fingers over my bare skin, his touch intimate and demanding. My awareness was filled with bombarding sensations. It was almost too much. He stroked me between my legs, touching my wetness, spreading it more over my pussy.

The sudden stinging pain took me by surprise, and my head reared up with another gasp. Oh my God. This spank was not gentle. Not like the first two. My left cheek was hot and burning.

I barely got my count out before he was handing out another spank on my left ass cheek, just as hard and fast.

Pain seared my skin. Master had one of his arms curled around my waist, holding me still as he continued to shower his punishment on my ass.

He didn't go slow. He wasn't soft. *This*...this was the punishment. And it *hurt*.

With each spank, I counted breathlessly. By the tenth, tears were running down my cheeks.

Master stopped, and I choked back a sob. My body was shaking, but I tried to be brave and strong for Lyov.

"You are quite extraordinary," Master praised, his lips feathering over my ear. His whisper had me calmed, and I relaxed into his hold. "Good girl."

His fingers were between my legs again, parting them and pushing against the lips begging for him. He pushed a finger inside of me, and I tried to hide my moan. Oh God. I could hear how wet I was. In and out, he moved deliciously inside of me. Slowly and at his leisure.

My ass was on fire and burning, but it was an exquisite ache as Master continued to touch the inside of my pussy. He pushed in another finger and started to massage my inner walls. My thighs clenched, and my eyes fluttered closed.

When he felt that I was coming close to a release, he pulled his fingers out and then…

The sting of pain against my ass took me by surprise again. I whimpered out the count as Lyov continued to deliver the spanking at his same punishing pace as before. Through the pain, I found a sweet, aching pleasure. And through the pleasure came the regret at disappointing him.

"I am sorry," I whispered as he handed me the last hard spank.

Finally, he was done.

And I was exhausted. My emotions were all over my place. My body was tight and in need, desperate for *something*.

I was being lifted and then settled on Lyov's lap. I flinched when my sore buttocks made contact with his thighs. Master held me close, and he brought my head to his shoulders. I buried my face into neck and *finally*…I took the deepest breath and everything was *right* again.

I smiled against his skin. I looked up and our eyes met. His gaze was hard but proud, and I reveled in that pride. "You were so good, Maria."

"Thank you, Master."

His fingers trailed up my neck, and then he cupped my jaw. Our lips met, and our kiss was unhurried.

When we pulled apart, Lyov gave me a look. I could see a dangerous gleam in there, and I instantly knew he knew the *truth*. "Maria. Did you purposely break my rule because you wanted me to punish you?"

I looked down, embarrassed, guilt clawing at me. "Maria, look at me."

My eyes snapped up. "Answer me," he said with a growl, displeased that I was avoiding his question.

I gave him a small nod in response. "I wanted…I needed…I mean…"

Not being able to say it out loud, I could only stare at Master in desperation, hoping he could hear my unsaid words.

I craved his control on me. I craved Master's dominance and the need to submit, to surrender, to let him play my body and mind as he pleased. To let him take care of me like I knew he would.

Over the last few months, Lyov spoiled me. I was a *good girl*, and Lyov was the sweetest and the gentlest. But I was missing his *other* side. The side I had seen at the auction, our first night together…the first time he touched me…the very first time I pleased him with my mouth and made him come.

I *needed* that side of Lyov. I needed him to be

my *Master*. And I knew the only way to bring it out was to play with fire.

I knew that Lyov understood me before he even handed out my punishment. He just wanted me to say the words, to admit what I wanted and why I did it.

The menacing look was back on Lyov's face again. He looked *beautiful* like this. Before I could think, he had me by the throat again, and I almost smiled.

There you are, my Lyov.

His lips curled back in a dangerous snarl, and his jaw clenched. "You. Played. A. Dangerous. Game. Maria."

"I'm sorry," I breathed again.

"No. You aren't." To Lyov, I was transparent.

"But don't worry, little one. You will be *very sorry* by the time I'm done with you and tonight ends," he rumbled dangerously, the sound vibrating through his chest.

I gasped, and then an intense heat went through my body. Without waiting for my response or giving me a chance to really think, Lyov was pushing me down on my knees, until I was kneeling between his spread legs.

In front of me, Lyov tugged at his belt and then unzipped his pants agitatedly—almost impatiently. My angry love was back again. A mixture of fear and anticipation slithered its way deep within me.

He pulled out his cock, and his hard length was fisted in his hand. Lyov gripped the back of my neck and pulled me forward. My lips parted instantaneously as he guided his cock past my lips.

I was exhausted and limp, but fire was burning through me. Lyov didn't waste any time. He didn't even wait for me to adjust to his girth or length. Instead, he started to thrust repeatedly, hitting the back of my throat each time.

I fought against the urge to gag. My lips were stretched tight over his cock. I couldn't do anything. I was without control as he used me.

My gaze was seeking his, and when we met, his eyes glittered furiously. Lyov angled my head up and to the side slightly. He pulled me more into him, and his ass left the couch until he was almost straddling my face, forcing himself down my throat.

I squirmed and fought against the invasion, suddenly finding myself out of breath. For the longest moment, he stayed still, rooted deep inside me, and I had to learn to swallow against him. When I struggled, he pressed harder, and then pulled out before pushing back in without giving me time to breathe.

My eyes watered, and he pulled out. The moist head, dripping with cum, rested against my lips. I calmed when his fingers tightened around the base of my nape. His hold let me know that he had me. He was telling me to give him control.

So I did. I opened my mouth wider and waited. He nodded, satisfied. Master withdrew before sliding his engorged cock back past my lips again. My throat was working against me, fighting to reject this big hard length so deep inside of me. It took everything in me to breathe through my nose and focus on his grey eyes.

Tears ran down my cheeks as he continued to

thrust in and out, fucking my mouth with abandon. He fucked it as if he were fucking my now clenching, dripping core.

Lyov was making a mess of me as I drooled and allowed him to use me. The sucking sounds filled the room as he continued to move his hips with a punishing rhythm. Pre-cum spilled over my tongue, and I tasted the saltiness of him. I hummed, and he swelled larger.

He thrust one last time inside. His face blurred, and I finally felt him. He erupted into my mouth without warning, and I greedily drank him. Cum spilled past my lips as I continued to suck and lick. Lyov released a long grunt, pushing deeper into my throat and staying there, even after spilling all his essence into the depth of me.

I continued to lazily lick and suck him, moving my mouth against his semi-hard length now.

He twitched, and I could feel him growing impatient with need again. Lyov growled like an enraged beast. Pulling out of my mouth, he stood up and gripped my arms, pulling me into a standing position too.

I wobbled and felt dizzy for a second. My vision was still blurred as I was walked backward. Suddenly, he swiveled me around, my back facing his front. My eyes widened when I saw the grand piano in front of me.

With Master's hand on my back, he pushed me forward and made me lean over, my bare front pressing into the hard surface. The top of the piano was cold, and my nipples hardened. Lyov's body pushed against mine, and I was rendered powerless.

BLOOD AND ROSES

My whole body was hyperaware, and the fabric of his clothes pressing into my sensitive skin made me moan.

Lyov bit my ear teasingly. "Horny girl. Desperate for my cock and to have her cunt filled."

I shuddered and moaned in response. His warmth left me, and I looked over my shoulder.

"Don't move!" he hissed.

I stayed immobile and breathed. My stomach fluttered, and there was something deep inside of me, waiting to erupt, *wanting* to erupt. I was shaking with it.

The next time Lyov pressed into my body, he was naked. His skin against mine felt so satisfying. I was primed and ready.

"*Please*," I begged with a whisper. It was so soft, it was impossible for him to hear it. But this was Lyov. He didn't miss anything.

"You will be begging me, Maria. Don't worry. Although we are not sure if you will be begging for me to stop or for more."

More. More. More. I want it all. Every little thing. I can take it all. Give it to me.

I felt him kneel behind me, and then he forced my legs open and wide. My cheek laid on the closed piano, my chest pressed hard onto its surface as I heaved for each breath.

I felt him near my dripping core. I clenched, and he chuckled. "Look at you, clenching this pretty pink cunt. It's a sight I want to see all the fucking time. I'll never get tired of it."

Slightly shy, I tried to close my legs. His fingers dug into my thighs as he held me open for him. "Oh no. You don't. You aren't allowed to move unless I tell you to."

I let out another moan when he pressed his finger right *there*. Oh my. It felt so good. And then he pounced. He dove right for my pussy. His face pressed into me, and I felt his tongue poking my entrance, before he was sucking on my clit and biting.

I *screamed*.

It hurt. It felt good. It...*confused*...I was so confused.

My mind swirled as he licked and sucked. "I love your taste. But fuck, I want this cunt wrapped around my dick. I am going to enjoy breaking you though, and watch you beg me to stop punishing this pussy," he hissed and groaned.

As quickly as he was there, he was gone. I was left empty and wanting again. But not for long. His front pressed into my body again, the heaviness of him pushing me more into the piano. I was practically crushed underneath his weight, and I was immobile. I couldn't fight even if I wanted to.

But I didn't want to fight. We both knew that.

The tip of his fat cock rested against my wet lips. He rubbed against my wetness, parting my pussy lips and teasing me to the point of complete insanity. I needed to come. I desperately needed release.

"*Master.*"

Me calling him Master did it. His fist wrapped around my hair, and he tugged my head back. His mouth found my neck as I felt him pressing against me.

"This will hurt."

That was the only warning I got before he rammed inside of me. So hard. So quickly. At the same time, he bit down on my neck.

It hurt. Oh, did it hurt. So good. So bad.

He glided easily through my wetness. I was stretched tight around him. Master felt even bigger than before. I had taken him inside of me many times, but this…this was different.

Lyov had me pinned into the piano with his cock forced deep inside my pussy and his teeth leaving their mark into my skin.

So deep. I was so full. I couldn't take any more.

But Master made me take more.

His fingers dug almost painfully into my hips. He leveled himself properly behind me, and then he pulled out before pounding back inside of me, buried to the hilt. *This.* I had absolutely no words.

"Fuck," he hissed.

I whimpered when he pulled out, almost fully. And then he thrust back in with the same painful thrust. I arched my back. Lyov released my hair, and his fingers wrapped around my throat. My head was pulled back, and finally, he angled my face until his lips met mine and he devoured me.

He picked up speed, and I could feel myself clenching and unclenching around him. It was building inside of me, that crazy wildlife fire.

I whimpered when Master pulled out and didn't push back in. But he only laughed mercilessly. "I'm not done with you yet, baby."

My breath caught, and nervous apprehension raced through every bit of me. His fingers delved between us. So much of my wetness had gathered there. He rubbed his fingers in them and then brought them…up…sliding through the cracks of my ass.

My eyes widened, and I gasped loud. *Oh.*

Both of his hands gripped my sore ass cheeks, and he pulled them apart. I felt him spit on my hole, and then he used my wetness to coat and lubricate the tightness there. Over the last few weeks, Lyov had used a plug on me. He said he was training me to take his cock.

I didn't realize that…*now*…

His thumb pressed into my hole, and all thoughts left me. Blank. I couldn't think.

I could hear our rapid breathing and the thump of our hearts. He massaged my inner walls there with two of his fingers. He spread more wetness and spat once more into my hole. Spreading my cheeks wider, he positioned the blunt head of his cock firmly against me.

His lips feathered over my ear. "Don't fight it. Don't fight me," he said hoarsely, almost *begging*.

I shook my head. "I won't. Take me, Master," I whispered.

Those were the only words he needed. In one thrust, he slowly entered me from behind, sliding deep into my ass. I cried out, my head rearing up from the piano. Lyov wrapped his hand around my neck again. Turning my face to the side, he silenced me with his lips again.

He stretched me impossibly full. The first few thrusts were gentle before he surged forward and slammed into me. I tried to process my emotions and all the sensations taking over my body, but I couldn't.

It hurt. With a bite and sweet kiss of pleasure. My head swam with ecstasy. He pulled out fully and then flipped me over so my back was against the closed piano now. Lyov hoisted me up until I was lying back, and I stared into his eyes. My arms wrapped around his shoulders.

Master looked *feral*. A ruthless intensity that had me moaning and whimpering. I was captivated by his dominance.

Lyov spread my legs, and he pushed them up toward my chest and outward. His arms curled around the back of my knees as he kept me there in place. In this position, my hips were tilted upward, both my pussy and ass open for him to use.

I stirred restlessly as Lyov's hungry lips kissed me into dizziness. His cock rubbed against my wet pussy, coating his length with my juices before he went back to my ass.

He thrust back inside without giving me time to think or adjust. I cried out and bucked upward. His gaze bore into mine as he flexed his hips and continued to thrust in and out of me. I was completely helpless and vulnerable. And it was everything I *needed*.

With his body over mine, he mounted me possessively. I clenched and then moaned into the pain.

I sobbed.

One of his hands came up to my neck, and there he was...my throat in his grip. "Trust me," he said in a guttural voice. *I do.*

His fingers tightened, and my eyes widened. Panic welled inside of me until I remembered his words.

Trust me.

My hand went to his face, and I caressed his cheek. Tears flowed down my cheeks, and he blocked my air. A breath. A gasp. And then *breathless*.

The room became hazy around me as I slipped beyond the pain and soreness of my body. Pleasure mixed with pain. Pain mixed with pleasure. There was no way to find the difference between the two. Where one ended, the other started. It repeated over and over again. A soft sigh escaped my lips, and I *surrendered*.

When I dove over the edge of unconsciousness, he let me go and pulled out of my ass before ramming into my pussy. I came back, gulping a long, heaving breath, and my mouth opened in a silent cry as I accepted his cock into me.

His lips desperately found mine, and we kissed. And kissed.

Finally, I came, something erupting inside from within me. A wall that had been built. It came down as I found my release.

Lyov came too, filling me. His thrust became jerky, and he throbbed inside of me.

Our repeated gasps. My moans. His deep groans. With each thrust, his grunts vibrated into my neck. His sharp sweet bite into my skin. His lips leaving wet kisses. The grinding of our bodies together in a perfect rhythm was a beautiful song. The way we fit together, skin to skin, his hardness into my softness, it felt like we had been made for each other.

He wasn't making love to me.

He wasn't fucking me.

He was *owning* me.

And it was perfection for us.

***

Lyov

I didn't stop thrusting inside her cunt, not even after we both found our release. I filled her up, and she milked me. We were wet and made a fucking mess between us. And fuck me, I wanted more of it.

It wasn't just a desire to fuck my Queen. No. It was a ravenous hunger, to devour every inch of her beautiful body until she was a sobbing limp mess on the floor.

And then I would fix her. Put all the broken pieces back together and start all over again.

She needed this, just as much as I needed it. I'd found my match.

I gazed into her hazy blue eyes. Tears were running down her red cheeks, and she was fucking *smiling* dreamily at me.

Beautiful. There couldn't be a more beautiful sight than this.

Maria's body slid down from the piano, and I pulled her to the floor with me when my legs couldn't hold us anymore. We both sunk to the ground. She laid on her back and spread her legs for me. I settled on top of her, and she wrapped her arms around my neck.

I thrust back into her, lazily and sweetly. *Just because.* I never wanted to leave her warmth. Our lips made love as I stayed rooted deep within her.

"I love you, Master."

A small hoarse whisper. I opened my eyes and found her staring up at me, a look of love and wonder on her face. For a brief second, I thought I misheard.

But she mouthed it again.

Then I thought maybe she was caught up in the moment. I had brought her into a place where her mind was neither here nor there. But then she smiled shyly and looked at me with the brightest blue eyes…the *happiest* eyes.

My chest ached, and I buried my face into her neck. *Fuck.*

I wanted to stop myself, but I couldn't. The words slipped past my lips before I could pull them back. I couldn't hide anymore.

"I love you too, Angel."

Her arms tightened around me, and I held her, silently promising to never let her go.

You and me, Angel. We will never end. We are forever.

Chapter 18

Maria

7 months later

His palm caressed my round bump. His fingers were tracing patterns over the firmness of my skin. I loved it when he did that. It soothed me, just like I knew it soothed our baby. Some days it felt like Lyov couldn't stop touching me and my baby bump.

Even though the pregnancy was unexpected and a surprise, it was not unwelcomed. In fact, I remembered Lyov puffing his chest out proudly when I announced it.

Now that I was carrying his child, he was beating his chest every now and then like a caveman. What a possessive beast he was. Lyov loved the fact that the world could tell I was his now. Only his.

His ring on my finger. His last name was mine. His child in my belly. And my heart in his hands. Our souls were entwined in a way that nothing could separate us.

I felt his smile on my neck when the baby kicked. Lyov tickled that side of my bump, and there was another kick in response. He laughed quietly, enjoying the playtime with our very energetic baby. The little one was happy in there, always responding to our touches.

My heart was filled with so much love that I thought it would burst. This was our *Happily Ever After.*

"I hope our baby has your smile," Lyov said before placing a kiss in the sweet spot behind my ear.

I hummed in response and placed my hand over his, our baby cradled in our hands.

"Have you thought of a name?" he asked.

I smiled at that. "Yes."

He tried to wait patiently, and I couldn't hide my giggle when he growled at my long silence.

"If it's a girl, I think…Sophia," I murmured. My heart ached at the whispered name. *Sophia.* My beautiful Sophia. If I had a daughter, then I would believe the higher powers had returned my princess to me.

"It's a beautiful name, Angel. I love it," Lyov agreed. His arm grew tighter around me, and I melted into his embrace. "And if it's a boy?"

"I was thinking…"

"Maria. Stop doing that. Just tell me. I'm kind of dying to know our son's name."

Turning around in his arms, I faced Lyov on the bed. We were on our sides, in the dark, awaiting sleep. I loved this. Our moments. Our late night talks.

My fingers traced his hard jaw and then his lips. He kissed my fingertips in response.

"Alessio," I whispered. "Our son's name will be Alessio."

That name, too, had a meaning.

Lyov wasn't silent for a minute. He stared into my eyes, and I could see the wheels turning in his head. "Do you not like the name?" I asked, feeling anxious that he would say *no* to my choice. Although by now, I knew that was impossible. Lyov could never say *no* to me.

"No. I like it. It's a very appealing name."

"But you don't seem to like it. I can tell."

He shook his head. His thumb caressed my cheek as he tried to soothe me and erase my worry. "I have no problem with it, Angel. I am just thinking what the *Family* would think. Alessio is an Italian name."

"Is that what you're worried about? Because it's not a Russian name?"

Lyov tried to shrug nonchalantly, but I pressed on. "Alessio means defender. It is a strong name, with an even stronger and more beautiful meaning behind it."

His lips twitched at my passionate response, and I lifted my chin up in defiance. "Then tell me about it, Angel. Tell me the meaning," he demanded softly into the darkness.

"There was a young boy at the abbey. He was only twelve. His name was Alessio. One of the helpers there, she ran away with her son from an abusive marriage. They found sanctuary at the abbey and helped us there. But he was sick."

I paused at the memory. He was a sweet boy. Always ready to help. Always so nice and respectful. I still remembered the day we found out he didn't have long to live. I still remembered his mother's cries and then her anguished wail when he took his last breath, surrounded by all of us.

"He didn't make it," I murmured with a shiver of pain. My body pressed closer to Lyov, seeking comfort against the assaulting memories. "He was so strong, Lyov. He fought so hard. He didn't want to die, didn't want to leave his mother alone. He was so mature at such a very young age."

Lyov's arms curled around me, and he pressed a kiss on my forehead, his lips lingering there sweetly. "That's why I want to honor him. The same way I would like to honor Sophia's memories one day if we have a daughter. They both deserve it."

Lyov cleared his throat before finally speaking. "We will name our son Alessio." He paused for a second before continuing. "I love it."

My heart soared, and I stared up at him in surprise. "Really?"

He raised an eyebrow in a mocking question. "Have I ever refused you anything?"

I bit on my lips, trying to hide my smile, but it was impossible. With Lyov, I couldn't hide my happiness, because he made me happy every day. "No. You have never. Thank you, Lyov."

His lips met mine in a soft kiss, and I sighed almost dreamily. He pushed his tongue past my parted lips, and he kissed me in a way that drove me

BLOOD AND ROSES

crazy. I returned his kiss with the same fervor, my tongue dancing and mating sweetly, almost lovingly. I moaned into his mouth as we pulled away.

"Don't ever thank me for loving you and for giving you everything you deserve, Angel." His rough voice was hoarse with emotions. His feelings—all his love for me—was clear in his gaze. His once unreadable icy grey eyes were now filled with so many unsaid emotions, with so much warmth and adoration that it left me breathless sometimes.

How did he do it? Leave me flushed and my stomach fluttering with just a look. My heart would do a pitter-patter dance every time I was in Lyov's presence.

"My name means Lion. I am a hunter. I like to possess and own things until they are solely mine. But I am also the protector of my pride, Angel. It's deeply ingrained in me. It means I protect those I love. That also means I am your protector because I happen to love you very much. *Fuck,* I more than *just* love you. Love is a weak word to describe what I feel for you. I am yours as much as you are mine. When I made you *mine*, I promised that you will never lack anything. There are no limits on the hell I would walk through to make sure you are always smiling...always happy. Do you understand that, Maria?"

There we go again. That pitter-patter dance was back, and my heart clenched. Tears stung my eyes, and I quickly blinked them away.

For months, I had been holding fear in a corner

of my soul. Fear that this would be ripped away from me. I panicked at the thought of *this* only being a dream and I would wake up in a cage again—back into the dark hole where I had ceased to exist, where I had only been breathing. Not *living*.

I cupped Lyov's face in my hands. "What did I do to deserve you?"

"I ask myself the same question every day, Angel. Pretty ironic, isn't it?" He laughed with a slight shake of his head.

I found myself smiling too. There was a kick between us, where our bodies were pressed together. It appeared the little one was demanding our attention again.

"There, there. It's time for you to sleep now," Lyov chastised gently, his palm finding its way to my round, rigid stomach again.

After a few seconds of dancing and moving around, the baby finally settled down. My eyes also started to droop, tiredness seeping its way into me.

"Alessio Lyov Ivanshov," Lyov whispered. "A strong name for a future King."

My lips parted, and I wanted to agree, but sleep took me under.

That night, I dreamed of a baby boy. He had blue eyes, like mine. But Lyov's smile and nose. I dreamed of holding him. And I dreamed of Lyov holding *us*.

It was perfect. It felt real.

And that was how I knew…my first born would be a son.

And his name would be Alessio Lyov Ivanshov.

Chapter 19

Maria

Lyov left early this morning with Boris and Isaak. Business. Work. The Clubs. I never asked for clarification. Partly because I didn't want to know. I didn't want the gruesome details of that side of Lyov's life. I knew what he did and how cruel he was in the position as the *Pakhan*. He built his empire of blood and the brutality that came with it. It was all dirty money.

But now he was expanding his empire. The human trafficking rings had been shut down after great difficulty. Lyov was scared that this would bring war upon our grounds. But they solved it rather peacefully after everyone realized Lyov wouldn't budge on the matter and there was no point in fighting him. He was the Master. The ruler. The King. The game belonged to Lyov Ivanshov and only him. His words were law, and everyone bent to it.

The Royalist was no longer active. It died the

night I sobbed for my Sophia in Lyov's embrace.

Now, Lyov was investing into other means. He promised me it would be safe, and I trusted him. He was a wealthy man. Powerful beyond words. Nothing was impossible for him.

My thoughts returned to the present when I stopped in front of Lena's door. I knocked and waited for her reply. We decided to go baby shopping today. Feeling excitement coursing through me, I waited almost impatiently, bouncing on my tippy toes.

A minute passed, and there was no response. I knocked again and called out. Leaning into the door, I pressed my ear there and tried to listen for anything on the other side. *Silence*.

But I knew Lena was in there because she was nowhere else.

Grabbing the handle, I twisted it around to check. It was unlocked, and the door opened. Uneasiness crept its way into my body, and my stomach twisted with a strange feeling.

I walked inside and paused on the room's threshold.

Something wasn't right.

The room was tidy, with bright sunlight soaking in the wide span of it. It was a deceitful look because the atmosphere in the room felt all *wrong*.

"Lena," I called out.

There was another few seconds of silence. My palms grew sweaty, and I hated this feeling brewing inside of me, a silent storm fighting to break free. My stomach tightened, and my happy baby stopped moving, as if the little one could tell something was wrong too. I cradled my bump, soothing both of us.

"Lena," I said again, looking around the room. "It's Maria. Are you okay?"

There was more silence.

Until I heard a whimper.

And then a sob.

It was pained, and my lungs clenched. I suddenly felt cold.

I followed the sound and realized it was coming from the bathroom. I moved through the room and opened the door.

The sight almost brought me to my knees. A small gasp escaped past my lips when I saw Lena curled on the floor, next to the toilet, whimpering and crying in pain.

Her eyes met mine, and they were filled with anguish. My heart dropped to my stomach, and I felt a cramp there. I could feel Lena's pain, and I quickly waddled over to her.

With some maneuvering, I finally knelt down by her side. I reached out to touch her, but she flinched and then let out another choked sob. My eyes scanned down the length over her body before pausing on her flat stomach.

My throat went dry, and my tongue felt heavy when I tried to speak.

"It hurts," she whispered through a scratchy throat. Her voice was almost unrecognizable. Gone was the happy, chirpy girl. In its place was a fragile, broken woman, crying out her loss.

My gaze fell on the blood that had pooled by her side. "Oh, Lena." I closed my eyes. My chest seized, and it hurt when I realized the meaning of this situation.

Shaking my head, I swallowed against my dry throat and opened my eyes. I needed to be strong for Lena.

"You need to get up. We'll go to the doctor. Nothing will happen. It will be okay, Lena." I grabbed her arm, trying to pull her up. She didn't budge. Instead, she curled more into her body, as if wanting to hide from everything. "Please, Lena," I begged.

She let out another whimper, and her sniffles filled the bathroom. Her hand went to her stomach, her fingers curling tightly around the fabric of her dress.

"It's…too…late."

"No. Don't say that!" I pulled at her again, feeling panicked.

"…too late," she whispered, closing her eyes.

Her dress had ridden up, and I could see blood coating her inner thighs. It appeared as if there were blood clots, a lumpy-looking thing between her legs, on the floor.

Bringing a hand up to my mouth, I tried to stop my choked cry. There was too much bleeding. And I knew she was right. It was too late.

We were both so happy last night, when we found out she was pregnant. We were going to be mothers together. Lena couldn't stop chatting about it…our babies.

She had meant to tell Boris the good news today.

"It hurts. So much."

Her broken words felt like lashes against my soul. "I didn't…have…a chance to tell…Boris. He was…going to be a…father."

My mind raced. My heart ached. I didn't know how to console Lena. I wished I had the proper words, but nothing could be said to lessen a mother's pain at losing her baby.

So I sat against the wall. I gripped one of her hands in mine, while the other stayed on her stomach. Giving Lena a gentle squeeze, I tried to comfort and soothe her with my touch. I thought of going to call Boris. She needed him at a time like this, but I also didn't want to leave her alone. When I tried to move, her hand wouldn't let me go. She made the decision for me.

Lena continued to cry until her tears turned silent. I thought maybe hours passed. Or was it just minutes? I couldn't tell. I lost track of time. It was tormenting to feel my baby's kick.

Eventually, I moved away from the wall and knelt next to Lena's head again. Touching her sweaty forehead, I tucked her hair away from her face and caressed her cheeks.

"Lena. You need to get up. We need to clean you up. Please," I said quietly.

She opened her eyes and stared into mine. Hers were dark—a mask of misery. Her lips parted as if she wanted to speak, but then she closed her mouth again. Silence.

I didn't say anything either, because words weren't needed. In fact, speaking hurt more than the silence around us.

Lena winced when she moved. I helped her into a sitting position, and her gaze went to the blood on her dress. Her expression turned bleak, and then she shuddered. With my help, she stood up on wobbly legs.

When I was sure she could stand while leaning against the wall, I took a step away and went to turn the shower on. I let it run, warming up the water to a temperature I knew Lena might like. I went back to her, where she was still standing, unmoving. Her arms laid limply at her sides as she just stared at the floor. I avoided the small pool of blood and stopped in front of her quaking body.

She let me help her undress until she was just in her panties and her bra. Lena's chin wobbled, and I could tell she was about to cry again. I knew the pain wasn't just emotional but physical too. I kept a firm grip on her arm and walked her into the shower. When she was under the cascading water, I took a few steps back, giving her privacy. I even turned around. "Do you want me to leave?"

Lena didn't answer, and I kept my back to her. After picking a new towel and a pair of underwear from her bathroom drawers, I placed them on the counter. There was still no sound except the water running.

I took a peek over my shoulders to see Lena standing still under the water, staring into the distance. She still hadn't moved from the position I left her. My shoulders slumped, and I took a deep breath, trying to ease the ache in my chest.

My feet took me forward, and then I stopped. I didn't know what to do. I wanted to help, but I was scared it wouldn't be welcome. And then I wasn't sure *how* to help.

Lena wrapped her arms around herself as her

small body trembled. Seeing her so fragile, so vulnerable, I made my decision without thinking twice. She *needed* me now, more than ever.

My dress pooled at my feet as I quickly disrobed. I left my underwear on and joined Lena in the shower. She barely acknowledged me until I touched her hands and tried to uncurl her arms from around her waist. Lena grimaced, and then she whimpered.

Her eyes met mine. "Maria." Her whisper was strained and hoarse, coming out from deep within her. I saw a hint of relief there, when she realized she wasn't totally alone.

We didn't speak as I lathered up her body and hair. She let me help her as I massaged her scalp. Her eyes closed, and she sighed, her body relaxing the slightest bit. That was enough for me.

After washing away the soap and shampoo, I let the warm water cascade around her. Lena breathed a long, deep breath, and she finally opened her eyes. Her hands gripped mine tightly, as if she was scared I would let go. But I didn't plan on doing so, *ever*.

Lena and I, we were a team. It had been like that since the very beginning—the first day we met and she decided we would be best friends. There was no separating us.

I pulled her out of the shower and wrapped a towel around her body. She shivered as I scrubbed her dry and then helped her into one of Boris's shirts and her pants. I did the same with myself, pulling on my dress again. We left the bathroom together, without sparing the pool of blood another glance. My throat felt heavy with a lump again.

The door closed behind us, and I helped Lena onto the bed. I went to kneel behind her on the mattress and combed through her wet hair until every single strand was untangled. She then laid down, and I joined her, pulling the comforter over us.

"*Thank you*," she croaked. Two simple words that meant a thousand things between us.

In response, I hugged her close, and she curled into me. "Thank you," she said again in my chest. Lena softly cried herself to sleep, and my tears fell down my cheeks silently. I rocked her gently until I knew she was asleep.

I am here, Lena. It will be okay.

One day soon, our babies would play together. That dream wasn't shattered. It was cracked, with a few pieces missing. But it was not forever gone.

Chapter 20

Lyov

"Well, congratulations are in order, Mr. Ivanshov. You are now the proud owner of a new hotel chain. How do you feel?" Isaak smirked as he brought his glass of scotch to his lips.

I flipped him the finger before taking a long drink from my own glass. I thought of all the things that had happened the past few months.

Just like I had promised my Angel, The Royalist had been shut down. Valentin gave me shit. Carlos didn't let go easily either.

It was a hard, dangerous game to play.

"You can't do that, Lyov," Valentin snarled.
"I can and I will. Watch me," I replied with the same steady cold voice. There was no room for argument. Solonik bristled at my tone, and I saw him wanting to end me, right then and there. His fingers were probably itching to take his gun out and pull the trigger, a bullet right through my heart.

But he was a pathetic man.

He knew he stood no chance.

He knew killing me would only bring war upon all of us. And there was no guarantee he would make it out.

That was why he never could become the Pakhan. The Bratva needed someone, a kingpin, without fear or weakness.

You see, Valentin Solonik was a coward. He was scared of death. He was scared of losing.

And lastly, he preyed on the weak—because he was never strong enough to fight someone more powerful than him. Me.

"Lyov." Carlos jumped in. His thick accent was laced with fury. God, how he must be dying to end my life too.

They couldn't, though. My men had their hands on their guns. They were alert. Solonik's men were ready too. Carlos's men were not far. But I had them all surrounded. If we started firing now, none of us would make it out alive. And today was not the day to die.

"Do you realize what you're doing? How this could affect us?" Carlos spoke in a low, menacing tone.

I shrugged. Carlos was not a man to mess with.

If I were the King, then he was no less. He was not a man to mess with. Carlos ruled the Mexican Cartel with an iron fist, and nobody could bring down his organization. Not even me. Not that I ever tried.

It was an unspoken truce. I let him do his own shit, and he let me do mine. As long as we didn't fuck each other behind our backs, then we had no problem.

"The Royalist is mine. Yes, I agree, you are my business associates, and you have invested a lot into this organization. Like I said, if the problem is money—then I will have it all deposited into your account. Count it as my agreement of peace. After all, we don't want to be enemies, am I right?"

Carlos stayed silent. He knew we couldn't afford to be enemies. He regarded me with questioning cold eyes, waiting for me to continue.

"We part ways from here, and we shall never cross paths again. You do what you want. Run your businesses how you want and I rule the Bratva how I want. But The Royalist is coming to an end. That is not up for discussion, gentlemen."

Carlos lifted his chin up in angry defiance. "Fine. You do whatever the fuck you want. Take down the Royalist for all I care. You seem to forget that I own my own rings—my own fucking arena. I am not the one losing here, Lyov. You are."

Touché, asshole.

I nodded. I knew that. I knew there were more human trafficking rings around the world and Carlos ran the biggest one after the Royalist. I also knew that this one was beyond my control. I could end the game from my side...but I had no power when it was being played from the other side.

We stared at each other until Carlos's lips curled back angrily. "I have nothing else to say."

I nodded again. "I guess this meeting ends here."

Valentin looked livid, but he stayed silent. His

dark eyes tracked my every move, and I knew he was a man not to be trusted. We might be from the same cloth, Russian, in the same brotherhood—but when it came to power and money, he would do anything. Even stab his own in the back.

I also didn't have to go far to know that when push came to shove, Valentin would extend his loyalty to Carlos instead of me.

Valentin's hands balled into fists at his side. His glare was made to kill. Too bad for him, I had thick skin and thick bones.

I liked to say I was…indestructible.

"Until next time," I said casually with a nod into their directions.

That was all that was left to say, and with it as my final word, I walked away. I wasn't scared of being stabbed in the back, though. I had my men with me, behind me, beside me—in front of me.

No one could kill the brain behind the game. The Master of it all.

Long live the fucking King.

Isaak brought me back to the present. I focused on him again. He *tsked* and raised an eyebrow mockingly. "You need to get laid. What's wrong? Haven't been getting it lately? I thought pregnant women want it all the time. Here I thought Maria would have tired you out."

"You're pissing me off now," I growled.

He shrugged. "When am I *not* pissing you off is the question."

Boris tried to hide his chuckle behind his fist. At my glare, he replaced it with a cough and looked

BLOOD AND ROSES

everywhere in the room except at me. Assholes.

"Maria should be giving birth soon, and she's been sick lately." I finally admitted my silent fears. Isaak and Boris lost their teasing look, and both harboured serious expression at my words. They knew how difficult Maria's last trimester had been. She'd been on bedrest for the last three weeks, and she'd grown progressively weaker.

I hated seeing her like this. Her skin pale and her small body curled up, so fragile and vulnerable. Maria had also lost the weight she had put on since I saved her from that living nightmare.

Fuck. I just wanted this to be over—soon—with both my Angel and my baby safe in my arms.

With a sigh, I started to get up. I chucked the rest of my drink down my throat, letting it burn and making me feel alive at the same time. "Let's call it a night. Maria must be waiting for me."

Isaak nodded and got up too. He clasped me on the back. "It will be okay. She's stronger than you think."

I knew she was. My Angel was so goddamn strong that she left me in awe every day. And this reason right here was why I was suddenly desperate to hold her in my arms. It had been a long day away from my wife.

Just when I was about to reach the door, it banged open, and I was forced to take a step back. Lena appeared in the doorway of my office, completely winded and a look of panic on her face. My blood instantly ran cold, and I lurched forward, pushing past her and running out of the office.

Lena was quick and followed me by my heels.

She was out of breath as she spoke. "Maria is in labor. I found her in bed, and it looks bad. She is…bleeding."

Her last word was choked out.

"Did you call the doctor?" I snapped. Fuck, I was going to lose it.

Lena nodded just as I reached my bedroom. I slammed the door open and found my Angel on the floor, curled up by the bed, whimpering. My heart sunk, and I was suddenly overwhelmed with a horrible sense of dread.

Maria moaned in pain, and I fucking lost it. Right then and there.

"Where is the fucking doctor?" I snarled at Lena. "Why is she taking so long?"

She didn't even flinch. I didn't waste her a second glance before sinking to my knees in front of my Angel and curling my arms around her body. I cradled her in my embrace. Standing up with her held closely against my chest, I put her on the bed. Lena threw the bedsheets away and settled the pillows comfortably behind Maria.

She moaned something under her breath before crying out. Her face was ashen, and her tears were my undoing. Maria gripped my hand, and she squeezed, rather strongly in her weak state. My breath left in a loud whoosh, and I wanted nothing more than to comfort her and take my Angel's pain away. But for the first fucking time in my life, I was clueless and utterly helpless as I watched her cry out in agony.

Huge sobs racked through her body, and she *begged*. Begged for me to make it stop. Begged for

BLOOD AND ROSES

me to save our baby. "Please, Lyov. It hurts…"

"I know, Angel," I soothed, leaning over her body and placing a kiss on her sweaty forehead. I pinched my eyes closed, trying to breathe through my clenching, burning lungs. But it was so fucking hard. It *hurt*. *I* was hurting.

I fought down the panic and forced down the terror. It was a torrent of unmasked emotions, and I had absolutely no idea how to feel or control them.

"I can't…lose…our baby," she whimpered through each labored breath.

My heart pounded, and I fought the urge to throw up. "You won't. Nothing is going to happen to *either* of you. I won't allow it."

My eyes drifted to her legs, and I could see the blood pooling between them, drenching the bedsheet underneath her. Why was she bleeding so much?

I stared up at Lena, as if taking some kind of courage from her—but she looked helpless herself.

"It will…be okay," I breathed, trying to convince all of us. But it didn't seem like it would be. It was at that moment that I started second guessing everything in my fucked-up life.

Dangerous thoughts bloomed in my mind, pushing me over the edge of insanity. I couldn't stop thinking about the fact that I was the one who got her pregnant…I was somehow responsible for my Angel's state of pain. It was stupid to think so, but the blame was heavy on my shoulders.

Finally, the midwife appeared, running into the room, looking out of breath. I felt the urge to claw at her perfectly put together, stupid face and tear her eyes and tongue out. She was supposed to be *here*. With Maria. Always at her side. But she wasn't when my Angel needed her the most.

Her frightened eyes met mine, and she *knew* she fucked up. Without wasting any time, she came to the bed. I closed my eyes, trying to tone down the alarm rising in my chest.

The midwife swore, and I heard her giving orders, asking for towels and a basin of water. I tuned her out, refusing to listen to any words around me. I could only focus on my Angel's whimpers and moans of pain.

I held her hand as her cries tore through my heart and split open my soul. Fear rippled through me at the thought of losing my Maria now. I wouldn't survive it. Not when she was so deeply ingrained inside my soul, rooted underneath my beating heart, and was there to stay.

Maria gasped out loud, and my eyes shot open. She tried to struggle into a sitting position, her hands flying to her stomach as she screamed.

"What's wrong? What's wrong with her?" I asked urgently to anyone in the room. My arms curled around Maria as I tried to soothe her in any way I could. "Do something," I finally pleaded to the midwife.

I didn't know how much time had passed. All I knew was that Maria's pain hadn't lessened. I couldn't stop touching my Angel. Her skin was hot and feverish, and her body wouldn't stop shaking. With each horrible contraction, she cried out in agony. Her small body was giving way, and I could tell she was growing weaker.

BLOOD AND ROSES

The midwife had ordered me to move behind Maria, supporting the upper half of her body in the cradle of my arms. She said it would be easier for Maria to push in this position. My Angel leaned heavily into my chest, her head rolling back against my shoulders. Maria's breath came out jerky. "…hurts."

I hated how small her voice sounded. Wounded and agonized.

My lips feathered over her cheek, and I placed a soft kiss there. She hiccupped back a sob. I brushed her hair behind her face and watched her blink her bright blue eyes open. They met mine, and I was ensnared once again.

Maria bit on her lips hard at another contraction, and I pulled them apart from her teeth. "You are hurting yourself, Angel."

"I can see the head. I just need you to push one more time, Maria," the midwife announced from between Maria's legs.

She nodded weakly against my neck. The next time her contraction hit, she screamed, and I saw her stomach ripple. My arms tightened around her quaking body as I supported her from behind.

"There you go. One more push," the midwife continued.

"You got this, Angel. Our baby is going to be okay. We're going to be okay. I love you," I whispered in her ears.

Another contraction. Another painful scream. Another push.

And then silence.

Maria stopped screaming. My heart stopped

beating. The roar of my blood rushing through my ears stopped. Everything was eerily...silent.

Until...

"It's a boy."

My heart soared. Maria sighed and dropped her head back on my shoulders, but I saw a whisper of a smile on her lips.

"Alessio," she muttered tiredly. I nodded in response, finding it hard to speak.

I kissed her lips, and she kissed me back, sweetly.

There was a commotion. Far away, I could hear the midwife asking to clip the umbilical cord.

A few minutes later, Maria and I heard something that made us pull apart.

"Why is he not crying?" Lena asked quietly from her position beside Maria.

I raised my head up and stared at the woman holding my son. She swallowed hard and gave a slight shake of her head. Maria let out a wail of sorrow.

I froze. My heart stuttered, and I could only stare.

"Do you want to hold him?" the midwife murmured.

Maria opened her arms, and our son was placed on her chest. She continued to cry softly, holding our unmoving baby. The midwife went between Maria's legs again. She said something about stopping the bleeding. Maria flinched, and my arms tightened around her.

My throat closed, and all words were lost from me.

BLOOD AND ROSES

I watched as Maria opened her nightgown and then laid him on her chest, skin on skin. She turned her face into my neck and cried.

My palm pressed against the baby's back. His skin was slightly cold, and I cradled both my wife and son in my arms. Maria looked down at him and softly, she started singing a Russian lullaby she had learned at the abbey in a low, melodic voice. Every night, while she was pregnant, she sang it to our baby.

My eyes focused on our son, and that was when I noticed it.

The rise and fall of his little chest.

My breath froze, and my eyes widened. I squeezed Maria's hand where our fingers were entwined. I breathed out a single word. "*Angel.*"

She stopped singing, and she noticed it too.

And then we saw it.

The smallest movement. Just a twitch of his little fingers that rested on his mother's breast.

"Lyov. He's moving."

Things happened fast then.

Alessio was taken away from us. The midwife examined him, and I saw her rubbing his back continuously, with small little taps.

And then he cried.

A loud, piercing wail that let us all know he was alive and very much breathing. His presence was loud and strong. *Alessio Lyov Ivanshov.*

He was cleaned and then swaddled before he was brought back to us. Maria's bleeding had also stopped by then, and Lena had helped clean her up. She left the room afterward, after tearfully kissing

243

Maria's forehead. "You did so good, sweetheart. I will give you three some time alone. And then it's my time with the baby boy," she said before pulling away and smiling down at Maria and me.

After Alessio was placed in Maria's arms again, I could have screamed in joy, but I fought it down. I was still holding my Angel, and now she was holding our baby. They were both delicate.

"He is so beautiful."

And that he was.

I leaned down and kissed his forehead. "You gave us all a scare. That was one hell of an entrance, Alessio," I said against his now warm skin. He hiccupped in response. His face twisted. His little hands balled into tiny fists, and then he bellowed loudly, almost angrily.

I couldn't help but laugh. *This*. This right here was…happiness.

"He is your son, after all," Maria sighed dreamily. "You Ivanshov men never do anything the easy way. Always dramatic. Always hungry for attention."

I kissed my Angel's lips next. "You were perfect. Thank you for giving me a son."

She hummed in response. "Thank *you*. For not letting me go. It was your strength that made me go through this without giving up, Lyov. I wouldn't have been able to do it without you."

"You will never have to do anything without me. We will always be together, Angel."

A vow was made. I never broke my vows.

They were always made with blood. But this time, it was made from the depth of my heart.

"Promise?"
"Promise."

Chapter 21

Maria

7 years later

I waddled out of the bathroom to find Lyov standing in the middle of the room, buttoning his black shirt. He smiled at the sight of me, and my stomach fluttered. No, that definitely wasn't my daughter kicking at my bladder like three minutes ago. This time…the fluttering feeling belonged to Lyov. Even after almost eight years of marriage, he could still have my stomach tickling with butterflies at just the sight of him and my knees weak with a single heated look of his.

I wasn't sure how he did it, but I never wanted this feeling to end. I wanted to savor it for the rest of my life. To have the love of a man like Lyov was a treasure.

I walked over to him, and he opened his arms for me, like always. I nestled into his chest and closed my eyes, sinking into the embrace of the man I

BLOOD AND ROSES

loved.

"How are you feeling?" he asked, placing a kiss on top of my head. "Is the little princess giving you trouble?"

I shook my head, overwhelmed with happiness at the mention of our baby girl. "No. She's being a good girl."

His arms tightened around me. I knew this was hard for him. After my difficult pregnancy with Alessio and the hard time we went through during his birth, Lyov couldn't bear the thought of me going through that pain again. I had tried a lot over the years to convince him to have another baby, but his answer had always been a cold hard *no* that sometimes made me flinch. Other times, I would just sigh and try again next week.

Until seven months ago, on a special day, I wore him down.

Apparently, Lyov had super sperm, considering I had still been on birth control pills that night.

But I remembered it fondly. It was a very *exciting* night indeed. I wasn't too surprised when I found out I was pregnant soon after, considering Lyov was on a mission.

A mission to fill me with as much cum as possible.

"Your eyes, Angel."

I smiled at his words and lazily opened them before peeking up at my demanding husband. "You want my attention on you all the time," I mumbled, although it was far from a complaint.

He shrugged nonchalantly. "What can I say? I am a greedy man."

I reached up and ran my hands through his silky black hair. God, how I loved touching him. I never tired of it.

"Like right now," he growled low in his chest. His hand ran down my side, over my round stomach, and then he parted my legs. Lyov cupped me between my thighs, and he smirked when my lips parted with a silent gasp. "I am greedy and starving for this pussy. Even though I fucked it very thoroughly two hours ago."

I bit on my lips, stopping the involuntarily moan he was trying to get out of me. Lyov and his filthy words. *That* I would never get used to.

"You know what I want to do right now?" he asked slowly.

I hummed in response, waiting for him to continue. "I want to bend you over this bed, spread your legs, and feast on this pretty cunt. Fuck, I would kneel for my Queen any day if it meant I could eat your pussy for breakfast, lunch, dinner, and dessert. And then I want to fuck you and watch you come real good on my cock."

This time, I moaned out his name. Lyov chuckled, knowing very well how to play with my mind and body without really touching me.

He leaned down and captured my lips with his in a hard, bruising kiss. I melted into the kiss and returned it with a greediness of my own. The whole world melted away, and I never wanted to escape from this bubble.

When we pulled apart, Lyov gave me that beautiful smile of his, the one that was just reserved for me and our son. And soon, our daughter.

BLOOD AND ROSES

That smile, it had the power to take my breath away. He was so handsome. In a dark, deadly, and beautiful way.

"Alessio must be waiting for us. It's his big day," I finally said. Lyov nodded, and his chest puffed, a very proud father. Our baby boy was no longer a baby. God, I never wanted him to grow up. I wanted him to stay just like this, little and pure.

This world would taint him.

Just like it tainted all of us.

I put Lyov's black tie around his neck and tied it, like every morning. He then shrugged on his suit jacket, and we walked out of the room, hand in hand.

Alessio's bedroom was down the hall, and we walked in to find him still faking his sleep. His eyes were squeezed tight, and he was hiding a smile. Lyov and I shared a look before we made our way to his bed. I leaned over and placed a kiss on his forehead.

His cute smile widened.

Lyov was on the other side. He winked at me before leaning over and tickling our little boy.

"Happy birthday," we both said at the same time.

Alessio howled with laughter as his father continued to tickle him.

My heart soared, and tears stung my eyes. My daughter kicked and rolled around in my stomach, sharing our happiness.

I never wanted this moment to end.

I never wanted to wake up from this dream.

This was *us*. It was so imperfectly beautiful that, in its own way, it was *perfect*.

I watched Lyov pull Alessio on his lap, and I listened to father and son talk.

In this moment, I fell a thousand times more in love with my husband than I was this morning. And every time, that love continued to blossom more.

His head lifted up, and our eyes met. A thousand unsaid words went through between us.

Thank you, Master. For saving me that night. For capturing me into your trap and giving me the wings of an Angel.

***

My fingers caressed Alessio's forehead, and I watched as my touch lulled him to sleep. He cuddled closer into my chest and sighed dreamily. My baby. My sweet boy.

I smiled, remembering our conversation just hours ago. He had asked why Lyov called me *Angel*. My sweet boy had been confused.

Lyov's kiss left me breathless, and I leaned into him. For the briefest moment, I forgot that our son was there and watching. Lyov pulled away and pressed his forehead against mine.

"I missed you, Angel," he whispered. He was only gone for a few hours. We had lunch together, and then he had quickly fucked me against the wall of his office before he left.

My smile widened, and I went to say I missed him too when Alessio interrupted us.

"Papa, why do you call Mommy 'Angel'?"

We both stared at Alessio. My husband laughed,

and I could feel my cheeks heating with a blush.

Lyov crouched down, and I listened as he asked Alessio what he thought the meaning of Angel was. I saw his small forehead crease in confusion, and then he replied something about angels being God's messenger. Helpers. Saviors.

Lyov nodded and then gave his own little explanation. Our own meaning of the word Angel. Lyov's reason to why I was his Angel. Now and always.

"Correct. But an angel is also someone who is sweet, kind, caring, and calm. The most beautiful woman on the planet. Someone who is amazing in every way. An Angel is the girl who makes your heart beat faster when she walks into the room. The girl you need wherever you go. The girl who makes you want to be better. An angel is someone who is your rock. The person you love with your entire heart. The person you can't see yourself living without."

There we went again. That pitter-patter dance of my heart.

When Lyov looked up, meeting my blue eyes with his grey ones, something stirred deep inside me at the look of love and protectiveness in his gaze.

I love you, I mouthed. And then I pulled our son toward me and into my arms.

"And one day, you will find your angel," I whispered.

Alessio still looked confused. He was too young to understand the meaning, the power of that word. I listened to him argue with the fact that he believed I was his Angel.

Oh, little do you know, my sweet boy.

I shook my head. "Your Angel is waiting for you somewhere. And when you do find her, don't ever let her go."

Lyov's hands gripped mine, and our fingers entwined. "Because if you lose her, then you will forever be incomplete," he added.

I watched as Alessio thought about our words for a second before he pulled away with a nod. Lyov pulled me off the couch and sat up before making me sit on his lap. He nuzzled my neck, and I giggled as his rough stubble tickled my skin. I rested my head on his shoulders, and he held me to him.

He listened to me intently as I talk about my day and how the little mischievous trio – Maddie, Alessio, and Viktor, would give Lena and I trouble all day long. Viktor, Isaak's son, was only a few weeks older than Alessio. He had been with us since he was only two months old, after his mother left him behind. After four miscarriages, Lena finally had Maddie. That day was one of the happiest days at the estate. The three had been inseparable.

Today, we had found Viktor hanging upside down from a tree, thinking he was Tarzan, before he fell on his head. These three were always finding something new to worry us about.

I couldn't ask for anything else, though. I had everything I wanted, right here. This was happiness. Being Lyov's wife and the mother of his babies.

Lyov's phone rang and pulled us from our bubble. He picked it up and listened to the person speaking from the other side. I guessed it must have been Boris or Isaak. That angry, murderous look on

BLOOD AND ROSES

his face told me it was very bad. He hung up and growled in frustration. I rubbed his chest, knowing that my touch could always soothe him.

Over the years, Lyov's Empire had grown. He was ten times more powerful than he was seven years ago. He owned more than half of New York, and his businesses continued to expand into other territories, countries. Hotels. Restaurants. The biggest enterprises—they were all somehow connected to the Ivanshov name.

An Empire of his own that was impossible to bring down.

And in the underworld? Lyov Ivanshov was the King. A name to fear. A name that had people bow in respect.

"What's wrong?" I asked, when he stayed silent.

Lyov took a deep breath before meeting my eyes. "I have to take care of some stuff."

I nodded, understanding what he meant. I got off his lap, and he stood up too. Pulling me into his arms, he held me tight into his body. His breath feathered over my lips before he took them into a long hard kiss. He kissed me with so much passion, so much love—and it was everything I needed in that moment.

When he pulled away, his intense grey eyes, the hardened look on his face, made me shiver. This man...he was the Master. No longer my sweet lover.

"It's only for a day. It will be quick. Fuck. I might even be back by morning. I promise, I won't be gone for too long. Go to sleep, and when you wake up, I will be there—by your side," he said.

I nodded again, silently. I watched as he

crouched down and talked to Alessio. My heart felt heavy, and I almost begged him not to leave us tonight.

When Lyov stood up again, he held my hand in his. I looked down at our laced fingers, and he squeezed my hand. He pulled me into him again before giving one last deep kiss. I melted into his embrace, but he pulled away too quickly for my liking. "Love you, Angel."

"I love you too, Lyov," I whispered back. My chin wobbled, and I tried so hard not to cry. Our daughter kicked in my stomach, as if sensing my sadness.

Lyov started to walk away, but I gripped his hand tighter, refusing to let go.

Until I had to.

I held on as much as I could, until the distance grew between us and our fingertips were only touching.

After the briefest second, and a look that said so much between us, we let go.

And then he was gone.

Lyov's words echoed through my ears. *Because if you lose her, then you will forever be incomplete.* I still remembered the fierce look he gave me when he uttered those words. I wished he didn't have to leave tonight.

With a heavy heart, I had let him go. And tonight was one of those few nights where I had to sleep alone without my husband. If only he was here right now. I *missed* him. I missed his touch. His smiles. His laugh. His sweet kisses. His heated eyes that were just for me. As much as I loved it when my husband fucked me, I also loved it when he made sweet love to me.

I closed my eyes and dreamed of being in Lyov's warm embrace.

Until there was nothing safe and warm.

My beautiful cocoon shattered when a loud bang jostled me awake and I sat up with a start.

Gunshots.

There were screams.

It reminded me of *that* night.

The night I was taken away…the night I watched the abbey burn in front of my eyes.

There were more sounds of guns going off. More screams. Some enraged. Some painful. I could almost vividly see the bloodbath happening from behind my closed doors.

With each loud bang, each scream—a chip of my heart fell away, and I was left bleeding from the inside.

History had a cruel way of repeating itself.

Chapter 22

Lena

I walked out of the bathroom, freshly showered, and found Boris on the bed, newspaper on his lap. He looked up and stared at me with his dark, gorgeous eyes. He was shirtless, and even after so many years, I found myself transfixed. God, he was sexy and mouth-watering.

He winked, and my heart melted. My panties too. Just like always. That was the effect my husband had on me. I joined him in bed. He pushed his newspaper away and rolled over until I was trapped underneath him. I sunk into the mattress, loving the feel of his weight against me.

"I missed you," he said. I hummed in response. We were only apart for six hours, but he was right. I missed him, too. Boris smiled and brought his head down. His lips brushed gently against mine, and I whimpered. He slowly moved his tongue on my mouth. I gasped, and he slid his tongue inside, softly brushing against mine. My husband kissed

BLOOD AND ROSES

me slowly, lacking the urgency he had a few hours ago.

Our tongues mated together, and I moaned. I felt him suck on my tongue, and I leaned more into him. My panties were soaked already, and I just needed him…to touch me more. My body moved underneath him, and he chuckled. "So impatient."

Boris nipped my lips in warning, and his chest vibrated with a low, teasing growl.

"Boris," I sighed into his mouth.

His kisses were a fire that burned me from inside out, and I never wanted him to stop. I felt him in every pore of me. I breathed him in, feeling the effect of him. His presence calmed me. Always. Whenever I was restless, my soul searched for him. And when I would find Boris, every anxious feeling would disappear into a soothing, calm wave. He settled me, and I found a way to balance him. He used to be an angry man at the world. Boris hated everyone…everything. He was a mad man. And then I held him, and it was magic.

We found our little fairy tale.

"I love it when you look at me like this," he said tenderly before kissing me again.

"Like what?"

"Like you love me. Like I am the only one."

Palming his cheek, I caressed him over his beard. "You are, Boris. You are everything. And I want you to always remember that."

He smiled that small smile he only gave me and Maddie. "I can't forget when you remind me about…a hundred times a day. Give or take. Whether it's that morning kiss when you wake me up. Or that special kiss in the shower that my dick loves so much. I love it even more when you stare up at me with those teasing eyes and you whisper *I love you* before taking me into your mouth."

We had been married for seven years. Been a couple for more than ten years, yet he knew exactly how to make me blush. His words ignited a fire within me that nobody else could. There were so many women he could have, he chose me. There were so many men I could have, but I chose him.

We chose each other.

"I think I am emotional," I whispered.

"When are you not emotional is the question, baby."

I slapped his chest, and he laughed. "Since you had Maddie, you are a walking emotion, Lena. Not that I am complaining. Not really."

I sent him a mock glare. "Who wanted to knock me up in the first place? Who made it his mission to fill me with cum every hour of the day? Who had a pillow under my ass and my legs up because he needed his cum to take *root*?"

My fingers trailed up his chest, and I pinched his nipple. Boris hissed. "I am sure it wasn't the bell boy or the pool boy," I mocked.

His black eyes narrowed, and his lips lifted up in a small snarl. There he was. My overly possessive husband. His grip tightened around my hips, and he pushed his body into mine, forcing my legs apart as he settled heavily between my thighs.

"*Me*," he growled. "It was me. *I* fucked you. It was *my* cock in your sore pussy. *I* filled you up and *I* gave you *our* baby. Not some stupid ass bell boy

BLOOD AND ROSES

or pool boy who doesn't know how to use his dick."

He glared, and this time it was me laughing. I bit on my lips and coughed, trying to hide my laughter. Boris finally lost his glare, and his lips tilted up in a smile. Leaning down, his lips feathered over mine. "Thank you. For giving me our daughter," he murmured into my lips.

A heaviness settled on my chest at his words. For years, there had always been something missing. A part of our soul. I had tried not to let it consume me. Boris tried to make me happy and told me he didn't need a baby. But I saw every time he looked at Alessio or Viktor. And his silent tears were the loudest every time we lost a baby. I heard them at the bottom of my core even when they were just filled with silence. "Thank *you*. For not giving up on me. For still believing in *us*." I could hear how heavy my voice was at the end.

Maddie was our fifth baby.

We lost four babies before her. After the fourth time, I bled...I gave up. I cried. I raged. And I said *no more*.

It wasn't until years later that Boris and I finally decided to try again. We were scared. My heart ached when I found out I was pregnant. I was scared to be happy. But then months went by and I didn't bleed. I had felt my baby kick. It was as if I could breathe again, and for the first time since I had found out I was carrying Maddie, I had a smile. Maria was happy. We were all happy. It was almost an aphrodisiac feeling.

"I will never give up on you, Lena. I will also never let you go," he said before his kiss turned urgent and needy.

I smiled into his kiss. "You are sweet."

"Oh, I'll show you *sweet*."

I moaned at the promise because I knew there was nothing *sweet* about what he was going to do to me.

Our clothes disappeared until our naked bodies were pressed together, feeling each other's warmth. His hand went between us, and my back arched as he played with my wet core. He pushed a finger inside and then two, humming as he did so. My swollen folds coiled tighter around his fingers, and he knew exactly where to touch me, where my sweet sensitive spots were. His lips found my sensitive nipples, and he teased me, his teeth grazing and biting.

His thumb found my clit, and he pressed and then circled in just the right way to drive me wild. My legs shook, and I panted heavily. My stomach clenched, and my insides convulsed with a small orgasm.

Boris brought his fingers to my lips, and he waited, his eyes dark and needy, holding me in this moment. I sucked my juices off his fingers, and I felt his length jerk between my spread thighs. He pressed harder into me, and I whimpered when he pushed past my entrance.

"I belong right here, baby," he whispered in my ear as he buried himself deep inside.

My hands left the bedsheet, and I clawed at his back as he thrust into me. "You feel so goddamn good." His groans filled my ears, and my moans filled the room. His thrusts quickened, and I

BLOOD AND ROSES

surrendered to this…to *him*.

I tilted my hips up, demanding more. Boris hissed in pleasure before pulling out. I whimpered at the loss, but he quickly turned me over and pulled my ass up. As much as he loved looking into my eyes while making love me, he also loved to have me on my knees and my ass up for him.

With one hard thrust, he was inside of me again. Boris slid in easily, and I could hear my wetness. His cock felt so big…so deep as he sheathed himself to the hilt. My breathing was shallow, and I knew I made him just as breathless. His hips jerked against mine, and he pumped harder inside me. With each stroke, I pushed against him, making me groan and driving him crazy. My body started to tingle, and I felt myself coming again. My fingers clawed at the bedding, and I cried out with each hard thrust.

Boris reached between my thighs, and his thumb found my sensitive clit again. He tugged at my little hard nub and rammed inside of me at the same time. My scream filled the room, and I felt myself gushing, milking him.

His thrusts grew urgent, and soon enough, he joined me. His essence filled me, and my eyes closed.

Through a hazy fog, I felt his lips whisper on the back of my shoulders. He placed four sweet kisses there. And I smiled.

Four kisses. I knew exactly where his lips had touched. Four black sparrows were tattooed on my shoulder, deep ingrained in me. My babies would always be here with me.

Four beautiful sparrows. I never wanted to add another one. I couldn't handle another loss.

Boris fell on the bed beside me, and I moved into his embrace. Half of my body covered his, and he held me tight. I inhaled his scent, feeling safe and loved in his embrace.

I love you.

***

I woke up with a start. A loud bang could be heard and then screams. Horrifying, painful screams. My eyes widened, and I sat up. My arm reached out for Boris, but he was already out of bed. My heart thundered at the sight of him, quickly pulling on his pants and shirt.

"Boris," I said quietly.

His eyes snapped up, and they held me place. Thousands of unsaid words passed between us. Tears filled my eyes, and I shook my head slowly. My stomach cramped, and my lungs tightened to the point I couldn't breathe. The estate was under attack. *God, no. This couldn't be happening.*

Another screeching bang jolted me, and I jumped out of bed. The trance between Boris and I was gone. I reached him the same time he reached for his gun. With one hand, he palmed my cheek. "It's going to be okay," he said quickly.

My throat felt heavy. "Don't leave me," I whispered.

"Lena…" Boris growled.

I couldn't move. I couldn't really speak. I felt…numb. Empty.

BLOOD AND ROSES

"Please."

His dark eyes stared into my crying soul. And then he shook his head. "Get Maddie from her room and hide. Don't come out, Lena."

"Don't leave me," I said again. Couldn't he hear my heart shattering? Why wouldn't he look into my begging eyes and stay?

"Lena!" he snapped, shaking my shoulders now. I saw the love in his eyes. I saw the pain there. His eyes told me he didn't want to leave, but his duty said otherwise. I also saw the fear in those eyes I loved so much.

Indescribable fear slithered into my soul. He was scared. Boris Ivanshov was never scared. Of nothing and no one.

"Baby. I need you to be strong right now. I need you to listen to me. Get Maddie and Viktor and hide. They are both in the next room. Don't step outside of this room. Open the adjoined door and get them. Turn the light off and hide in the bathroom."

I started to shake my head. Why wouldn't he listen to me? *Don't leave me!*

He placed a gun into my palm. "If someone comes in, you shoot first. Don't ask questions. Don't speak. Don't wait. You shoot."

Pain. That was all I felt. It...hurt so much.

"Boris..."

I gripped his hand tighter when he tried to let go. He made a pained sound at the back of his throat, and my chin wobbled with the effort not to scream or cry out. His fingers entwined with me. He squeezed my hand, and I choked back a sob.

Pulling me closer, he placed the sweetest kiss on my lips.

And then he let go.

I reached for him, but he took a step back. *No.*

Our gazes met. *I love you,* he said.

Don't go! Please don't go, I said. *Don't leave me. Don't leave us. Stay. Please.*

But the moment was once again broken by the sound of gunshot. Boris didn't look at me again, but he turned around. I watched my husband walk away and out of our room.

Right into the arms of bloodshed.

A single droplet of tear silently fell down my cheek. *Stay with me*, I wanted to beg. But it was too late.

He was gone. My heart cried. My soul bled and wept.

I never wanted to add another sparrow on my skin. But…fate was cruel.

Silence filled my ears, and then I heard his voice. His vows the day he made me his.

You are burning. You are out of control. You are sweet and wild. You have the heart of the storm and the soul of love. You are fire. And you are everything that I love. You and me…forever, baby.

Little did we know…forever didn't exist, just like fairy tales were just stupid dreams.

Chapter 23

Maria

"Mommy?"

The voice of my sweet boy brought me back to the present, and my fear skyrocketed into my system. My blood ran cold, and my eyes widened in realization. If anything happened to Alessio…

No, I shook my head. I refused to let anything happen to my son. Without thinking twice, I was already pulling him out of bed. There was no time. The screams got louder. The gunshots sounded closer.

"Mommy, what's happening?" Alessio asked, his little voice trembling.

My lungs clenched, and I didn't know what to say to my little boy, how to appease his fear. *God, Lyov…where are you? We need you.*

I knelt down in front of Alessio. My stomach tightened, and then my baby girl went still, as if she was hiding away. I looked around the room, searching for a place to hide Alessio. My whole body shook, and the insides of me were twisted in knots. My eyes drifted to the bed.

Another loud bang rang through the walls of the Estate. "Alessio, listen to me carefully. I want you to hide under the bed. Okay?"

I could hear the tremble in my voice, the panic. My stomach dropped, and my lungs squeezed together. "No matter what happens or what you see or hear, you don't come out. Do you understand?" I whispered, grabbing his shoulders and giving him a little shake when he didn't respond. I hated the look of terror in his blue eyes, the same eyes as mine— the eyes Lyov loved so much.

At the thought of Lyov, I choked back a sob. I couldn't die today. No, I *just* couldn't. What would Lyov do? I was his Angel. He *needed* me. We needed each other.

Alessio finally nodded, and I breathed out a shaking sigh of relief. He would be safe. I would make sure of it even if that was the last thing I did. Tears stung my eyes. I tried not to cry, not wanting to scare and worry Alessio any further, but the tears slid down my cheeks before I could stop them. They were the hardest tears I had ever cried.

Pulling Alessio in to my chest, I held him closely. So tight. I wish I could burrow him into my embrace and protect him from this bloody, tainted world. I peppered his face with kisses. His chubby cheeks. His eyes. His nose. His forehead. I couldn't stop loving on my sweet boy. Deep inside of me, I feared it would be the last time I could hold my baby in my arms.

When I pulled away, Alessio gripped my wrists

BLOOD AND ROSES

tightly into his little hands. His hold tightened. He was so strong for his young age. There was no mistake that he was an Ivanshov.

"Mommy, what about you? Why am I hiding under the bed?" he questioned slowly.

I wished I had the answers for you, my sweet boy. But I didn't.

Another loud bang came through, and this time, my whole body jostled. My mind went back to *that* night again. *No. No. No. Stop, Maria. Think of Alessio. Think of your baby girl. Your little Princess.* I needed to be strong for my babies. I couldn't lose my mind right now; I couldn't go back into being that broken girl.

No. I was Lyov's Queen. And a Queen never cowered in fear.

"Alessio. Don't ask me questions, okay? Please, baby, just listen to Mommy. Hide under the bed and don't come out. Not until Papa, Lena, or Isaak come looking for you," I said. I could hear the desperation in my voice. Alessio opened his mouth to argue; I could see it in his eyes. I shook my head, and he went silent.

"Please, my baby. Promise Mommy that you won't come out," I begged this time.

Alessio finally nodded, and this time, I cried. Pulling him into my chest again, I gave him a final kiss on his forehead before whispering, "I love you. I love you so much, my sweet boy. Never forget that."

As we pulled apart, I could hear the noises closer to the door. They were right outside. I heard Boris. He bellowed something loud. I could hear fighting from the other side. My heart accelerated, and it beat heavily, almost painfully against my ribcage.

Quickly, I pushed Alessio toward the bed. "Go, my baby. Don't come out. Don't make any noise—no matter what. Do you hear me?" He crawled underneath the high bed, and I pulled the corners of the bedsheets down so he was perfectly hidden from view.

I separated my sweet boy from me. I suddenly felt sick, and my throat started to close up. Just when I stood up, the door banged open. My heart thumped, and I closed my eyes for the briefest second. My breathing stuttered.

You will never have to do anything without me. We will always be together, Angel.

Bringing my hand up, I choked back an agonized cry. *Where are you, Lyov? Please come back.*

The intruder *tsked* from behind me. Taking a deep breath, I faced him. The villain of my happily ever after.

My gaze found his face, and the world came to a screeching halt. Everything went chillingly silent. A dark cloud settled around my once happy bubble. My blood ran cold, and my eyes widened at the familiar face. My hands grew clammy, and my heart twisted.

"Maria. How lovely to see you *again*."

That voice. It once haunted me. Many years ago, he belonged in my nightmares. He was the face I saw behind the bars of my cage as he reveled in my suffering and threw pieces of bread at me.

"Alfredo," I replied, my voice surprisingly cold and hard. This man was part of my misery. He had

BLOOD AND ROSES

sat there in a pretty suit and watched me break while laughing.

I saw Boris behind Alfredo. His face was harsh and badly bruised, bleeding. He seemed out of breath, his wide chest heaving and his face twisted in pain with each laboured breath. I could tell he had fought through hell to be here. But before I could rejoice in slight relief that Boris was here, everything crumbled around me. My heart thundered and then shattered at the sound of a gunshot going off and then Boris falling limply to the floor.

NO!

I wanted to scream. My lips parted, but my agony was silent.

Alfredo smirked, his face a mask of evil. "I am surprised Lyov left you unprotected."

You are stronger than you think, Maria.

I lifted my chin up and stared into his black, soulless eyes. "Why are you here?" I asked.

"You know exactly why I am here, sweet Maria."

Sweet Maria.

Sweet slave.

Bile rose in the back of my throat, and I suddenly wanted to throw up. I felt *sick.*

Get on your knees and suck my cock, sweet slave.

The memories assaulted me with such pain, and I almost doubled over. My gaze went to the dagger in his hand, and I saw the emblem. The Italians' emblem. The Abandonato.

Alfredo Abandonato.

Oh God.

My eyes widened in realization. But oh, how late I was. So very late. So very stupid.

My head lifted up, and our eyes connected. He laughed, a cold, merciless laugh. He saw it in my eyes. He saw it in the depth of my soul. He *knew* that I figured it out. Only I was eight years too late.

Alfredo was *there*...when I was owned by Valentin. He would come to Solonik's house, to the little parties that he would throw every now and then, to show his collections of slaves.

Alfredo took part during those *parties*. He was an active member of that society.

But Alfredo was an Italian. He was a Boss. He was not meant to be there. The Italians and Russians never crossed paths.

My heart hammered, and I closed my eyes briefly. *Oh Lyov.*

Solonik betrayed the Russians.

He was in partnership with Alfredo. Valentin planned it—*this*. He was the mastermind.

"A little too late, aren't you?" Alfredo *tsked* with fake sadness. "Lyov will never know the truth now."

His mocking words *hurt*. God, did it hurt. So bad. Sharp knives were being stabbed into me, digging holes into my soul and leaving me to bleed.

I didn't reply. Angered by my silence, just like always—he wanted my tears, my cries of agony—Alfredo lurched forward and grabbed me by the hair.

His black eyes were hard and cold. I saw death in them. *My* death.

He spat into my face, his fist twisting painfully

into my hair before violently pushing me away. My feet twisted under me, and I went down hard. My stomach hit the ground, and this time, I screamed. My Princess.

I squeezed my eyes shut as indescribable pain went through every inch of my body. But that wasn't what hurt the most. My nose tingled and my chest heaved with a laboured breath. Darkness clouded around me. What hurt the most was the bleak and bitter realization that there was…no escape.

From the corner of my eyes, I saw Alessio trying to move, trying to come to my rescue. My sweet protective boy. He was so much like his father.

I gave him a slight shake of my head, silently begging him, and he stayed still. I saw his tears. I saw my sweet boy cry, and my tears fell.

Turning around, still on the floor, I held my stomach and looked up at the man who could be my downfall. I pleaded with him, even though it was the last thing I wanted to do. I pleaded with the devil, because I didn't want to leave my Lyov behind.

"Please, don't do this. I beg you. Have mercy."

His laughter boomed around the room, and I flinched, choking back my cries. He knelt down next to me, and his filthy hands *touched* me. His fingers traced a line up my neck, my jaw, and then he thumbed my lips roughly.

His touch then continued down, toward my breasts. He circled my nipple, and I wanted to claw his eyes out. Alfredo raised an eyebrow seductively, and he pinched my nipple to the point of pain, and I cried out.

"I can show you mercy if you agree to come with me. Be my whore and then maybe I'll show you mercy."

I let my head fall back on the floor, and I stared at the ceiling. My body was cold and numb, my emotions in turmoil. My broken heart was like a shattered vase, all the fragile pieces scattered around. The broken glasses pierced my soul, without consideration and almost mockingly.

Lyov had been able to gather the shattered pieces of my heart before. He had slowly pieced them back together. It had not been a perfect mold, but it was perfect enough for us.

But *now*...those shattered pieces? They couldn't be fixed or put together.

They burned into a bright fieriness until nothing was left but the ashes of it.

Alfredo leaned down, closer to my face, and murmured in my ear. "It could be just like before, sweet Maria. Although this time...I will take your cunt. Hmm, maybe I will let you come too. I'll make you *enjoy* it. I'll *make* you cream and squeeze my dick."

No. I could see it in his eyes. The dark, evil glint. He would just use me in the most sadistic ways. He would fuck me until the sheets were red with my blood.

By the time Lyov found me, I would only be a corpse.

A man like Alfredo would never let me survive for more than a few hours, for his enjoyment. And then he would take great pleasure in ending me.

BLOOD AND ROSES

My sweet princess, what would become of her then?

Never again. I would never bow for men like him again. I'd rather die as Lyov's Angel…a Queen, rather than as a slave.

"Never," I spat. "I will never allow another man to touch my body. I only belong to Lyov. I would rather die than have you touch me."

Alfredo grunted in response, and he raised an eyebrow, surprise at my outburst. "Is that your final decision?"

I kept my eyes on him, unflinching. My silence was my answer.

"Well, okay then," he said.

He stood up and pointed the gun at me. "Why are you doing this?" There was a break in my voice, and I hated it.

"Don't you know, Maria? The best way to bring a man down is by his weakness. And you, my sweet, are Lyov's weakness."

My breathing faltered. Lyov called me *Angel*, and I always thought of myself as his guardian Angel, the wings that would protect him just like he was my shield. I vowed to be his strength.

But it was in that moment when I realized that I was more his weakness than his strength.

I was his downfall.

I saw Alfredo's finger on the trigger. My palm cradled my rounded stomach, and I felt my baby girl kick one last time. I wanted to rage at the unfairness. I wanted to hate Lyov for leaving us. But I *couldn't*.

The fault wasn't ours. The fault lay in the cruel

game of fate.

For eight years, our lives had been divine and so full of love. But we had been dancing within the arms of death, escaping through it, but for how long? Time ran out, and it was my blood they wanted.

Time slowed and silence took the shape of life, surrounding me with a sharp coldness. Everything flashed before my eyes, my whole life. Everything, every little piece of me was unfolding and scattering around…floating far, far away. I watched it all from a distance. Not exactly here or there, but somewhere in the middle.

I thought of my parents. The accident. I thought of the abbey and all the sisters. I thought of Sophia and my unborn princess.

I thought of Lena. Isaak. Boris. Viktor. Maddie.

My sweet boy. Alessio. I remembered the day he was born. His first breath. His first cry. His first word. His first steps, the first time he walked toward his papa. I remembered how proud Lyov looked that day. I remembered how he had held Alessio close and kissed his forehead.

I thought of my Lyov. Our first look. His first words to me. His first touch on my skin.

My name means Lion. I am a hunter. I like to possess and own things until they are solely mine. But I am also the protector of my pride, Angel.

That also means I am your protector because I happen to love you very much. Fuck, I more than just love you. Love is a weak word to describe what I feel for you.

BLOOD AND ROSES

There are no limits on the hell I would walk through to make sure you are always smiling...always happy.

I thought of my cruel, heartless made man. And then I thought of my sweet lover.

My gaze flittered over my left hand, my wedding ring. It was very simple, with only a single small diamond in the middle. There was nothing fancy about it. Just elegant and perfect for me.

Our wedding. My beautiful white dress. Lyov had twirled me around the dance floor. Then he had leaned down and placed a kiss on my neck, over my thrumming vein.

I thought of Lyov standing at the end of the aisle as he waited for me to walk to him, on shaky legs. I held on to Isaak and made my way to my love. Our unbroken vows to each other.

I, Maria Andersen, take you, Lyov Ivanshov, to be my husband. I promise to be true to you in good times and in bad. I will love, cherish, and honor you all the days of my life.

I, Lyov Ivanshov, take you, Maria Andersen, to be my wife. I promise to be true to you in good times and in bad. I will love, cherish, and honor you all the days of my life.

Lyov's smile.
Lyov's grey eyes.
Lyov's love.
Lyov's heart.

In honesty, in sincerity, to be for you, a faithful and loving husband.
In honesty, in sincerity, to be for you, a faithful and loving wife.

Our entwined, singing souls. Never to be apart, for we were one. The stars had aligned, and we were meant for each other since birth. It was fated. It was destiny. There are no accidental meetings between souls.

I give you my hand and my heart as a sanctuary of warmth and peace. I promise to be worthy of your love.
I am my beloved's, and my beloved is mine.

His sweet kisses. His lips making love to me. He had touched me where no one else could. In the deepest part of me, my wounded soul. I had been crying from inside, begging for someone to see and save me. Lyov saw and he took me away, far, far away into our castle, where he was King and he made me his beloved Queen.

I will respect, trust, help, and care for you; I will share my life with you; I will forgive you as we have been forgiven; and I will try with you better to understand ourselves, the world, and God; through the best and worst of what is to come, and as long as we live.

Lyov's body on mine, pressing into me. Making sweet love. Our bodies tangled intimately. His breath as it breathed into me. Our wedding bands heavy on our fingers, with our hearts beating to the same beautiful rhythm.

For richer, for poorer. In joy and in sorrow, in sickness and in health, as long as we both shall live. To have and to hold from this day forward. Always and forever. There will never be another, for my Angel is the only one. This is my solemn vow.

There will never be another, for my Master is the only one. This is my solemn vow.

His love for me. My love for him. Our love. My heart only ever wanted one thing. My heart only ever had one thought. One need. Despite everything I could have, all my heart ever wanted was Lyov. A piece of him—a single cloth of his love, even it was ripped or used. But he gave me more than that. Lyov gave me all of him—every fragmented, dark piece of him.

I am now Maria Ivanshov.
You are mine.
I have always been yours.
Just like I am yours. Always will be. I belong to you, Angel.

Sometimes, I had felt like I didn't belong, a lost soul. But then I would lay my head on Lyov's chest, his heartbeat strong in my ears, and he would hold me tight. I would then breathe, a slow shuddering breath of realization his embrace was my home.

Your heartbeat is so strong. I like it. It makes me feel...warm.

I remembered his whisper in my ears. I could hear it as if he were speaking it right now. I could almost feel his touch, his voice caressing my skin.

It's yours, Angel. You are the first fucking woman to lay her head on my chest. I have held no other in my arms like this. So hold me close and hear my heartbeat. And let me feel yours in return.

It wasn't his collar or his chain that kept me close to him. No, it was all in his gaze. The way Lyov looked at me, I had been bound to him in the most beautiful way. He had made me *his* with a single look.

It hurt. It hurt so much.

The agony was more than being made to crawl around with a collar around my neck, for the sadistic, ugly pleasure of men.

The thought of leaving my family behind—my Lyov, this pain...it came from the pit of my soul, the marrow of me.

It hurt knowing that our dreams would be shattered the moment Alfredo pulled the trigger.

This time, when our princess is born, I want to be the one to cut the umbilical cord. And I want to hold her first. Last time, you got to hold our son first.

I want to take you to see the world, Angel. Just me and you.

BLOOD AND ROSES

I want to kiss you at the sunrise. And I want to make love to you in front of the sunset.

It hurt even more because I had to break the promise I made to Lyov.

Angel, I didn't realize I was alone until I met you. I had been missing a piece of me, I was somehow...empty in the inside, but I didn't know.
Master, from now on...you will never be alone. I will always be here for you.
Promise?
Promise.

My dark, angry Prince Charming had come on his black horse. He had swept me up, saved me, and dragged me into his violent world, where I planted roses and made them bloom with every breath I took. It was a twisted fairy tale, with a beauty within the thorns.

My eyes clouded with tears, and I felt those droplets slide down my cheeks.

We will never end, Angel. Not even God can separate us. This...this is my vow to you. Right here and now.

Lyov was wrong. No matter how powerful of a King he was, this was not in his control. If only I had told him this, if only I hadn't let us drown in such a beautiful reverie.

I saw our last kiss. Our last touch. Our last hug. The last time our bodies had entwined in the most intimate way. I heard his last words.

Through blurry eyes, I saw Alfredo's fingers move. My eyes closed. But my lips smiled.

You have a beautiful smile, Maria. I want to see it on you every day.
I will always smile for you, Master. Promise. Forever. Until my last breath.

The trigger was pulled. A loud bang. My chest heaved. My last heartbeat belonged to Lyov.

I thought we would live happily ever after. But there was no happy ending in this life. I found this out the hard way, as the blood flowed, red as roses…

I love you. I love you so much. Do you hear me, Lyov? I love you, Master. My Lyov. Please don't forget that. Please keep fighting. Please protect our son. Don't let him go. Love him the way he deserves. Please be strong, my love. Please. Please. Please. For your Angel.

A breath. And then breathless. Silence. Darkness. Cold.

Our fairy tale was now just a distant memory. So very far away and out of reach.

"Till death do us part."

Chapter 24

Lyov

Beat. Thump. Beat. Thump.
Something was wrong.
Beat. Thump. Beat. Thump.
I could feel my heart beating in my ears and the pulse racing in my neck.
Beat. Thump. Beat. Thump.
There was something heavy sitting on my lungs. My heart pounded and clenched, and I didn't even fucking know why.
Beat. Thump. Beat. Thump.
I didn't get carsick, but right now, I was about to throw up.

My chest grew tight with a strange feeling, and I rubbed it, hoping to elevate the burning sensation there. I felt on edge, and my stomach churned as if sensing something *wrong* was going to happen.

"Isaak, I need to go back," I announced without thinking.

He looked in the rear-view mirror, confused. "What?"

"Go back," I said through clenched teeth, still rubbing my chest. The pain wouldn't alleviate. When he wouldn't do what I said, the frustration built inside of me. Mixed with fear and agitation, it was a weird, fucked-up feeling. Why was I even scared? I didn't fucking know. I just felt unsettled.

All I knew was that in this moment, right now…I had to be home. Nothing felt right. Being away felt wrong. So, so wrong.

My lungs clenched, and it fucking hurt.

"Fuck! This can wait. Turn the goddamn car around!" I roared. Isaak hit the brake hard, and he turned his head to look at me, sending me a confused, yet somewhat dark, angry look.

"Lyov, we got a call that there was an attack at the club. The place was lit on fire. There are people…"

I stopped his tirade of words with a low growl. His mouth snapped shut when I leveled him with a dark look of my own. "I don't give a fuck. Let the others take care of it. I need to get back home. Now."

He was silent for a second, just staring at me. "Is something wrong?"

My fists clenched, and I looked outside at the dark night. Everything felt eerily strange, as if a balance was broken. "I don't know," I said, my throat suddenly feeling tight. "But right now, I need to be with my wife and son. I could tell Maria didn't want me to leave tonight."

It had felt wrong, leaving her when she so desperately clung to my hand. As if she couldn't bear the few hours of separation. Fuck, even I

BLOOD AND ROSES

couldn't. A few minutes away from her felt like hours. Hours felt like months. Every time I was away, not in the proximity to touch her or stare at her smile, in those beautiful blue eyes—it felt like I couldn't breathe.

Sometimes, it wasn't just *love*. It was so much more.

I was obsessed with my Angel.

Eight years together didn't lessen what I felt for Maria. *No*, I just fell deeper into her beautiful trap every day. Every morning I would wake up and see her beautiful face first thing. Hear her voice and then watch her smile sleepily at me, her eyes sparkling with something akin to adoration and so much love.

With a heavy sigh, from the corner of my eye, I saw Isaak nodding. He didn't say anything else; he just put the car into gear again and drove back to the estate.

The whole drive back was filled with tense silence. I leaned back into my seat and closed my eyes, trying to control my somewhat irregular breathing. I just didn't understand, and it frustrated me even more.

Finally, the car came to a stop. I didn't waste any time getting out of the car. Something was wrong. I knew it for sure this time. My guards weren't present. There were always four of them at the gates.

Today…not even one of them was here.

And the rest of the entrance…empty. Silence. Where the fuck was everyone?

Isaak swore behind me, but he stayed close to

my heels as I ran into the house.

Red. First thing that filled my sight.

Blood. Bodies. Death.

The air smelled of sweat, blood, and death. My estate looked like something akin to a horror movie. A fucking massacre.

This wasn't the same house I left behind. No, this...this was all *wrong*.

My heart stammered, and I ran blindly upstairs, ignoring everything else...everyone else. The cries of pain, the bellows of agony and anger...of fear, I blocked it all out.

Except...my Angel.

"Maria!"

My voice didn't sound right. There was fear in it. Horror. Distress. Panic. Everything that wasn't Lyov Ivanshov.

Right now, I wasn't the King of the underworld.

Right now, I was just a man who desperately needed to hold his Angel. I was a husband who feared—the last time he had touched his wife was hours ago—that he would never get the chance again.

My heart raced as I ran to my room, where I knew Maria would be. With each step, it was harder for me to breathe. The blood. The dead bodies. Fuck.

I was silently praying to the Higher Powers. For the first fucking time in my life, I prayed as I ran. *Let her be safe. Let Alessio be safe.* They were all who mattered.

None of my prayers mattered, though. I was too late. And after all, the prayers of a Devil could

BLOOD AND ROSES

never be accepted. I made hell my home. Heaven was far from my reach, let alone that my prayers would make any difference.

The door was open.

My lungs clenched. My heartbeats became faster, harder, and erratic. There was a turbulence of emotions in me.

I walked inside, and my legs weakened before giving out under me. I sank to my knees. My breath left me. My heart was in pieces.

My body trembled with the force of reality. My brain tried to register the scene in front of me, while my soul slowly withered into nothingness. The world swirled around me, and my stomach rolled with a sick feeling, fighting the urge to throw up. It felt like a clawed hand was around my throat, restricting my air. I couldn't breathe. I fought for it, gasping, but I just couldn't…breathe.

My lips parted, and a roar of agony ripped through my throat.

No. No. No.

This was just a fucking dream. I slapped myself on the head, hitting myself over and over again. *Wake up. Wake up, damn it.*

I closed my eyes and continued to scream, hoping it would pull me from this nightmare.

But when I opened my eyes again, I only saw blood.

Blood covering my Angel.

Blood everywhere.

My Angel's corpse.

"Maria." Her name came out as a whimper.

Everything else faded away. It was just her and

me. Just me and my broken Angel.

I crawled to her, slipping on the bloody floor. Falling beside her too-still body, I wrapped my arms around her. I held her on my lap, her blood seeping into my clothes.

Blood never did anything to me. Fuck, I lived for it…to spill the blood of others. But not my Maria. I couldn't bear it. It made me sick, and I crumpled at the pain.

With a hand, I held her face. "Please, open your eyes, Angel. Please. Don't do this to me."

I shook her body, but there was no response.

Silence. She was too cold. So cold that I would never be able to warm her again. Her warmth had left her…me…us. And now, I was cold too. Cold and so empty.

Pain had a way of evolving. You felt it in every pore, down to your bones, and the depth of your heart—your soul. Sometimes it started slow and then your body would slowly go numb.

Pain was an emotion that thrived from weakness, no matter how much you were meant to be strong and powerful.

When it came to pain…to the hurting part of your soul, there was no escape. And just like that, it filtrated me like a virus, a sick feeling that felt like I could never rid of. My lungs contracted, and my chest felt like it was being dug on, knives cutting through, deeper and deeper. Slashing with no remorse, carving a sculpture of pain without any sympathy. My heart was being wrenched away, and I watched it bleed, shrivel, and die.

Just like my Angel.

BLOOD AND ROSES

No. This couldn't be happening. Not like this. Not this way.

I bellowed out another scream as I pulled her body closer into my embrace. Burying my face in her neck, I cried. "Wake up. Please wake up. You can't…leave…me."

But she did…my Maria left me. I was too late.

My throat felt tight and heavy. Raw from crying and screaming. Maybe I was like this for hours, clinging to Maria's still, cold body. I held onto her until I was numb…until nothing made any sense to me. Until my ears became deaf. My eyes lost their sight, except of her beautiful face. Everything else was just a dark hole.

I caressed my Angel's face, moving her hair behind her ears. Her lips were parched and cracked, bloodied. But there was a whisper of a smile on them.

That hurt. Fuck, did it hurt. My soul was stabbed and torn open, leaving nothing except a hollow depth.

I leaned forward and placed my forehead against hers. She loved it when I did that. She would always smile, and her eyes would sparkle.

My lips feathered over hers. She always kissed me back.

She didn't kiss me back this time.

Kiss me back, Angel.

I sobbed into her lips, pressing harder and hoping to feel her move…hoping to feel her kiss but *nothing.*

How could fate be so cruel?

"You promised not to leave me…" I whimpered,

my voice cracking over each word. "You promised me forever."

Our memories flashed in front of my eyes. The first time I saw Maria. The first word. The first touch. Our first kiss. I thought of *us.*

I saw all the happy moments we went through. When we married. When we said our vows. When we found out we were going to have a baby. Every night she played the piano for us. Every time I made love to her. We had wanted this. A family. Our family. Our happily ever after in this fucked-up world.

We were so happy.

We were meant to always be happy…we were meant to have our Princess. To watch our babies play together, grow, and marry. We were going to be grandparents. We were going to be together, grow old…live our lives *together*. As one.

Not apart.

Not alone.

But our ending didn't happen like we wanted.

My clouded thoughts broke through at the screams penetrating the walls of my room, now my living hell.

I looked away from Maria, long enough to see Lena coming into the room, sobbing her heart out. She fell down to her knees beside another body, and she cried to the moon. I realized it was Boris.

Another love was lost.

Another broken love story.

Another tainted story.

The walls became my solace as I kept my Angel in my embrace. I refused to let go, watching the walls, which were now tainted in blood.

Hours must have passed, maybe.

Isaak came to kneel beside me. I refused to acknowledge him…until he tried to separate me from my wife. My hand lurched out, and I gripped his wrist, feeling his bone almost crunch underneath my hold.

He didn't even flinch. His hardened expression was gone. In its place…I saw pain. Not because I was about to break his fucking hand…but because he felt *this* loss too.

"Lyov," he tried to say but couldn't really speak. His mouth snapped shut. He looked down at Maria's body, his gaze staying on her stomach for a second longer before he closed his eyes tightly. Bringing his fist to his mouth, he choked back a sob too.

I knew what he was seeing.

Maria's stomach torn open.

Our baby no longer lived there, safely cocooned in her mother's womb.

I heard Lena's voice, and I forced myself to watch as she came forward. Sinking to her knees a few feet away from me, she picked up the tiny body and held my baby in her arms. Tears streamed down her cheeks. Lena looked so…broken. Fuck, I knew what she was feeling right now.

"She is beautiful," she whispered. She cried softly, holding my princess closer to her chest. "Do you want to see her?"

I shook my head. I couldn't. I just…couldn't. Not without Maria. We were supposed to look at our Princess together, while she breathed, lived, and cried.

Not cold, still, and silent. "Take...her...away."

The realization sat heavy on my shoulders, and whatever was left of my heart crumbled. My head hung low, and I closed my eyes.

I didn't just lose my Angel. I also lost our princess. I would never know what the color of her eyes were. Or if she had her mother's smile. Would she pout like Alessio if Maria and I didn't cuddle her exactly the way she wanted?

In that moment, I was scared to think of Alessio. If I lost him too...then what would I have left? As if Lena could tell my thoughts, she softly called out, "Alessio."

My eyes opened when I heard her gasp. She quickly handed my baby to Isaak, who left the room, and Lena pulled a trembling Alessio from under the bed. His face was ashen and caked with dry tears. His expression was a mask of shock and fear. His little legs were shaking so hard Lena had to hold him up. His pants were wet, and I knew it was probably piss.

Alessio didn't make a sound. He stared into the distance. Lena quickly placed a hand over his eyes, shielding his gaze from the horrifying scene in front of him. She ushered him out of the room and followed suit.

I looked down at my Angel again. My fingers couldn't stop caressing her cheek, touching her cold, velvet skin.

I knew this would be the last time.

"I don't want to let you go, Angel. I...can't. Fuck, I just can't...I can't...live...I can't…breathe," I cried into her neck. "This is all…my fault…I shouldn't…have left you. I shouldn't have…all…my fault. I…am sorry…so…so sorry…please…come back."

I only got silence in response.

From now on, I would never hear her voice. No matter how loud I would call for Maria, I would only get silence.

I had forced fate. And this was the outcome.

Angels don't belong in this world…in my world.

Chapter 25

Lyov

They buried my Angel a week ago. It had been seven days. Seven. Fucking. Days since I last held my Maria.

She now laid in the dark, cold ground, far, far away from me. I didn't attend the funeral. I was hidden deep in the trees and then walked away when they lowered her casket to the ground. My feet took me nowhere; I just walked mindlessly around in a world that my Angel no longer breathed in.

Our princess was buried beside her, too. I lost four people that night. I lost my friend. I lost my wife. I lost my daughter. And I lost my son.

Alessio hadn't a spoken a word since that night, when Lena had pulled him from under the bed. He wouldn't talk. He wouldn't react to anything. He was just a living corpse. Like me. Alive yet dead inside. Breathing, yet just surviving…not living.

I almost wished I'd died that night. Maybe the

BLOOD AND ROSES

pain would be easier. Maybe then, I would be with my Angel. Maybe then, we could have our happy ending. Maybe then, our love wouldn't be so broken and empty.

My thoughts were interrupted by a knock on my door. Through the darkness, I watched as Lena walked inside without waiting for my reply. She knew there would be no response. My doors had remained closed for the last seven days. Nobody was allowed in. I guessed I wallowed in self-pity and dreamed of days when my Angel was still alive. I dreamed of the days when I would wake up beside her and see those vivid blue eyes staring into me. Her beautiful smile and her infectious laughter. I dreamed of when my Angel was still alive and she would hold me in her embrace.

Except, no matter how much I would dream of these beautiful moments, I would always wake up into this nightmare.

Even with the light off and the room basked with darkness, Lena found her way to my bed. She sat down on the edge. I closed my eyes, refusing to acknowledge her presence.

I didn't want to talk. There was no point. What was there left to say?

Nothing. Absolutely nothing.

"You didn't eat," Lena said quietly. I didn't respond. She let out a sigh, and I could almost feel her shoulders drooping.

"I want to be alone," I finally said after a few minutes of silence.

"I want to be alone too, but we can't always have what we want, right?" Her voice sounded so empty, so unlike the old Lena I once knew. She was broken too. But I chose to ignore the fact that she lost her love too. I couldn't handle thinking about her *hurting* while I was so deep in pain.

My eyes snapped open, and I glared at her through the darkness. "What the fuck do you want?" I barely even recognized my voice. It was rough and gravelly after days of not speaking. It sounded…raw and pained.

"I don't want anything, Lyov. I am just here to *give* you something."

I waited, but finally she moved. My fist tightened when she touched my hand. Gently, she opened my clenched fingers and then laid something cold in the middle of my palm. She closed my fingers around it again. "This belongs to you."

With that, Lena got up and left the room.

Silence fell upon me again. I shifted around in the bed and turned on the lamp. I opened my palm, and in the middle, I found a ring.

Maria's wedding band.

Lena must have kept it when…

I shook my head, refusing to think of it. My eyes burned with unshed tears as I stared at my Angel's ring, the same one that she never took off. The same one that had my name engraved on the inside of it.

I looked down at my left hand, where my wedding band was still present. The word *Angel* was engraved on the inside of it. Matching rings for my wife and me. She had my name, and I had hers…*Angel*.

I choked back a sob and fisted her wedding band,

so tight that my knuckles turned white and my fingers started to hurt. Closing my eyes, I laid against the headboard. My head hurt. And my heart...the ache never disappeared, not since the night I found Maria in a pool of her blood.

Darkness swallowed me, and I fell into another bottomless pit. The next time I woke up, the ring was still held tightly in my fist. I opened my fingers and found it hard to breathe. Fuck. I hated this. I hated being weak. I hated *this*...this feeling of helplessness and emptiness.

I leaned forward, over the edge of my mattress, and opened the drawer of my nightstand. I found the silver chain that I kept in there. Placing Maria's ring onto the chain, I lifted it in front of my face and watched the ring dangle perfectly in the middle.

Forever, Angel. I promised you forever.

I placed the chain around my neck, and the cold ring laid in the middle of my chest. My beating heart thundered, and a painful, silent tear fell down.

I wished I could go back and change the past. I wished I could go back and protect my Maria just like I had promised. But I couldn't. What a fucking failure I was. The *King*, yet now...I was nothing but a stupid, broken soul.

My gaze went to the open drawer, and the pain turned into fury. Seven days. I lived seven days without my wife with only two emotions. Anger. And pain.

I took out the crumpled note from the drawer and stared at the words. My blood roared in my ears, and my veins thundered in my neck. Every pore of me vibrated with the need to shed the blood of those who had destroyed my life.

The note I found on Maria's body had sealed their fate.

Let that be a lesson for you.

Fucking Italians.

The Abandonato.

The men who were captured revealed the truth. Alfredo was behind the attack. Alfredo killed my Angel.

Oh, he would pay.

His death would be slow and painful. I would end him, and with him, I would bring his empire down.

Eight years ago, I made wedding vows.

Now, I made a vow to end *this*.

The Italians started a war.

The Russians would end it.

And a bloodbath was the only answer.

Chapter 26

Lyov

22 years later

It took Alessio three years before he started speaking again after witnessing his mother's death. Since that night, my boy was never the same. Not the innocent, sweet boy Maria used to love, coddle, and cherish. He changed the night he watched his mother's blood flow, saturating our lives with its painful meaning.

Three years after Maria took her last breath, Alessio made his first kill at only eleven years old. I wished I was a better father. Maybe stopped him when I could have. I wished I had kept him away from this fucked-up life. But I didn't. Life had fucked me up so I could only see my pain and revenge. I didn't understand Alessio. I didn't understand his fear, his sorrow…and his emptiness. Only because I was too blinded by my own.

Life had hardened Alessio Ivanshov into a

ruthless, merciless King. He built the Empire I turned into ash with his own bare hands.

I wished I could have done a lot of things differently. But now, as I watched my son wrap his arms about his woman, his Ayla, his Angel…I wouldn't change anything.

Some would say it was fate. Destiny.

Maybe this was meant all along.

Maybe I was meant to lose my Angel.

So Alessio could find his.

I had given them both a hard time. I believed that Angels didn't belong in our world, and by pushing my anger and sorrow at losing my wife on Alessio, he almost lost his Ayla.

But now they were happy. They were together, with a baby on the way.

A princess, Ayla said.

It hurt to think about it, to think about their happiness because mine had just been an incomplete, broken story. Even after twenty-two years, the realization that I would never hold my daughter…the ache in my heart only worsened.

I watched as Alessio laced his fingers with Ayla's and they walked toward the woods that led to the streams and a field of flowers. A sanctuary, a piece of heaven in this hell.

I watched as my son leaned down and kissed his woman on her lips. Ayla threw her head back and laughed. Even from far away, I saw Alessio's lips tilted up in a smile. The way he looked at her, it reminded me of the times when I would look at my Maria. I was sure I had the same look in my eyes, on my face. That look of love and absolute

BLOOD AND ROSES

adoration. A look of protectiveness. A look that said *this* woman…she was *mine*.

They walked further into the woods together. My hand came up, and I touched my silver chain from under my shirt. My fingers rubbed over Maria's wedding band. I could almost feel her presence, as if she was right next to me. I could feel her smile…her warmth.

I imagined she was *here* right now, standing beside me, watching over our son and his Angel.

I gripped the ring tighter. "They are happy, Maria. Alessio found *her*. And I think…I think they are going to live happily ever after. Just like you always wanted for him."

Alessio and Ayla disappeared into the trees, and I couldn't help but smile. They were *beautiful* together.

Leaning against my window, I stared outside at the back garden where my Angel had spent most of her time. I would always find her, hands buried into the soil as she planted more and more flowers.

The thought came to a screeching halt when something else caught my eyes. Silence filled my ears, and I forgot about Maria. I forgot about the flowers.

I only saw the shadow following behind Alessio. Someone who shouldn't have been there.

Shock coursed through me. My heart kick-started, and every instinct in me told me something was *wrong*.

Just like *that* night…twenty-two years ago.

My instincts were never wrong. Without thinking, I turned away from the windows. My legs were shaking almost, but I ran out of my room. A deep sense of fear was instilled in me.

I ran down the hall and the stairs. I heard Isaak yelling. I heard other men running behind me, following me as I ran toward the woods. But I didn't stop. I didn't stop once because something was wrong.

They were in danger. Alessio. Ayla. Their baby.

Something deep within screamed and urged me to run faster, to save them.

Finally, I broke through the trees. From a distance, I saw Alessio first. He was only a few feet from Ayla. She had her hands over her stomach and tears running down her cheeks. She looked scared. Alessio looked scared.

And then I saw *him*. The Devil of their story.

His gun was pointed at Ayla's stomach. And I heard his words. Loud and chilling. Hurtful to my ears. He was going to hurt their Princess.

NO!

I didn't think. I didn't stop. I had to save them.

Never again. This family wouldn't lose another Angel…another Princess.

In a flash, I saw Alessio running to Ayla. I saw him standing in front of her. I knew he would take the bullet.

But this…this couldn't be the end of their story. This couldn't be another broken love story.

And I couldn't lose my son.

My feet took me forward. Time slowed. The chirping birds…and the flowing water…everything disappeared into silence.

In my head, I saw a brief flash of black hair and

blue eyes standing in the distance. It happened fast. I was far away from them, and then I was in front of the gun.

Even the gunshot was silent.

Everything...was...empty. Silence.

I was falling...falling...and falling.

I saved them.

I saved his Angel. I saved their princess. I saved my son.

Darkness engulfed me, and I sunk deeper into it, waiting for the pain. But nothing hurt. I felt...peaceful.

I love you, Master.
I love you, Angel.

Epilogue

Lyov

I used to think I was unbeatable…indestructible. But every man has a weakness.

Sometimes, I wanted to curse the day I met Maria. The day I gave myself to her, the very soul of me—I placed it in her hands. I wanted to hate the day I gave her my heart and felt her body under mine. I wanted to forget her warmth, her shivering skin underneath my wandering touch. I wanted to forget to laugh. Her smiles. Her love.

I wanted to go back to the beginning and wished I hadn't laid eyes on her…hadn't looked into the blue eyes of a tempting siren. Because then, I wouldn't be *here*—utterly broken and weak.

She was the light that shone during my darkest hour. My Angel became my Queen, who stood by me as I built a stronger empire. And now…everything was burning into ashes. I was powerless to stop it.

But even though I wanted to curse the day I laid

eyes on my Angel, I really couldn't. No matter how much I wanted to hate it all…I really couldn't.

Our memories were all I had left. They kept me alive, even when I was *dead*.

You are in my arms right now, and I don't need anything else. I can feel your love in the way you touch me. The way you look at me.

You are mine, Maria. And I will always be forever yours. I. Love. You. Fuck, those words aren't enough.

Then show me. Show me how much you love me. Don't let me forget, Lyov.

I knew she wasn't coming back. I knew I would never catch a glimpse of my Angel again, would never hear her laugh or drown in her eyes…or feel her touch on my skin. But there was a hole inside my stupid heart. It made me hope…that for the briefest moment, if I closed my eyes and opened them again, she would be here. My Angel, in front of me, opening her arms for me so I could sink into her embrace.

It was a hopeless dream, yet I couldn't help but close my eyes.

I remembered when she would look at me, my heart would beat wildly. When she would smile at me, there was something that deep within me, feeling that smile all the way down to my toes. I didn't want this moment to ever end. A fragment of imagination was what kept me going. I held on to those moments even when they hurt and left me even more pain afterward.

So I closed my eyes and hopelessly dreamed that when I opened them again, my Angel would be here. That our fairy tale wasn't bloodily tainted.

My eyes opened.

Silence.

Emptiness.

Nothing.

Just…empty. Alone yet again. It fucking hurt, and I clenched my eyes closed again, choking back a horrible sob. The droplets of tears slid down my cheek, almost burning in realization.

My Maria was never coming back. No matter how many times I closed my eyes and dreamed of her…it was all broken.

Her blood had flowed…red as roses.

My palm laid over my bandaged chest, feeling my heartbeat. The bullet I took to save my family, it didn't kill me. It almost hit my heart, but it missed.

I thought I had died. I remembered seeing my Maria, but then she disappeared, and I was thrust back into the present, alive, breathing.

It wasn't my time to go yet. It wasn't my time to reunite with my Angel yet…but one day soon. Maybe I was kept alive all this time for this. A purpose. Maybe I was meant to be here, to save Alessio and his family.

So many years ago, I failed mine.

This was my second chance.

I hadn't had a chance to save my Angel, but I saved my son's *Angel*.

I couldn't save my Princess, but I saved Alessio's,

A full circle of life. I found my redemption, and

BLOOD AND ROSES

it felt like I could finally breathe a little.

My gaze found our portrait on the wall. My Angel was smiling down at me.

I miss you in ways that nobody could comprehend. No even words can understand.

I wanted to beg her to come back. *Come back, Angel. Stay just a little longer. Let me kiss you one more time. Let me feel your arms around me. Let me love you. One last time.*

But I knew she was somewhere so far, far away, way beyond my reach.

What a funny way to live our vows...*till death do us part.*

No. Not even death could separate us.

Maria was mine. Always would be. And I was hers. Till my last fucking breath.

There would be no other. For my Angel was the only one.

And *that* was my vow.

My Angel had wanted a fairy tale. I had given her that. I was her salvation. She was my redemption. Except as much as our fairy tale was beautiful and mesmerizing, it had a sick, twisted ending.

Angels deserve happily ever after.

Monsters like me don't. My darkness became hers, and our life became tainted.

We didn't live happily ever after.

I touched the portrait and traced her beautiful, smiling lips.

But when I did have her in my arms...when we had each other, when we were together, we were happy. Love stories like ours didn't have *endings*.

It lived on forever. As beautiful and as flawed as it was.

Until we meet again, Angel.

THE END

Or is it?

You can turn the next page for an excerpt of the next book in the *Tainted Hearts Series.*

Sneak Peek

The Mafia and His Obsession: Part 1
(Tainted Hearts, #4)

HIM

Some say we were cruel. Disgusting human beings. Heartless. Ruthless.

I would agree.

But I liked the word barbaric better. Unsympathetic. Sadistic. Vicious.

After all, we were killers.

We were born into this life. Since the very beginning, we breathed it.

From first breath…till our last.

His whimpers snapped me out of my thoughts. Was that piss I smelled?

Most probably. They always turned into disgusting carcasses when their death flashed in front of their eyes. Too bad for them it was always too late.

He opened his mouth to speak, but I never gave

him a chance. My fingers tightened around the knife before I drove it down, right in the middle of his throat.

The man gurgled his last breath as his blood poured around him…and on me. Shaking my head in disgust, I spat on him.

"Foolish. They know the consequences, but they still try and play us," I sneered at him.

His chest expanded as he took his last breath…and then silence. Nobody spoke a word as we stared at the dead man, his eyes still open. Still staring into mine.

The only difference was that his were empty, while mine were still very much alive, glowing with power.

I heard Phoenix talking over the phone while I stood up. My handkerchief was already out of my pocket, and I cleaned my hands, trying to remove the blood. My face was next. It felt sticky where the blood had splattered.

Disgusting filth. I need a fucking shower now.

Why didn't Alessio do it himself?

Oh, wait…because he didn't want to get his hands dirty this time. His Angel was waiting for him at home.

Like that made him the lesser evil.

He was just as fucked up.

We were all fucked.

But we had her to bring us some light. A little bit of happiness. Some smiles…some occasional laughter. Some scraps of love.

She gave it all to us, without expecting anything in return. She loved so much and so hard that sometimes our hearts were not big enough to take it all.

Someone swore behind me. My eyebrows furrowed in confusion as I was brought back to the present.

Annoyingly, I had been lost in my thoughts too much lately. Very bad.

I'm going to get killed if I don't get my shit together.

"Boss," I heard Phoenix warn.

What the fuck was he warning Alessio about? I turned around, facing the others.

Only to come face to face with Alessio pointing his gun at me.

"Seriously? We don't have time for this," I said, my eyes on the gun. He cocked his head to the side, his eyebrows lifted in amusement.

"Can we do this later? After we have disposed of the body? C'mon, man."

I rolled my eyes, knowing Alessio wasn't going to do something stupid. He wouldn't. Not after everything.

Turning my back to him again, I put my life…everything in his hands. I gave him my full trust.

That was my first mistake.

I heard the gunshot first. It rang so loud in the silent alley. My heart thumped in response.

Then I felt it. The indescribable pain and burn that came after the bullet pierced my body.

He shot me.

He actually shot me.

In the ass.

What the ever-loving fuck?

He did not just fucking shoot me.

I swiveled around to face him, ignoring the pain. Trying so hard to ignore the fact that I had just been shot in the ass. I had a hole in my ass cheek!

This wasn't some *Deadpool* bullshit. And I sure as hell wasn't some super mutant who could pop bullets out of his ass.

Yeah…he's a dead man.

"Ayla's going to be pissed when we get back home and she finds both of us shot," I drawled, reaching behind me.

I never got a chance to get my gun. He was now aiming at my chest, right over my heart.

I froze. My muscles locked as I stared at Alessio in surprise. He wouldn't…

Raising my hands in surrender, I took a step back. "Alessio, we can talk about this."

At least not my heart. He could shoot anywhere but the heart. Or my dick.

"No. We can't," he simply replied. His eyes appeared darker than usual, anger glistening in them. Alessio was a madman when he turned angry.

He would blur the lines between right or wrong. Nothing mattered to him except his revenge. He would do anything and…everything.

In that moment, I was on the other side. Not beside him. But against him. For the first time since I had known him.

Instead of our guns pointing at some other bastards, his gun was pointed at me. And only one reason made sense.

"Did you think I wouldn't find out?" he hissed. I

saw his fingers tightening around the gun. His index fingers laid on the trigger, waiting for the right moment, dragging out the suspense.

He loved the chase, the adrenaline in making others shake and whimper in fear. Except I wasn't shaking or whimpering.

That probably pissed him off more.

"I was going to tell you," I answered.

Lies. I wasn't.

Because there was nothing to tell. Nothing was what it seemed to be. Every action, every word, had a meaning behind it.

Nothing in our world was the perfect image. Everything was in pieces, and we had to put all of them together to find the truth. A piece in the puzzle to get the whole vision.

Everything was a lie.

Everyone was a lie.

Every fucking day was a game to play. A game we had mastered.

Believe nothing. Whatever you see or hear is a lie.

That was one of the lessons learned and a lesson to remember.

"Let me explain," I tried to convince him. Anything but another bullet in my body.

"You know damn well that I never give anyone a chance to explain," he snapped. Thrusting his gun toward my chest, his lips curled in disgust. "And you aren't any different."

"Boss," I heard someone say. There was a warning in his tone. Maybe he was trying to save me? We were a brotherhood after all.

Alessio smirked, just the corner of his lips turning up, and I just knew. My death had just been signed, and I had no choice over it.

The veins in my neck throbbed. Blood rushed to my ears until the only thing I could hear was the pounding of my heart.

Their voices sounded like they were underwater as my dreadful life flashed in front of my eyes. This was it.

The end.

BANG!

I closed my eyes as the gun went off, sounding so loud, so evil to my ears. The connection of the metal and my skin was quick. So quick that I could have missed it.

But when the pain came later...there was no escaping it.

Sweat dripped down my forehead as my blood dripped down my body. The cold bullet penetrated my chest, and I prayed it didn't hit my heart.

A laughable thought that was.

Alessio had perfect aim. If he wanted me dead, shot in the heart, there was no escaping death.

He was death.

My eyes fluttered open as I regarded my boss for one final time. His hand dropped to his side, still holding the gun.

The anger in his eyes was gone, replaced with hurt and pain. His expression changed to one of regret. "I didn't want to do this, but you gave me no choice. You fucked up. And you fucked up bad."

I knew that!

I wanted to scream, but my lips felt numb. My

throat grew tighter as the pain spread across my body. It felt like I was burning from the inside as the ground turned darker with the red shade of blood.

Through blurry vision, I saw Alessio pointing the gun at me again. I closed my eyes, waiting for him to end this. Waiting for this indescribable pain to finally end.

The fired round seemed to float through fragile air, my ears barely registering the gunshot. It pierced my chest without consideration, without real meaning or relevance.

A sacrifice made from my part. A sacrifice I was willing to make. For my family. For her.

The small wounds leaked blood similar to how crying eyes leaked tears.

I sank to my knees, my body too weak to hold myself strong any longer. I gasped for breath, pleading for air.

Maybe I heard him whisper sorry. Maybe it was my mind playing tricks on me, but there was no mistaking the anguish in his voice.

I wanted to open my eyes, to give them a final look. A final goodbye. But my weakness won over.

"The only reason why I can regret this is because Ayla will be hurt. She is going to cry, and I won't be able to do anything," Alessio said. His voice sounded nearer but still so far away.

I was drifting. Falling deeper and deeper into the dark abyss.

Suddenly everything went completely silent. All movement around me slowed down to an excruciating pace. I could feel my pulse pounding through me as visions flashed behind my closed eyes.

The images swirled before me right until the end, leaving that last scene of her imprinted upon my mind without the oxygen to sustain it.

Her smile. Her laughter. The look of love as she gazed up at him. Never me. Always him.

I bled out, losing consciousness faster…falling faster…until I hit hard ground.

I was jostled, and pain racked through me. It felt like my unbeating heart just started again, pumping blood through my body.

I died. I knew I died…then the voices…

What's happening?

I opened my mouth to speak, but no words found their way out. The burning sensation in my chest never ended. It hurt more and more every second.

"He's flat lining!"

The noises grew louder over the pounding of my heart.

"Don't let him die!"

New voices. They didn't belong to Alessio or any of our men.

"Fuck! I need him alive, damn it!"

No. I was dead.

"He needs to live," the voice hissed.

"You need to live. Do you hear me, son?" It sounded nearer now.

Was he talking to me?

My body was moved, pushed, pulled, and I bore down on the agony.

What the fuck was happening?

Leave me alone, I wanted to scream. I was with

her…at least in my death moment, she loved me.

But now some stupid bastards were taking me away. I could see her fading…turning away from me.

I reached for her, but it was too late. She was gone, fading into the darkness. She left me alone again.

"This is what happens when you choose the wrong side."

Huh?

"Fucking Ivanshov. They would pay for this. All of them."

No.

"I told you to join us, but you didn't listen. Now bear the pain of being betrayed by your *brother*. Over whom? Some fucked up Italian *blyad*."

Don't fucking call her a whore.

Anger swirled inside of me before realization finally dawned.

They were speaking Russian.

Ah, fuck my life.

"Don't worry. You will get your revenge. They all betrayed you. You will live and get your revenge."

His words penetrated through my mind, and I held them close, wrapping myself around the words.

They all betrayed you.

Other words were mumbled, but I ignored them.

You will live and get your revenge.

I smiled internally. *Oh, yes I will.*

I was going to live…fuck death. It was not my time yet.

"Get him to the estate. When he wakes up, we

will put our plans into action. The time has come for my heir to join me."

The smile turned into a smirk. It was time.

Blood would be spilled, and only the strong would live. There can only be one conqueror. Everyone else was going to be ten feet under the cold, hard ground.

Deceit. Betrayal. Lies. Traitors. Hate. Revenge. Fraud.

We lived with them every day. We breathed them. We played them. And we welcomed them.

The game had begun.

AUTHOR'S NOTE

Wow. I actually truly don't know where to start this. I am so overwhelmed right now as I write this part of the book. When I first wrote *The Mafia and His Angel*, there was a small flashback of Maria and Lyov, where the meaning of *Angel* is explained. Since then, I felt the connection, the love, and the chemistry between these two characters. They became so much more than just characters to me. They breathed, they had feelings, they loved. Every time I wrote a scene of Lyov, I was left wondering…how was he when he was in love? And that was how *Blood and Roses* happened. Lyov started speaking to me. And Maria made her sweet innocent appearance in my head. I couldn't stop myself from writing their story, and I truly believe they deserve their story to be told.

Lyov and Maria made me fall in love with them. And then, they obliterated me. *Blood and Roses* was meant to be a very short story, a novella of only about thirty thousand words. But it turned out much longer, and I believed this was how it was meant to happen. I can't imagine trying to fit their love story in just a few words. They are worth so much more.

I wished I could have given them a happy ending, but even though I am a storyteller, their love story was not in my hands. Like Lyov said, it was fate, and this was how it was meant to be. It hurts, I know. It truly hurts.

This is just another part of the Tainted Hearts Series, and now we are moving on to the next. I can't wait to write about the other couple, and I can't wait for you read them.

Acknowledgements

I think first and foremost, I want to thank Lyov and Maria. This story wouldn't have been possible without their forever presence in my little head. They spoke, and I wrote. I am so sad to be ending their story now, for I wished I could write more of their sweet love story.

I want to thank Vivvi. My girl. My boobito. You are everything. Thank you for being there for me. Thank you for always pushing me up when I am falling down. Thank you for loving my characters, my babies, just as much as I do, if not more. Actually, saying thank you is not enough. I am so glad to have you in my life.

My parents, thank you for your never-ending support and love.

To Jessica and Chelsea, my girls. What would I do without you? Seriously, I would be drowning if it wasn't for you two keeping me afloat. Thank you for being there and supporting me through all this craziness. It has been a wild ride, and you have stuck with me till now—thank you will never be enough. Cheers, to so much more now.

The biggest thank you goes to my publisher. Thank you for giving *Blood and Roses* a chance. I am holding my book right now because you think it is worth it. So thank you.

To my editor, Toni—what would I do without you? Seriously. You are a life saver, and I am so glad you didn't hunt me down, tie me to a chair, and make me write this book faster without procrastinating so much. Your patience has been so amazing. *Thank you.* I am so glad we worked together on this book. You truly did wonders.

Thank you to everyone else who had a hand in making this book—my proofreader, formatter…you guys are stars.

To Deranged Doctor Design—this cover is EVERYTHING. You painted my vision. Thank you.

To the bloggers and everyone who took their time to promote Blood and Roses, you are awesome! My big thanks to you.

And I wanted to leave this for the end, because this is the important part. A huge thank you to every single one of my readers. My lovelies. Your never-ending support and love has taken us on this path. From the first word to the last, you have been here with me. I am proud we took this journey together. You have loved Maria and Lyov as much as I have. I am so thankful for that. Thank you for standing with me, even through my craziness. To all the fan accounts and groups out there, thank you! All the beautiful edits and posters you have made, they are my inspiration and motivation. I am going to say it loud and clear. "You freaking rock!"

About the Author

Lylah James lives somewhere in Canada. She is usually pretty busy, but she uses all her spare time to write. If she is not studying, sleeping, writing, or working – she can be found with her nose buried in a good romance book, preferably with a hot alpha male.

Writing is her passion. The voices in her head won't stop, and she believes they deserve to be heard and read. Lylah James writes about drool worthy and total alpha males, with strong and sweet heroines. She makes her readers cry – sob their eyes out, swoon, curse, rage, and fall in love. Mostly known as the Queen of Cliffhangers and the #evilauthorwithablacksoul, she likes to break her readers' hearts and then mend them again.

FOLLOW LYLAH AT:

Facebook page:
https://www.facebook.com/AuthorLy.James/

Twitter page:
https://twitter.com/AuthorLy_James

Instagram page:
https://www.instagram.com/authorlylahjames/

Goodreads:
https://www.goodreads.com/author/show/16045951.Lylah_James

Or you can drop me an email at:
AuthorLylah.James@Hotmail.com

Or check out my website:
http://authorlylahjames.com/

You can also join my newsletter list for updates, teasers, major giveaways and so much more!
http://eepurl.com/c2EJ4z